"*Searching for Jimmy Pa* ....gerous magic that arises when pop culture is mixed with traditional folkways in the rural South. From power chords to delicate noodling of our heart's innermost strings, Hallberg's debut demonstrates breathtaking range."
—George Hovis, *The Skin Artist*

"When a troubled teenager from eastern North Carolina decides that iconic guitar player Jimmy Page must be the father she's never known, she sets off on a quirky coming-of-age journey with special appeal for 70's rock fans, spanning two continents, three decades, and a deep dive into Led Zeppelin history and lore."
—Ellyn Bache, *Safe Passage*

"Steeped in rock and roll lore, *Searching for Jimmy Page* is the coming-of-age tale of a motherless daughter making sense of her grief, and finding the strength to save herself from the flood of loss that threatens to wash her future away. Hallberg's prose is sumptuous and rich with detail, and readers will fall in love with tenacious Luna. *Searching for Jimmy Page* is a heartbreaking and hopeful debut."
—Meagan Lucas, *Songbirds & Stray Dogs*

"Multi-generational secrets, the semi-mystical music of Led Zeppelin, and the tidal pull of a southern family combine to create literary magic in Christy Alexander Hallberg's *Searching for Jimmy Page*. Luna Kane, a troubled but determined young orphan, believes she is undertaking a journey to learn the truth about her father, but along the way she gains deeper insights about her long-lost mother and finds not merely Jimmy Page, but herself. A beautifully written and engaging first novel."
—Kim Wright, *Last Ride to Graceland*, winner of the Willie Morris Award for Southern Fiction

Rock on!
All the best,
Christy Alexander Hallberg

SEARCHING FOR
JIMMY PAGE

CHRISTY ALEXANDER
HALLBERG

Livingston Press
The University of West Alabama

ISBN 13: trade paper 978-1-60489-291-8
ISBN 13: hardcover 978-1-60489-292-5
ISBN 13: e-book 978-1-60489-293-2

Library of Congress Control Number 2021941897
Printed on acid-free paper
Printed in the United States of America by
Publishers Graphics

Hardcover binding by: HF Group
Typesetting and page layout: Joe Taylor
Proofreading: Kaylnn Ward, Joe Taylor, Caitlin Saxton,
Brooke Barger, Claire Banberg

Cover Design: Nic Nolin

AUTHOR'S NOTE

Searching For Jimmy Page is a work of fiction. Unless otherwise indicated, all the names, characters, businesses, places, events, dialogue, and incidents in this book are either the product of the author's imagination or used in a fictitious manner. As such, the book should not be read as a factual account of events or as biography, especially with regard to Led Zeppelin and Jimmy Page personally.

Livingston Press is part of The University of West Alabama,
and thereby has non-profit status.
Donations are tax-deductible.
6 5 4 3 2 1

SEARCHING FOR

JIMMY PAGE

For my mother,
Frances Baker Alexander,
who never owned a tie-dye skirt or Tarot cards
but loved "Kashmir" and "Immigrant Song"
and helped me cover my bedroom walls with Led Zeppelin
posters when I was a teenager

PART ONE:

"FOUR STICKS"

CHAPTER ONE

THE NIGHT my great-grandfather died, frigid air howled through the pines and swirled down the chimney of his shack near our fallow tobacco fields in eastern North Carolina. My grandmother and I kept vigil at his bedside, a battery-operated space heater oscillating at our feet, kerosene lamps lofting shadows on the walls. He'd refused to install electricity and insisted the fireplace remain unlit at night. He claimed spirits talked to him through the flue at the Witching Hour. So did birds, especially owls. He said they were good omens, unless they flew inside your house. *Owl in the house means death's coming*, he'd say.

I lolled my head against the wall, bare like all the others, no family portraits or prosaic artwork or thumbtacked greeting cards with snapshots of my great-grandfather's progeny tucked inside. The shack was cluttered with clothes and other debris from a fading life, but the walls were naked. He preferred it that way, no memories or illusions, except the ones that came to him at night.

At the stroke of twelve he wrapped his knotty fingers around my wrist and squeezed. "Can you hear it?" he asked, his voice like winter wind crackling through kindling. An icy shiver ran through me. He had not spoken since that balmy summer night when I was nine years old, when the river ran dry and the pines began to cry. The night my mother committed suicide—an abomination, he'd called it. A sin against Providence. He'd sat expressionless in his rocking chair while Grandma delivered the news, his face bathed in candlelight, then hobbled into the woods and chanted my mother's name, like an incantation, a prayer for deliverance. Then he'd spoken no more.

I inched closer to him, close enough to smell the implacable stench of the dying. "Hear what?" I asked timorously.

"Owls," he said. "Like music."

My body fluttered as if I were falling out of oblivion, slowly, unwittingly, the air prickly and thin. Long ago, I'd heard a song about owls crying in the night, the singer's wail primeval, in sync with marauding guitar licks, the beat like jungle drums. I felt them vibrating inside me just then, like a distant echo from another life, one that still included my mother.

"Can you hear the music?" he persisted, struggling to raise his head.

Grandma implored me with her eyes. "I can hear it, Granddaddy."

He gave a shuddering laugh. "Ain't in your head, girl."

"Where then?"

I waited, watching his chest rise and fall, his fitful breaths grow shallow—the caesura between life and death.

"It's in your soul," he finally said. He nudged his Bible beside him, giving voice to verse: "Ecclesiastes 6:10: That which hath been is named already."

He dropped my arm and exhaled, his face pallid and drawn. Grandma and I stood over him, bearing witness, sleet pelting the windows, that song about the owls, its searing guitar, haunting me, like fragments of memory I'd buried with my childhood—grainy images of my mother in her yellow bedroom with her lavender incense and votive candles, her black and white photograph of a Rock star standing on a stage at Kezar Stadium in 1973, dressed all in white, lips pursed, unruly dark hair framing a beatific face, guitar strapped over his shoulder, arms spread wide, as if he were awaiting crucifixion. The two of them were intertwined in my mind's eye, like ashes wafting in a summer wind, waiting for water to receive them. I was born of water and moonlight, and of her and of him.

Grandma stopped the clock on the mantle to mark the moment of my great-grandfather's passing, as if halting time held power—*then* forever *now*.

She handed me a flashlight then draped her overcoat around me, the scent of Jergens lotion and talcum powder lingering in the fabric. "Go on home, honey," she said. "I shouldn't have brought you here."

"You didn't," I said faintly.

I'd followed her from our farmhouse at dusk, trudged the quarter-mile past the barn and hog pen, through the woods, where the footpath ended, as if I'd heard my great-grandfather's keening call.

"Go home," Grandma said, prodding me toward the door. "I'll be along directly."

I wrenched away from her and stared at my great-grandfather, the withered shell that remained, searching for some part of him that still looked vital—the outline of his body beneath the quilt, legs splayed as if the cat he used to own were nestled between them, his arm dangling over the side of the bed. Grandma tucked it underneath the quilt her mother had made, tattered and yellowed with age, the same quilt that had covered her while she lay dying over half a century before, cancer ravaging her breast, flies swarming the window screens, attracted by the fetor of rotting flesh, all because her husband had believed he could heal her with ritual and prayer. I harbor a picture of that night in my mind's eye—my great-grandmother's bewildered stare, her mouth a perfect O—a last word half-spoken, an oracle undelivered. Now he was dead, his jaw unhinged, spittle on his grizzled chin, his only child by his side—the daughter whom he only recognized after she'd tell him her name, the name he'd given her seventy years ago.

"Do like I say," Grandma said sternly.

I stood there breathless, my great-grandfather's milky eyes—fixed and dilated, seeing nothing, seeing everything—boring into mine.

Grandma cupped my chin in her hand. "Don't look back," she said with urgency in her voice.

I never had before. Not after my mother died. Like my great-grandfather, I had not spoken her name since. I had not heard her voice in a brooding summer rain or felt her hand clasping mine in a sibylline dream or seen her face in the shadow of a stealthy Hunter's Moon. I had erased her and the sainted sinner who conjured music and magic from an electric guitar, his photograph in my mother's bedroom, her unfaithful talisman. I'd never looked back. Never. Until that winter's night in February 1988, when I was eighteen years old, the past summoned like fire in my great-grandfather's shack, phantom owls crying in the night.

It was inevitable. Perhaps it was even Providence.

Now would return me to *then*.

The tale demanded to be told.

CHAPTER TWO

WHEN I was nine, my mother gave me a leather-bound journal with gold-tipped pages and placed a pen in my hand.

"Write," she said, her long blonde hair feral in the dusty breeze.

"Write what?" I asked.

She hiked up her tie-dye skirt and squatted next to me on the splintered wood floor of my grandmother's front porch. I sat Indian style, my bare legs splotched with mosquito bites, the heart my mother had scrawled in red Magic Marker around the stitches on my right calf barely visible in the speckled sunlight. I'd tumbled into the hog pen while attempting to walk the top of the fence like Dorothy in *The Wizard of Oz*. My realization that I couldn't fly once airborne had been more shocking than the bloody gash I'd sustained when I hit the ground.

"Come on," she said. "Tell me a story."

"Uh uh," I said. "You tell me a story, the one about my name."

"You've heard that a million times."

"So?"

"So, so, suck your toe. All the way to Mex-e-co," she sang in her butterscotch alto.

I rolled my eyes. "You're stalling, Claudia." I'd always

called my mother by her given name. She'd asked me to. Not *Mama* or *Mommy*, like my schoolmates, who marveled at my idiosyncrasy. I couldn't understand why they referred to their mothers as designations rather than distinctives.

A gust of wind carried the pungent smell of tobacco from the field across the dirt road. It was harvest time. Uncle Jack had hired a crew of local high school boys to help, and I could hear them whistling at Claudia above the distant din of the tractor. She stretched her legs then plopped into the cane-bottom chair under the ceiling fan. I couldn't tell if she was oblivious to their flirtations or simply bored with them. Either way, she never engaged.

"Once upon a time on a crisp autumn night," she began in a hammy voice, "a fairy princess flew out her bedroom window and—"

"Where was she going?" I interjected, feigning ignorance.

"To visit the wise old man who lived in a shack in the woods."

"Howcome she couldn't wait 'til morning?"

"It was important. And stop interrupting," she groused, swatting my leg with her bare foot. "When the fairy princess got to the wise old man's shack, he was communing with the spirits who'd come calling."

"He was talking to the fireplace," I said petulantly.

Claudia groaned. "He was talking to the spirits," she insisted. "Then the fairy princess gave him a slip of paper with a question on it."

"What was the question?"

"She wanted to know what to name her soon-to-be-born child."

"You mean she wanted him to ask the fireplace."

She gave an enigmatic grin then rolled the sweating bottle of Pepsi across her forehead, unblemished and makeup-free, as always. "Anyway," she continued, "he read the question, then he wrote something on the paper and handed it back to the fairy princess. Then she set off for home. When she got to the edge of the woods, the full moon—the Hunter's Moon—came out from behind the clouds and lit up the whole yard. It was like the sky had burst into white-hot fire. She could see past the hog pen and barn and the clouds and stars, all the way to the edge of the universe."

She leaned her head back and stared at the ceiling, as if she were gazing through the wood and shingles into a fulgent fall sky. "Then the child's name came to her," she said dreamily. "Luna, Roman goddess of the moon, bright and beautiful and strong." She winked at me. "And you are."

"So are you, Claudia." I crawled over to her and wrapped my arms around her legs, damp with sweat. "You're not like anybody else."

She sighed and handed me the bottle. I secretly preferred Mountain Dew, but since Claudia drank Pepsi, I'd forced myself to acquire a taste for it. I took a slug, then managed a hyperbolic belch and burst into giggles.

"I don't need manners," I said smugly. "I'm a goddess, just like you said. I'm not like anybody else, except you." I pointed to my sutured calf. "See? I've got a red mark on me, just like you've got a red birthmark on your tummy. Now we're both marked. I'm just like you."

Her hazel eyes went stony. "Listen to me, Luna. You're not marked. Hear me?" Her tone held fear, dread. "You're not marked."

"What's wrong, Claudia?"

She jerked my chin up and glared at me. "Don't ever say that again. Understand? You're not like me."

I pushed her hand away and scrambled on my hands and knees to the top of the steps. The taste of bile filled my mouth, as if my innards had shuffled without warning. My heart was pounding in my belly, lungs throbbing in my throat.

She padded toward me, her jingle bell anklet making a tinny sound. "Say it."

I shook my head defiantly.

"Say it, Luna."

"I'm not like you," I whimpered.

She knelt beside me and stroked my hair, both of us silent. Her touch felt tentative, her hand cold, spiritless.

I listened to her jingling inside the house, then upstairs to her bedroom and locking the door. The music came next. That song about owls crying in the night, the rainbow's end, rivers running dry, running red. The song she would play whenever she'd disappear inside herself, alone in her room. Always that song. Over and over.

"You need to get her a doctor, Mama," I overheard Aunt Lorraine tell Grandma during one of Claudia's previous episodes. "Or maybe send her somewhere for a little while, let somebody who knows about this kind of thing get her straightened out once and for all."

I was hiding behind the drapes in the living room, eavesdropping while they talked in hushed tones in the kitchen. Uncle Jack was upstairs trying to coax Claudia out of her room. I could hear him talking to her through the door in his husky voice. Uncle Jack was a burly man, ursine and coarse. When I was a child, he reminded me of Grizzly Adams.

"Send her where?" Grandma said sharply. "Some asylum with padded walls and a bunch of crazy people roaming around drooling and moaning? You really think that's the place for your sister? She just gets a little depressed is all."

"What in the world has she got to be depressed about? She's twenty-eight years old, living at home rent-free, never worked a day in her life, except whatever piddly jobs she does on the farm. I should be so lucky."

Aunt Lorraine sat at the Formica table, pushing pie crumbs around her plate with her fork. She lit a cigarette and inhaled languidly. She was thirteen years older than Claudia—the clichéd homely elder sister, with a purposeful gait, as if she were marching off to battle, a cigarette perpetually dangling between her fingers, nail polish in perfect three-part harmony with her lipstick and shoes, tightly permed cropped brown hair dyed a shade too dark for her pasty complexion. She resembled an aging Morticia Addams, sans come-hither eyes and sleek figure. Claudia was the golden child, and Aunt Lorraine knew it.

She flicked her ashes in her plate. "You think it's good for Luna to see her mama like this?" she said primly. "It was one thing when she was little, but she's not a baby anymore. It's bad enough the child doesn't know her daddy from a field hand, which is probably what he was."

"Don't start that again, Lorraine."

"Don't tell me you haven't thought of it. Mark my words, she'll start asking questions about both of them soon enough." She clucked her tongue. "Sometimes I think she'd be better off away from all this."

"You mean better off with you." Grandma wet a dishcloth and wiped down the table contentiously, as if she were scrubbing scuffmarks off the floor. "These spells don't happen often anymore. You're overreacting."

"I think you're *under*reacting." Aunt Lorraine sipped her iced tea then traced the rim of the glass with her fingertip, emitting an eerie trill that sent a shiver through me. "Maybe it was hormones at first, after she got pregnant, then postpartum depression," she said. "Maybe if she'd seen a doctor then she'd be fine now."

"Doctor Hollis said there's nothing wrong with her a little rest and patience won't take care of."

"Doctor Hollis is a quack. You need to find her a specialist. Soon as she started acting funny that winter, you should have taken her to Duke. I don't care what Daddy said, God rest his soul."

The music stopped and I heard Claudia's upstairs door creak open. I leaned into the silence—upstairs and down—the gathering sway of momentary stillness when possibility and certainty collide.

"Feeling better now?" I could hear Uncle Jack ask, in the conciliatory tone he reserved for children and injured animals. "Your mama says you been in there since yesterday. What in the world you been doing?"

I pictured her tipping her head and peering up at him coquettishly, the way she did whenever he would tease her. "Nothing," she said whimsically. "Just wishing on a star."

He chuckled. "Well, come on down and get something to eat."

"Not yet," she said. Her voice was distant again, inscrutable, as if she were slipping back into that haunted place no one could enter, not even me.

Uncle Jack cleared his throat, then said in a whisper barely loud enough for me to hear, "We're not staying, Claude. I'll get her out of here in a minute."

"Then I'll come down in a minute."

He hesitated. "All right then."

He clomped into the kitchen in his brogans and sat down heavily across from Aunt Lorraine. "All's well upstairs, I reckon, except that incense could choke a horse."

"I told you not to go up there," she said icily.

"Take it easy, Lorraine. I got her to come out, didn't I."

Her mouth twitched, as if she were struggling to contain her contempt. "Wasn't your place," she said.

"Well, why didn't you give it a try?" he said, drumming his fingers on the tabletop.

She stubbed out her cigarette and glared at him. "Because I don't coddle her the way you do."

"No, it's tough love all the way for you where your little sister's concerned. You might take another tack. This one is about as useful as a urinal in a convent." He pushed his chair back, the legs screeching across the floor, and plucked his car keys from his pocket. "Thanks for dinner, Margaret," he said to Grandma. "I'll be in the car, Lorraine."

Grandma waited for the mudroom door to slam then said, "One day you're gonna push that man too far."

Aunt Lorraine gave a grave smile. "He's never been close enough for me to push him anywhere."

"That's ridiculous, Lorraine," Grandma said. "If anything,

it's the opposite."

Aunt Lorraine rinsed her dishes then placed them in the drying rack. "I think you should let us take Luna," she said artlessly, her back to Grandma. "We've been thinking of moving to Morganton to take over Jack's daddy's farm, now that his health is failing. We can give her a new start. She'll forget all this in time."

I heard the floorboards creak upstairs. Claudia was standing on the landing, listening to her sister betray her, waiting to see if her mother would follow suit. My eyes darted back to the kitchen. I was waiting too.

"At least consider it," Aunt Lorraine pressed.

Grandma set her jaw and bustled about fixing a plate of food for Claudia, her silence response enough.

"Well then," Aunt Lorraine said, her tone hard. "Tell Luna I said goodbye." She collected her purse then stalked out.

Claudia breezed downstairs and stopped abruptly in front of the curtain, tapping her sandaled foot on the hardwood floor. "I think I see the moon behind a cloud," she said in a sing-song voice that reassured me the spell had once again been broken. I was terrified that one day she would dissipate with the lavender-scented air inside her room and never return.

"What a strange cloud it is," she said. "Long and wrinkled, like it fell from the sky one day and someone made a tent of it."

I forced a laugh. "It wasn't a tent. It was Dorothy's house after the cyclone blew it to Munchkin Land and it fell on the Wicked Witch of the East."

"And now it's a cloud again?"

"Nope, now it's a curtain."

She whipped open the drapes and scooped me into her

arms, swinging me around until we collapsed in a dizzy heap on the floor. "Why not a cloud?" she said. "Or a house or a rainbow? Anything but a boring old curtain."

My throat tightened. "Will you live with me over the rainbow?"

She kissed my cheeks, one at a time, like posh British people do, she'd told me.

I swallowed hard. "Will you, Claudia?"

"Oh Lunabelle," she said, sweeping her arms across the room. "I already do."

I climbed onto her lap and buried my face in her hair, tears stinging my eyes. I wanted to tell her. I wanted her to know what I'd always believed, what I believed until believing anything seemed a moot point. She was a goddess, an angel, mythical and infinite. To me she was.

.

CHAPTER THREE

I SAT next to Grandma on the front pew of Grace Holiness Pentecostal Church and waited for the choir to finish singing "What a Friend We Have in Jesus." My great-grandfather's pine casket loomed large at the front of the sanctuary. He'd carved it himself decades ago and stored it in the shed behind his house, *Do Not Enter* painted in red on the door, a padlock ensuring no one did. It took Grandma and me the better part of a day to find the key after he died.

"I don't know who in the world he thought would steal a coffin," Grandma had griped as we emptied his dresser drawers, tossing soiled napkins and moth-eaten sweaters into trash bags. She'd always done his laundry and brought him his meals, but he'd refused to let us do more than a cursory cleaning or in any way manipulate his space.

I plopped into his rocking chair and twisted the string of my hoodie sweatshirt around my finger. "Maybe we should just let the place be," I said, poking the bulging tip of my pinkie when it turned purple. "Leave it for those freaking spirits in the fireplace."

Grandma had given a hollow smile and handed me another trash bag. "This has to be done, honey," she'd said stoically. "The sooner the better."

I squirmed in the pew during the preacher's fire and

brimstone sermon. I hadn't been inside a church since Claudia's funeral. Once Grandma realized my refusal to accompany her to Sunday services was nonnegotiable, she'd respected my decision, just as she had Claudia's after her father's fatal heart attack, a few months before I was born. *I never really joined in the first place,* Claudia had told me. *And I didn't want my child speaking in tongues before she could even say her name.* She'd agreed to let Grandma take me to Easter and Christmas Eve services, but that was the extent of my sojourns to the House of God, until Claudia died. Aunt Lorraine had insisted on a church funeral. Grandma had been too distraught to protest, and I'd been too sedated to care. Immediately following her service, Grandma and I ventured off alone to scatter her cremated remains in the Tar River, just as Claudia had always wanted. *Everything is made of water,* she used to say on bleak rainy days, quoting a philosopher whose name escapes me. I'd said the words in my head as Grandma let a torrid summer breeze commit my mother to the shallow water, the current drifting toward the Pamlico Sound, silent and solemn.

Shortly afterward, Uncle Jack's father died and he inherited his family's dairy farm in Morganton. He and Aunt Lorraine sold their white clapboard house down the dirt road from ours and moved to the other side of the state. Grandma rented out our fields and sold the hogs and most of the equipment, and she and I settled into a quiet routine. We never spoke of Claudia, not even in whispers. We never entered her room, not even on pretext. She was dead. And it's always best to bury the dead, especially those who chose to be dead. Sooner the better.

****

Road construction on I-40 had kept Aunt Lorraine and Uncle Jack from my great-grandfather's funeral. They pulled into the driveway just as Grandma and I plodded into the mudroom, our faces flushed from the icy air. Aunt Lorraine scurried inside, carrying a bag of paper plates and cups and a box of cupcakes—for the reception, she said.

"There won't be a reception," Grandma said.

"Why not?" Aunt Lorraine lit a cigarette, her face pinched and disapproving.

"Daddy hadn't seen a living soul except family in years. He wouldn't want a bunch of folks coming by now. He wouldn't know any of them from Adam, anyway." She looked tired, old, her face vacant, her skin like gray gossamer. The lines around her mouth formed parentheses, enclosing thin lips and slightly crooked front teeth, like asides, supplementary information about a life marked by resignation and loss. She poured herself a cup of coffee then sat down to eat one of the cupcakes.

Uncle Jack barged through the back door hauling two suitcases. He dropped them on the linoleum floor emphatically and massaged his biceps. "You'd think we were staying a week, Lorraine."

"I never know what I'll need," she said.

I'd moved my necessities to the living room, where I'd bunk on the sofa until they left. There were three bedrooms in our house, and all three were occupied—two by the living, one by the dead. I'd sacrificed mine for the occasion; the other two had not.

Grandma glanced at the clock above the table. "Y'all must be hungry. The Ladies Auxiliary brought over a hamper of food this morning. Dig around in the refrigerator and fix yourselves a plate." She patted my knee. "Go on, honey. You need to eat something."

"I'm not hungry," I muttered. I'd felt as if I were waffling in a gray fog since my great-grandfather's death, viewing everything around me through cloudy eyes. Even food looked gray. The sight of it left me dizzy.

Aunt Lorraine combed her fingers through my hair. "You finally cut off that rattail, I see. Looks much better. You always did have beautiful hair, dark and thick. Don't be surprised if you have to color it before you're twenty, though. Everyone on Mama's side of the family turns gray early. Lord knows what my mop looks like underneath thirty years of Miss Clairol."

Uncle Jack slopped potato salad on a plate with cold fried chicken and macaroni and cheese and sat down next to me. "How's the fundraising going for your senior trip?" he asked. "Where's she going, Lorraine? Spain?"

"Mexico, Jack. She's going to Mexico."

"That's right, Mexico. How you coming in the money department?"

I shrugged, anxious to escape the familial chitchat for the refuge of my room. "Okay," I said. "I'm still working after school at KFC. I've almost got enough for the deposit."

"Got a passport yet?" he asked.

"It came a couple weeks ago." I tried not to look at him. Uncle Jack ate with his mouth open, and a renegade particle of some vegetable or meat would invariably wind up stuck between his front teeth.

"Sounds like you're on top of things," he said.

Aunt Lorraine fished an envelope from her purse. "We figured you could use this now rather than later, what with your deposit due next month and all." She handed me the envelope and kissed my cheek. "Happy almost-graduation, sweetie."

"I thought we were gonna wait until tomorrow," Grandma said. "Today hardly seems like the right time."

"It's the perfect time, Mama. We could use a little pick-me-up. Go on, Luna."

I tore open the envelope and unfolded a check. "Thanks," I said, proffering a grateful nod. I wrapped my arms around Grandma then gave Aunt Lorraine and Uncle Jack polite hugs.

"You're gonna have a wonderful trip, sweetie." She ran her fingers through my hair again. "You know, it might be even better if we do something with this hair. How about I take you to the salon tomorrow."

I stiffened.

"Lorraine, why don't you fix yourself a plate and sit down and eat," Grandma said tersely.

Aunt Lorraine threw up her hands in mock surrender. "I didn't mean anything by that, sweetie. Do what you want with your hair. It was just a thought."

Uncle Jack popped open one of the suitcases and brought out a slim square-shaped package crudely wrapped in Happy Graduation paper.

"Heavens, Jack, let's save something for graduation day," Grandma said.

"We're not together all that often anymore, so let's celebrate now. Luna will have a lot going on that weekend." He passed me the package. "I got it the other day. Reminded me of . . . Well, see for yourself."

Grandma scrunched her brow. "What in the world, Lorraine?"

"Don't ask me. I don't have any idea what that is."

I ripped off the paper. A glacial shudder ran through me.

Aunt Lorraine squinted at the record album I held in my hands then slammed the plastic pitcher of tea on the countertop. A tsunami of amber liquid washed over the rim and drowned what was left of the chicken. "My god, Jack. What were you thinking?"

Grandma craned her neck to get a better look. "What is it?"

"Calm down, Lorraine. It's just a record."

"You know perfectly well it's not *just* a record. Give it to me, Luna. Don't look at it."

I clutched the album, my body numb.

"Will somebody tell me what it is?" Grandma insisted.

"It's a record by that guitarist Claudia was so crazy about," Uncle Jack said. The late afternoon sun streamed through the sheer curtains above the sink, spotlighting the man's face on the cover. "Remember? Jimmy Page," Uncle Jack said.

Grandma squeezed the edge of the table, what little color that remained in her face leaching away.

"Actually, it's not gonna be released until the summer, but a friend of mine's got a son who's a hotshot music critic for some magazine in New York. He gets advance copies all the time. I saw this at Fred's house and—"

"Stop it, Jack," Aunt Lorraine hissed.

He crossed his legs at the ankles and stroked his beard, a stance he took whenever he was about to launch into a diatribe. "For nine years we've acted like Claudia never existed. It's time we stopped this foolishness. Her baby's about to graduate high school. Claudia would wanna be a part of it. She'd wanna be remembered at a time like this. Seems like when I saw the record it was some sort of sign."

"What does shoving that man's music in Luna's face have to do with remembering . . . Claudia?" Aunt Lorraine sputtered her name as if she were hocking a wad of my great-grandfather's chewing tobacco into a spit cup.

"Because besides Luna, she loved *that man* and his music more than anything else. It's his first solo record, and she'd have been over the moon about it. She'd have given it to Luna herself."

My eyes wavered over the close-up of Jimmy Page in a black and gray striped jacket and black shirt, holding his guitar erect in front of him, a blur of light encompassing him, the blur of movement, lateral movement—a blazing star shooting sideways. His lips are taut, eyes fixed in a basilisk stare.

Fixed, but not dilated.

I felt a seizing vertigo, the gold and white paisley wallpaper suddenly a sickening morass.

"Don't you remember that *song*, Jack? The one she used to play when she had those spells? Why would you—"

"That's a Led Zeppelin song, Lorraine. It's on one of their records, not this one."

"But he's part of that song. Don't you see?" she said

pleadingly. "You brought that song back into this house."

He sighed heavily. "Honey, that song never left this house."

" 'Four Sticks,' " I said blankly. "That song is called 'Four Sticks.' "

****

The fog enfolds me, cold, vacuous, soundless. I'm vanishing in a supernova in slow motion—one cell, one breath, one heartbeat at a time—falling backward, back to the beginning. In the beginning there is truth, knowledge, and light. There is music, my mother's voice, her face, her laugh.

I'm in her room—with the yellow walls and lavender incense burning on her dresser and the black and white photograph of Jimmy Page on the wall above her bed. He's young—late twenties, I think—ethereal, luminous, even in black and white.

Claudia is here, swaying to the music, that jungle beat, that feverish guitar. Her shadow flickers in the moonlight streaming through the curtains.

Listen to the song, *she tells me.*

I shake my head.

Ain't in your head, girl, *she says in my great-grandfather's craggy voice.*

I search the room. Underneath the bed. In the closet, wire hangers dangling like bones with the flesh stripped away.

Jimmy is watching, keeping vigil from above, his arms outstretched, waiting.

Glory be to the Father, *I say.*

Claudia reaches for me. Her arms are red. Her hair is red.

Glory be to the Daughter, *she says.*

And to the Holy Ghost, *I say.*

She's crying.

When the river runs dry, Mama . . .

Her tears are red.

When the river runs dry, Mama, in your room with the yellow walls and lavender incense burning on your dresser and the black and white photograph of Jimmy Page above your bed and your shadow, swaying to the music, flickering in the moonlight streaming through the curtains. When the river runs dry, Mama, how do you feel?

****

I awoke on the sofa, Grandma fanning my face with a copy of *Good Housekeeping*, Aunt Lorraine and Uncle Jack squabbling in the hall over whether to call 911. Music rang in my ears, like phantom pain from a severed limb.

"Luna," Grandma said. Her voice was tangled in the music.

I blinked my eyes. The gauzy glow of the floor lamp made my head swim.

"She's coming around," Uncle Jack said. "Put the phone down, Lorraine."

"She should still see a doctor," she said.

"Hell, I took harder knocks than that every day at football practice when I was her age. She'll have a goose egg fit to burst for a couple days, but she'll be fine."

Grandma tossed the magazine back on the coffee table and lifted my shoulders from the pillow. Aunt Lorraine slipped a bag of frozen peas behind my head then eased me back down.

"I need my journal," I sputtered. Not the one Claudia had

given me when I was nine. I'd torched it in a burn barrel in the backyard the day after scattering her ashes. My journals now were crude wire-bound notebooks I hid underneath my mattress and in a box in my closet.

Grandma looked perplexed. "You need your journal? Why?"

"I have to write about it before I forget."

She sat on the edge of the sofa next to me and stroked my arm. "Forget what, honey?"

"Where I was."

Aunt Lorraine knelt beside me. "What do you mean where you were?"

I thought of the *Outrider* album, Jimmy's stare on the cover, scuffed green and white linoleum as old as Aunt Lorraine shifting underneath my feet, rising to catch me, to cradle me, lull me to sleep.

"You didn't go anywhere, honey," Grandma said. "You've been right here all along."

A bitter sob rose in my throat. *No*, I thought, *I've been to Oz and back.*

****

Aunt Lorraine stashed the album in her suitcase after I fainted and forbade Uncle Jack to mention it or Claudia again. *We'll go back to the way things were before*, I heard her tell him. *It'll be all right if we just pretend this never happened. It never should have happened.*

The day they left, I swapped a Siouxsie & The Banshees record for *Outrider*. At first I just sat in my closet and studied the nondescript black disc, his name—Jimmy Page—stamped on the label in the center like the eye of a hurricane. By dinnertime I'd placed it on my turntable. I wasn't ready to play it. Not yet. I would wait—for what I wasn't exactly sure. I wasn't superstitious. I didn't believe in premonitions or talking fireplaces. I didn't believe that my eyes—anthracite, smoldering, Claudia had described them—evinced evil, as a classmate had once claimed. I didn't even believe in evil, as such. Yet something—instinct or delusion—told me to wait.

That night, Grandma and I sprawled on the sofa and watched Edward G. Robinson shoot up a black and white town on the classic movies channel, my legs draped across her lap. She hadn't spoken of the fainting incident since it happened. I was ambulatory and clear-eyed; that was indication enough for her that she needn't phone Dr. Hollis.

"It's nice to have a little peace and quiet again," she said during a commercial for tampons. She usually found an excuse to run to the kitchen for something or make idle conversation until such as that passed.

"Aunt Lorraine's anything but peaceful or quiet," I grumbled.

Grandma swatted my leg. "She means well. And she loves you. You're the only baby she's ever had."

"She doesn't know me. She wants me to be some girly girl, with pink lipstick and geeky hair. It's like she thinks I'm a doll she can dress up."

"That's silly."

"Bullshit."

"Luna, stop cursing. I swanny, I don't know where you learned to talk like that. Not from me, I'll tell you that much."

Edward G. Robinson collapsed in a barrage of gunfire, mortally wounded. *You should have come out when I told you to*, Sergeant Flaherty said. *Mother of mercy*, Rico gasped, *is this the end of Rico?* I watched him die with his eyes open, campy music playing in the background. The actor would die another death decades after the movie was filmed, the kind of death you're supposed to have—in a warm bed, loved ones at your side, one of them, the most loved, holding your hand, whispering your name, your eyes closed in hermetic pageantry, skin untarnished, translucent, bloodless.

There is no blood in a good death.

"Tell me something about Claudia," I blurted. Her name felt foreign on my tongue. The letters had a sound and meaning all their own, the syllables out of sync and strident.

Grandma watched the credits roll on the screen, the prominent vein in her neck bulging.

"I don't even have a picture of her," I continued, my heart thundering. "I can hardly remember her face." I clicked off the TV and sat up. "Her hands. I remember her hands."

Grandma was still staring at the screen, as if she were waiting for the picture to come back on and Edward G. Robinson to resurrect and walk off into a Hollywood sunset.

"You have her hands," she said flatly. "Same long fingers and slender wrists. I tried to get her to take up piano when she was in grade school. Even got her lessons with the church organist. She went a month and quit. Didn't wanna learn scales—you know, the basics. She always did wanna fly before she could walk."

I imagined her sitting at the upright Baldwin in the corner of the room, bored by the prosaic practice tunes the organ lady had assigned, searching for the notes to the dulcet intro of "Stairway to Heaven" instead, though "Stairway to Heaven" hadn't even been recorded then. In my entire life, I never heard her play that piano.

"Was she crazy, Grandma?"

"Where'd you hear that?" she said sharply.

"Was she?"

The timer on the washing machine buzzed. Grandma headed to the mudroom to add the softener, the canvas soles of her slippers clip-clipping across the floor. I pulled the afghan she'd made for my eighteenth birthday over me and gingerly laid back down. The knot on my head smarted when I put pressure on it.

She's not right in the head, Mama, I'd heard Aunt Lorraine say of Claudia once. Why the head, I thought now. Why not a toe or a fingernail? Why not the birthmark on her belly that looked like a little red dot? You could remove a birthmark. You could clip a nail. You could even amputate a toe without much detriment. But a head? Especially one as ineffable as Claudia's. You couldn't do without a head.

Grandma pulled a load of towels from the dryer then trudged upstairs to bed. She was exhausted, she said, worn out from the whirlwind of weekend activity, the extra bodies in the house, and the one we'd buried in the frozen ground a few miles away. I dozed fitfully through another old movie then dragged upstairs to my room. I flipped on the overhead light and immediately glimpsed a photograph on my bed that had not been there before. I recognized the shot, remembered the moment I'd clicked the shutter button. My first camera, a Polaroid. We were in the electronics department at Dawson's.

Claudia is leaning against a display cabinet, arms akimbo, her golden hair swept up in a bun, cerulean sweater as frayed as her jeans. She's gazing into the camera. Gazing at me, through me, through the swinging glass doors behind me, into the morning light, the morning sky, and whatever lay beyond. Now she is beyond.

"I see you," I said aloud. "I see you, Claudia."

CHAPTER FOUR

TO SLIP inside another's soul, if only for a moment, to share that space, relive the memory. To know the whats and the whys. How to do it? Where to start? A door had yawned open inside me. I'd seen my mother in her room, touched her, heard her voice—powerful, numinous. I wondered, when Dorothy awoke in Kansas, a goose egg fit to burst on her head, did she ever cross the rainbow again? Did she even try?

"What the hell are you talking about?" my friend Connie said, gazing at me nonplussed.

"You heard me," I said resolutely.

"You want me to get you mushrooms. As in 'shrooms." She pinched the bridge of her nose and shook her head. "How am I supposed to do that, for fuckssake?"

Mrs. Neville cut her eyes at us from the front of the classroom. We were supposed to be peer-reviewing our essays on *Wuthering Heights,* a superfluous task since I'd written both mine and Connie's. For quid pro quo, she'd agreed to do my math homework for the week. Both of her parents were CPAs. She had fractions and decimals in her genes.

"Denzel Gaynor has a crush on you," I whispered. "Maybe you could ask him."

"He's not a dealer."

"I know, but I heard him bragging about doing 'shrooms

with his cousin once. He'll know how to get some."

"Jesus, Luna. You're weird enough sober. Besides, I thought we agreed we'd stay way the hell away from shit like that." She hunched over my paper, pretending to mark nonexistent errors. I felt a sudden urge to touch her hair. She had a spongy black afro she'd boldly grown after our African American history teacher gave her a 45 of James Brown's "I'm Black and I'm Proud" when we were sixteen. She'd shown me how to comb it with her pick, and I'd let her braid my rattail before I cut it off.

"I'll only do it once," I said. "I promise."

"Why do you wanna do it at all?"

I slipped my hoodie over my head and slumped in my seat. "The situation calls for it."

Mrs. Neville tapped her dog-eared copy of *Wuthering Heights* on the podium and admonished us.

"We're discussing the insufficiency of quotes in her essay," I said glibly.

"And the complete lack of any in hers," Connie added.

"Well do it quietly. And take that hoodie off your head, Luna. No hats in school." She glared at me until I complied then returned to her book.

I lurched my desk closer to Connie's and scrawled *please* at the top of her paper.

"What situation?" she muttered.

"I can't tell you," I said.

Her eyes slid off me to the black and white checkered floor, and I knew I'd hurt her feelings. We'd been inseparable since eighth grade when she'd joined me in pummeling Kevin Irwin for blowing spitballs at us on the school bus. He and his cohorts had singled us out—Connie, for having the audacity to be an affluent black girl in a small Southern town whose public schools had only integrated the decade before; me, for daring to swap white lace granny dresses for black hoodie sweatshirts and black lipstick, pigtails for rattails, the moon for its nemesis after my mother died. At first, the kids had shied away from me, as if tragedy were contagious. Then came the taunts about Claudia. They could overlook her out-of-wedlock pregnancy—most of them had one or two shotgun weddings in their own families. But suicide, with its violence and complete disregard for the Will of God, they couldn't abide. My mother had committed the most unholy of sins, and her blood had marked her daughter more conspicuously than a Scarlet Letter. Eventually, they moved on to more tangible fodder, like my clothes and hair, and relegated Claudia to forgotten local legend. Connie had most certainly been privy to gossip about her, but she'd never broached the subject with me. I'd never talked about my mother with her or anyone else, and I wasn't prepared to start now.

"Please, Connie. Just this once."

She heaved a dramatic sigh. "I'll see what I can do."

****

Denzel slipped me the mushrooms in the school parking lot the next afternoon. Just like that, a simple exchange of cash for a paper bag of unchartered territory, as if we were trading lunches in the cafeteria—chicken salad for mystery meat.

"How long will it take to kick in?" I asked.

"Average person, 'bout a half hour. Skinny girl like you,

probably less." He brought his pudgy hands to his mouth and blew on them. I could feel the steel gray cold of his breath on my face. "Make sure you wait 'til after your grandma goes to bed," he said.

"She'll be gone most of the evening. Some church thing." I opened the bag and studied the contents. "Looks like regular mushrooms. You sure they're the right kind?"

He snickered. "You'll find out."

I felt my chest tighten. "How will they make me feel?"

He seemed to ponder the question. "Unbelievable," he finally said. "Like a god."

God the Father, and the Daughter, and the Holy Spirit.

We were all three in my room that night.

I'd lined up photographs of Claudia on the windowsill. I had several of them by then. Each night I'd find a new one on my bed, sometimes with a keepsake of Claudia's—her jangly anklet, her favorite rhinestone ring, the apotropaic crystals she'd bought at the county fair from a sideshow fortuneteller. Grandma had become Boo Radley. We never spoke of the treasures that magically appeared in my room those winter evenings of 1988. But we did speak of Claudia. Grandma allotted five minutes once a day for me to ask questions about her. That was as much as she could take. I never asked about my father, the man with no name or face or form. Sometimes I doubted I even had one. I never asked why Claudia had left us the way she did. I didn't have to be told those two questions were taboo, and I didn't want to risk Grandma's silence again.

I turned up the volume on my stereo. I'd played the entire *Outrider* album twice already, but I couldn't hear the songs. "Wasting My Time" sounded like "Four Sticks" in my head;

all of the songs sounded like "Four Sticks"; all three of the vocalists Jimmy had used sounded like Robert Plant singing "Four Sticks," including Robert Plant singing "The Only One," a track on *Outrider*. All I could hear was owls crying and those drums and that guitar and a crystalline wind howling in my head. Or maybe it was my mother's breath in my ears.

I hear you, Claudia.

I didn't know memory came in colors, that it could pulsate through your body in fulgent shades of red and orange, then fade like jeans to dusky blue. Or that the word, swirling in the back of your throat, tasted like rusted metal, like the corroded bicycle rack I'd once kissed on a grammar school dare. I didn't know it could take the form of fire and water, or whirl and twirl and churl inside the song blasting through my stereo speakers.

The unraveling of subterranean spaces . . .

I pressed my palms against my cheeks. I felt my head expand and grow light. *Light as a feather, stiff as a board.* How amazing to fly and still remain on terra firma.

I sat on the cold wood floor and sweated. The votive candles on my bookshelves flickered, flames dancing like tribal fire. The space heater hummed. It sounded like "Four Sticks," too.

The room had become sepulchral. I felt like Annabel Lee in her tomb by the sea. I kept watch for Claudia. I wanted to play Jimmy's record for her. She'd parse each song like a surgeon's knife, examine the innards with microscopic precision—the colon of "Emerald Eyes," kidneys of "Prison Blues," liver of "Hummingbird," cerebral cortex of "Liquid Mercury," Jimmy's guitar the lifeblood pulsing through the veins. She'd put a pen in my hand and say, *Write, Luna. Get it all down. Don't listen to the owls. Don't listen to the dead.*

But you are the dead, I'd say, her gilded shadow glinting in the flames.

Then I'm not really here. Say it, she'd insist.

You're not really here.

Except she was. I could smell her mango-scented shampoo, taste her butterscotch voice.

"This is not a dream," I bellowed.

Are the walls of my room still yellow? she asked.

"I don't know."

Is Jimmy's picture above my bed?

"I don't know."

Go and see, she said.

"I can't."

Go and see.

"We don't go in there."

Why not?

A flood of Technicolor memories swept over me. Grandma holding me in her lap on her bed, a quilt wrapped around us, both of us shivering in the stifling summer heat. Policemen with their notepads and probing eyes. Aunt Lorraine mounting the stairs, reaching the landing, approaching Claudia's door. A policeman—a friend of Uncle Jack's—pulling her aside. *Don't go in there, Lorraine.* Her face, dazed, oblivious. *Why not?* she'd asked. *Because they ain't cleaned it yet.*

I squeezed my knees to my chest. *There's no place like home there's no place like home there's no place like home.*

That's why people leave home, Luna, Claudia said.

"I can't go in there."

Yes you can. Take the record and play it on my stereo. That's where it belongs.

I rocked back and forth on my heels.

You can do it, Luna. She waited. *Do it.*

I crawled to my stereo and lifted the record from the turntable, then slipped it back inside the Siouxsie & the Banshees album sleeve.

That's my Lunabelle. Go on.

I crept through the doorway into the hall. It looked smaller, darker. Another sepulcher. I was sweating, my hair damp against my neck.

Just a few steps farther, she said. *Straight ahead.*

I felt my way along the wall, like a blind girl in a funhouse.

That's it. You're almost there.

My fingers brushed the door. The wood was cold, sardonic. I wrapped my hand around the knob.

Open it.

"I can't," I stammered.

You've come this far.

I turned the knob.

Go on.

I gave the door a nudge. I knew it would be swollen after all those years, that the hinges would creak and groan like Marley's ghost. I gave it a harder shove and it yielded.

Turn on the light, Claudia said. *I want to see.*

I don't want to see, I thought. *I want to drift in this liminal space, in limbo, between heaven and hell. That's salvation enough.*

What are you waiting for? she said. *You asked for this.*

"No I didn't," I cried.

Yes, you did.

"Well I don't want it anymore." My head was fuzzy. *I'm going to faint again*, I thought. *I'm going to crack my head on the floor and get trapped in this nightmare forever.*

Turn on the light, Luna. I want to see my room.

"I'm fucked up," I said. "I don't want to see it—not like this. I'm too fucked up."

I tossed the record into her room, then slammed the door and slumped to the floor, my head spinning. I hadn't asked Denzel how long the high would last. I would have to be patient. I would stay there in the darkness, eyes closed, still, quiet, floating like an embryo, and wait for the rainbow's end.

CHAPTER FIVE

CONNIE AND I sat on the hood of her Chevette in the KFC parking lot and passed a can of Coors back and forth. We'd just finished our shifts, and the smell of sweat and fried chicken lingered on our clothes and in our hair.

"So how'd it go?" she asked, leaning in to me, as if she were awaiting the revelation of a top-secret message. She'd held out until now—longer than I'd expected.

I took a swig of beer then lit a cigarette, the searing red embers glowing in the dark.

"Come on, tell me. Denzel said you'd probably freak out. You should've let me come over and babysit."

"I didn't want company."

She snatched the cigarette from my lips and flicked it into a mop pail beside the dumpster. "I thought you quit."

"I did."

"What's with you lately?"

I gazed at the moon. It was full that night, pellucid, with a silver-limned halo. *Don't eyeball the moon,* my great-grandfather used to say. *Do, you get youself some bad luck.* I was fettered to his folklore, just as I was fettered to my hometown—the backroads leading from Main Street to our farm, where Uncle Jack had taught me to drive; the public library where Claudia discovered Arthur Rimbaud and Henry

Miller and read me poems by Sylvia Plath and Adrienne Rich, the two of us huddled together on one of the plush sofas; the roller rink where I had my ninth birthday party; the strip mall where Connie and I perused albums in the Record Shack and gorged on donuts at Jerry's Sweet Shop; the Homecoming dances in the high school gym I was never invited to; Fourth of July fireworks on the Town Common, Uncle Jack carrying me on his shoulders, shielding me from the boisterous crowd; paper sailboat races on the Tar River with my Brownies troop, the same river that would harbor my mother's ashes a year later; the road that twined between the hospital and Highway 264 then on to I-40, westbound, in pursuit of Manifest Destiny, just like Jack Kerouac, Claudia would say. She'd drive us in her VW Bug to the city limits and park on the side of the road and watch the cars streak by. *Where are they going?* I'd ask. *To freedom*, she'd say. *Is that a place, Claudia? Yes, baby. Where is it?* She'd pop a Led Zeppelin eight-track into the tape deck then pull back onto the blacktop. *Anywhere but here,* she'd whisper.

"Do you ever think about leaving Full River?" I asked Connie. "Starting over someplace else?"

She cocked her head. "Yeah, when I go to college."

"I mean now."

"And screw up my chance to be a mogul on Wall Street? Hell no." Connie zipped up her coat and stuffed her hands in her pockets. She'd planned her future when she was twelve years old. UNC-Chapel Hill for undergrad, NYU for grad, then on to Wall Street, where she'd rule Goldman Sachs by the time she was thirty. Failure was inconceivable. Her parents had made sure both of their daughters believed that.

"I don't know," I said. "Expect poison from the standing

water."

"What?"

"It's from William Blake."

"Oh shit, we've got a test on him and that other dude on Monday."

"Keats," I said. "It wouldn't hurt you to read some of this stuff. You might like it."

"Yeah well, it wouldn't hurt you to do your own trig homework. Besides, I hate all that ode shit. Who writes an ode to an urn?"

A line of cars pulled in from the boulevard and snaked around the building to the drive-thru. I pitched the empty can into the mop pail with my soggy cigarette.

"I needed 'shrooms because I wanted to see my mom," I said. The words penetrated the crisp air like a lanced wound. I wanted to grab them, choke them back down, undo my undoing.

Connie's eyes fluttered. "What do you mean?"

"Something happened the night my great-grandfather died," I said. "Something that has to do with my mom."

Connie let loose a stupefied whistle and dug through her backpack for another Coors.

"Take it easy," I said. "Big Brother's watching."

"They can't see dick from way over there." She retrieved another beer and handed it to me. She'd filched a six-pack from her dad's cache. He didn't keep count and she wasn't greedy, so he never noticed when one went missing every now and then. "You never talked about your mom before," she said, then hesitated. "Is it true she shot herself?"

I grimaced. "I don't wanna talk about that."

I cracked open the beer and took a sip, felt the bitter sting as it raced down my throat. The bitter end. The bitter beginning. I couldn't figure out the taste of the middle, that amorphous gully in the marrow of loss.

"A couple days after my great grandfather died, my uncle gave me this record, and I passed out and had some sort of—I don't know what it was. My mom was there. I could see her, feel her, hear her." I watched Connie's expression shift from surprise to incredulity. "I know it sounds crazy," I said. "I hadn't even really thought about her since she died. It was like I'd totally blocked her out. Now all these memories keep surfacing, only most of them are kinda freaky, like they don't seem real but I know they are. At least I think they are." I took another pull on my beer. "Anyway, I just wanted to see her again after that, and I couldn't think of any other way."

"Holy shit," Connie said under her breath. "You really passed out? As in hit the floor passed out?" I took her hand and placed it on the knot on the back of my head. "Damn. Must've been a hell of a record."

"You've heard of Led Zeppelin, right?" I said.

She shrugged. "Yeah, I guess so."

"My mom had a thing for the guitarist, Jimmy Page. She thought he put messages in their music about them, especially in this one song, like they were star-crossed lovers or some bullshit like that."

Connie tapped her fingernails on the can. She had a congenital inability to fathom anything but the literal, the logical. "What kind of messages?" she asked dubiously.

I should stop right now, I thought. Change the subject, talk about something banal, the weather maybe—*it's fucking cold, colder than usual this winter, remember the last time it was this fucking cold it snowed over two feet and that old lady who lived between Full River and Grimesland froze to death in her trailer. Which do you think is worse, freezing to death or burning to ash?* Talk about anything else, or better yet, don't talk at all. I was betraying Claudia somehow, betraying my family's silence. *We'll go back to the way things were before. It'll be all right if we just pretend this never happened,* Aunt Lorraine had said. *Do you think the dead can see the living,* I thought, *does their vaporous skin still smell of lavender and moonlight, can they follow you from one room to another, command you to enter with a butterscotch whisper?*

I combed my fingers through my hair, found the knot and pressed it hard. I wanted to feel the pain. I wanted to remember it. All of it. *Before* was rooted in *now*, a stopped clock on a dead man's mantle. Silence wasn't a panacea, a vehicle to oblivion. Not anymore.

Connie nudged me. "Come on, Luna. What kind of messages?"

"I don't know exactly," I said, surprisingly calm. "She'd get all weepy talking about him sometimes, though."

"No kidding? So they actually met?"

"Yeah—well, I think so. She used to talk about going to a Led Zeppelin concert in Raleigh or Charlotte. Could've been Greensboro. As far as I know, she never traveled outside North Carolina, so it had to have been someplace in-state."

One of the assistant managers emerged through the back door and waved at us. We hid our beers inside our coats and waited for him to jog to his car then peel out of the parking lot.

Connie handed me what was left of her beer. "You finish it.

I gotta drive."

"Just pour it out," I said. "I gotta eat dinner and do homework when I get home, and I'm already buzzing."

She grumbled something about not wasting perfectly good beer and took a gulp. "So when was that concert?" she asked, wiping her mouth with the back of her hand.

"I'm not sure," I said. "Wait, winter 1969. She told me she got the ticket on her birthday. Late February 1969. Funny," I said, marveling at the circularity. "She would've been the same age I am now when she went to that concert."

Connie slapped my thigh. "Christ on a stick, Luna. Your birthday is in November."

"I know when my birthday is. So what?"

"So you would've been conceived in late February of '69, and you said your mom told you she met Jimmy Page in late February of '69."

I pushed her hand away. "I didn't say for sure she met him. I just said she went to a Zeppelin concert."

"Why would she think he put messages about them in a song if they never met?" She hopped off the car and began to pace in front of me. "Can you imagine? You could be a Rock star's kid."

I snorted. "Denzel slip you some 'shrooms too?"

"No really, think about it."

"Connie."

She was gesticulating ardently. "Seriously, do the math."

"Connie, get a grip. Jimmy Page is *not* my old man."

She looked at me with a mix of revelation and bewilderment. "Well then," she said, "who is?"

My eyes flashed, radiant with anger. Bone-deep anger. Then something else. A sort of emptiness. One that had always been there—nameless, inchoate, now tangible. I felt nothing, except the nothing.

"Oh shit, I'm sorry, Luna." She sat back down, wrapped her arm around my shoulder, pulled me close, the butterfly comb in her afro scraping my cheek. "It's the beer," she said. "I'm really sorry."

We sat there for another few minutes in silence, the cold seeping through the seat of our pants, the tips of our noses raw, then she drove me home.

She put the car in park in the gravel driveway and let the engine idle, headlights illuminating the tire swing hanging from a pecan tree by the car shed.

"You okay?" she asked. She was unusually contrite, solicitous even. She knew she'd crossed a line. She'd listened to my confession then tried to force more. She leaned back against the headrest, her hands on the steering wheel. "Look, just forget everything I said. What do I know, anyway?"

I clutched the door handle and fixed my eyes on the tire swing. Claudia used to push me on it. Higher and higher. Until I thought I was flying. If I concentrated hard enough on that tire swing, could I fly back to the moment I was conceived? See my father's face looming over Claudia's, breathe his scent—a piquant blend of sweat and desire? Could I feel the second I became a possibility, the moment he became a mystery? What if I could conjure him like memory?

"Luna?"

I blinked back into myself. "I'm fine, Connie. Really." I gave her a quick hug then hurried inside.

"That you, Luna?" Grandma called. "Come on in and set the table."

She was standing at the kitchen counter rubbing garlic on the pork chops she was about to broil, the sleeves of her cardigan pushed up to her elbows, her salt-and-pepper hair already pin curled for the night. Loretta Lynn sang about a cheating husband on the radio.

Grandma sniffed the air then drew a disapproving breath. "You been smoking again?"

I dropped my backpack on the floor. "Do you know who my father is?" I asked curtly.

She braced herself against the counter, her back to me.

"Grandma?"

"What time is it?" she asked coldly.

I glanced at the clock. "Almost seven."

"You've got five minutes. Starting thirty seconds ago."

"Who is he?"

She slid the pan of pork chops into the oven then drained a pot of potatoes.

"You said I've got five minutes, so tell me. Who is he?"

"Four minutes."

"Damn it, Grandma, you've gotta know something. Didn't you ask her when you found out she was pregnant?"

She whipped around, her face a rictus of indignation. "Of course I asked. We all asked. Your Granddaddy Hyram would've shot a no-count field hand he suspected if I hadn't stopped him."

"So he was a field hand?" I asked.

Her eyes filled. "She wouldn't say."

"Well, were there other boys who used to come around that winter?"

She sighed impatiently. "Boys were always around. They'd

flirt with her on the farm in the summer, and the ones who didn't move on would chase after her at school. Used to make Lorraine pea-green with envy. Jack's the only one who ever paid Lorraine any mind." Grandma squeezed her eyes shut and shook her head. "Claudia dated a few of those boys. I recall one she carried on with the summer before you came along. Hyram put a stop to that after he caught them together at the end of the season, though. There were a few boys after him, but she wasn't all that interested in any of them, far as I could tell, and I never saw her with anyone after she got pregnant."

"So you're saying my mother was a slut."

Grandma slapped me hard across the face. "Don't you use that kind of language when you talk about her. Hear me? You don't know what happened."

She'd never hit me before—not once. Not when I wrote *fuck* in black Magic Marker on the cloakroom floor in sixth grade. Not when I absconded to my dugout in the woods with my favorite piglet after I read *Charlotte's Web*. Not when I shaved my head when I was fourteen just because. Never.

"Luna, I . . ." She wrung her hands, as if she were trying to wipe away the evidence like Lady Macbeth. "I'm sorry, honey."

"Doesn't matter," I blustered. "I don't care about any of it anyway."

I bounded upstairs to my room and locked the door.

"Luna, come back here," Grandma called. In a minute she knocked lightly on the door. "Let me in."

I wiped my nose on my sleeve. "Go away."

I could hear her breathing hard in the hall and worried she'd overexerted herself. "I'm fine, Grandma," I said softly. "Just leave me alone for a little while."

"If I do, will you promise to come down to dinner in a bit?"

I flopped on the bed and hugged my stuffed Snoopy, a present from Santa when there still was Santa, and the Easter Bunny and the Great Pumpkin, and my mother. They were all gone now. Only Grandma remained.

"I'll come down for dinner," I said. "I promise."

I waited until I heard her footsteps on the stairs then pulled my journal from underneath my mattress and flipped to the list of remaining questions I had about Claudia:

Did she want me?

Did she love me?

Am I like her?

Why was she so sad sometimes?

Why did she leave me?

I grabbed a pen from my nightstand drawer then wrote down one last question:

Who is my father?

Maybe Grandma wouldn't or couldn't tell me, but someone had to know. Who was my father? A field hand, a drifter, a boy Claudia knew in school? A Rock guitar god she met at a concert like a backstage groupie?

That was preposterous.

But what if it wasn't?

What if my father was a god?

CHAPTER SIX

THE FIRST time I saw Jimmy Page in living, pulsing color, I was six years old. Claudia had taken me to the drive-in to see Led Zeppelin's concert movie, *The Song Remains the Same*, filmed largely at Madison Square Garden in 1973, when Jimmy was twenty-nine. In an opening scene, before the concert begins, a man with dark hair and jeans sits on a blanket in an English garden playing a hurdy-gurdy, swans floating in the lake nearby. The camera approaches him from behind. Closer. Closer. The music stops. Closer. He pivots around and stares into the camera, his eyes a bubbling, glowing red.

I hid my face in my hands.

Claudia nestled her head on my shoulder. "It's just a fantasy, Luna. It's not real."

I peeked at the screen through my fingers. "Who is he?"

"The man in the black and white picture in my room. That's Jimmy."

"Uh uh," I said ardently. "It's the devil."

She clucked her tongue. "There's no such thing as the devil."

I watched Jimmy emerge from a plane with the other three band members, climb into a waiting limo, speed along a highway into New York City, then burst onto the stage like a dark angel with a six-string.

Claudia bolted from the car and began to twirl in the mottled light from the projector, her tie-dye skirt flapping in the breeze. She reminded me of a radiant Julie Andrews spinning on a verdant hillside in the Alps, alive with the sound of music.

"Look, Luna," she called. "He's beautiful."

He *was* beautiful, ethereal, with wavy dark hair that grazed his shoulders and a pre-Raphaelite face, like the ones I'd seen in Claudia's art history books. He tore through "Rock and Roll" with a febrile zeal that countered his delicate features. The ambiguity frightened me.

Claudia thrust her arms out, as if she were about to take flight. I closed my eyes, picturing her twirling in a ray of light, her yellow hair—blazing yellow—flowing down her back. She was flying, like those doves at the beginning of the film.

"Look, Luna." She opened my door and led me to the front of the car. Someone blew a horn. Someone else threw a cup of beer at us. Lascivious snickers. Catcalls and sneers. The air taut with sordidness.

"Claudia, we're in trouble!" I cried.

She clasped my hand and twirled me around, like those corny dancers with plasticine smiles and shellacked hair on the *Lawrence Welk Show*, Grandma's favorite Saturday night program.

Get back in your car, freak!

"We're in trouble, Claudia!"

I jerked away from her and urged her back inside the car. She watched Jimmy through the dusty windshield, transfixed. I watched with her, a box of half-eaten popcorn on my lap. He was a wizard, manipulating invisible energy around the

Theremin in "No Quarter," beguiling a doubleneck guitar in "The Rain Song," black shirt open in the front, stars and half-moons on black pants, cryptic silver pendant dangling from his neck.

I gazed at him, unsettled, my insides churning.

The scene shifted from Jimmy to Robert Plant, galloping on a steed toward a dreary castle with an eagle perched on his arm like a shield. The band had interspersed fantasy sequences throughout the film. In Robert's, he's a gallant knight who rescues a beautiful princess in a turret.

"Did you know that guy—like you knew Jimmy?" I asked cautiously, unsure if I wanted to hear the answer.

She smiled, her lean profile spectral in the flickering light. "How do you know I don't still know him?" A chill ran through me. "There are lots of ways to know someone, Luna. You can be face to face with a person and not know them at all. Or you can hear their voice in your head and know their soul."

The eerie bass line of "Dazed and Confused" began to thrum.

"I wanna go home," I said.

She eased back in the seat. "Not yet."

Halfway through "Dazed and Confused," a roadie hands Jimmy a violin bow from the shadowy wings of the stage. He stands alone under a spotlight and strokes the bow across the strings of his Les Paul. Slow, sensual, like a seduction. The scene shifts from Madison Square Garden to a blustery moonlit night in the Scottish Highlands. An ascot-clad Jimmy climbs a mountain. An old man, the mythical Hermit, like the one from Claudia's Tarot cards, stands alone at the crest, ominous music droning in the background. Jimmy reaches for the old man, who morphs into Jimmy himself, clad in a hooded gray robe, lantern in one hand, violin bow in the other. He sweeps it overhead like a saber while the scene fades back to Madison Square Garden—Jimmy in a halo of white light, back arched, bow commanding guitar strings. Intense, fast. Robert Plant's voice, a plaintive wail, in sync with the music. At the climax, Jimmy tosses the shredded bow into the audience like a discarded lover then launches into a blistering guitar solo.

"You see," Claudia said. "He's not the devil. He's just searching for the light."

"What light?"

"Knowledge. Truth. The things we're all searching for."

Her eyes were glassy. She was fading away. By the time we got home she'd be gone, locked in her room with Jimmy's black and white picture above her bed, "Four Sticks" blasting on her stereo. I would sit by the door and wail, *Claudia, let me in. Tell me the story of my name. I'm the moon and you're a goddess. Tell me. Tell me.*

"Why'd he turn into that old guy?" I asked frantically.

She gripped the steering wheel. "Because he found the light."

CHAPTER SEVEN

I USED to cut myself after Claudia died. Small slashes on my chest where no one could see. The pain was welcome, invited, each incision an ablution, a cleansing of knowledge and truth—what she'd done, what I'd seen. I climbed down the mountain one nick at a time, away from the light, away from the bow, the music and magic, the taste of her name on my lips. I burned her paintings and photographs, trashed board games and crayons and coloring books, doused clothes she'd bought me from yard sales and thrift shops with motor oil, flushed gold stud earrings she'd given me down the toilet then let the holes grow up, mauled my long hair with Grandma's pinking shears. I excised her from my life, along with any recognition of the girl I'd once been—her girl—and then I forgot her. Gradually, then completely.

I forgot Jimmy too. The last picture of him I'd seen was from 1979, the year before Led Zeppelin disbanded. Claudia had a copy of a music magazine with a story about their forthcoming album, *In Through the Outdoor,* released the month after she died that summer. He was thirty-five, still handsome, but gaunt and ashen. His royal blue shirt and white trousers billowed on him. Gone were the days of the black satin dragon suit and seraphic beauty. Rumor had it he was a junkie. Claudia placed the picture on the floor of her room and surrounded it with white candles and her healing crystals. She laid four Tarot cards above him—the Hermit, Temperance, Strength, and the Nine of Cups. For wisdom, healing, and happiness, she said. She played "Stairway to Heaven" and we sat with him, concentrating on the cards until the candles burned out.

He'd aged nearly ten years by the time I saw him again, on the cover of *Outrider*, but he looked much more robust. Claudia would have been pleased. *I told you*, she would have said, *the magic worked*.

"You look like him," Connie said, glancing from a poster of the cover of *Outrider* to me. We were conducting the examination in the Record Shack since Aunt Lorraine had taken the *Outrider* record sleeve home with her. She'd probably trashed it by now without ever discovering I'd switched the albums.

"Think so?" I said.

She studied his fuzzy image. "Kinda. It's hard to tell. You have another picture of him?"

I thought of the one above Claudia's bed. "No," I said.

"Why's the photo so blurry? Is he trying to hide some hideous scar? Does he have pockmarks, or something?"

I snatched the poster from her and returned it to the P slot in the bin. "He's good looking. You should see pictures of him from the early '70s."

"Maybe he hasn't aged well. He used to do smack, right? That shit'll rearrange your face."

"Trust me, he's cute," I said. "Which should be proof positive he's not my father."

"Don't start that. How many times have I told you you're pretty?"

"I know," I groaned. "I've got great hair."

She pulled one of the butterfly combs from her afro and adjusted it behind my ear. "You *do* have great hair. But I miss your rattail."

"I'm thinking of getting a Mohawk. My aunt will shit."

"Let her shit. You've got your own thing going. Fuck what anybody else thinks."

She reminded me of Claudia right then. *Don't listen to them, baby,* she'd said. *Fuck what anybody else thinks,* Connie had said. That's easy to say when you're beautiful. Like Claudia. And Connie. She bore an uncanny resemblance to Thelma from *Good Times,* with her plucky hair and silky skin and curvy body. I looked more like Patti Smith.

"No you don't," Connie chimed. "Whoever Patti Smith is. Okay, yeah, you're skinny, and it wouldn't hurt you to get a little sun, but . . . I don't know. You've got this look, like a fairy—enchanting in a way. It's in your face, but mainly your eyes, underneath all that black eyeliner and shadow, that is." She smirked. "Jesus, you got me talking all poetic like you."

I wondered how poetic she'd be if she saw the scars on my chest. I hadn't cut myself in years. The scars had largely faded. But they were still there, like a ghostly afterimage. I'd never told anyone about the times I would steal away to my dugout, nestled in a copse of trees near my great-grandfather's shack, and drag the razor blade across my skin—charily, just enough force to summon tiny beads of blood, enough to feel the sting, the rush. I'd press my finger against the wound then wipe the blood on a blank page in my journal, the date duly noted. No further entry. No *Today I feel X* or *Tonight I eyeballed the moon and got myself some bad luck* scribbled below. The red smear was enough.

Once Connie and I became friends I traded razor blades for cigarettes, a less salubrious habit, and one more difficult to hide, but I found that addiction the less desperate of the two. After that fortuitous moment in the back of a shabby Pitt County Schools bus when we were fourteen years old, bloody snot spewing from Kevin Irwin's mangled nose, I *was* less desperate. But I became just as addicted to smoking as I'd been to cutting. *It's a nasty habit you'll be sorry you started*, Grandma had said when she first smelled the telltale signs on my clothes. When I was sixteen, the mastectomy of her right breast and grueling course of chemo that followed compelled us both to quit. But the return of Claudia had rekindled my craving. This time I couldn't seem to shake it—or Claudia.

"I think you should buy that *Outrider* poster," Connie said. She was flipping through a stack of Janet Jackson albums looking for *Control*, switching her hips to the music on the store stereo. Connie owned whatever space she occupied. She moved swiftly, vibrantly, even when she was standing still. She was *esprit de corps* in motion, and I was in need of both. Maybe that's what drew her to me—a need to feed a need, to make a fraction whole.

"Let's go, Connie," I said, nodding toward the group of girls from school at the checkout counter, all of them dressed in spandex leggings and oversize sweaters and booties. One of them caught sight of me and flashed a mordant smile.

"Why do you let them get to you? In ten years they'll all be fat golf widows. But you, you'll already have bagged a kazillion dollar book deal."

I sucked my teeth. "Yeah, right."

Christy Alexander Hallberg

"Did you or did you not just publish one of your short stories?"

I swished my hand through the air lackadaisically. "It was just some stupid magazine."

"Oh please. You're a great writer, Luna."

I stuffed my hands in my pockets—my mother's hands. *You have her hands*, Grandma had said. Claudia had placed a pen in them when I was nine and told me to write. It was the only thing I was ever good at. In those first months after Claudia died, I didn't speak a word; instead, I wrote—vignettes, snapshots from a thwarted life, sepia and still. Then came the cryptic journal entries steeped in red. Later, short stories set in a small Southern town about an ancient soothsayer and a tortured young girl, Providence hot on her trail. One such story had caught the eye of an editor at *Teen* magazine, and I'd won a coveted spot in the 1988 winter issue. The day the magazine arrived in the mail I'd taken it to my dugout and sliced it to shreds with a razor. It was the closest I'd come to cutting myself in years, and the rush was palpable. I taped the sliver of paper with my byline on it in my journal. No further entry. The carnage was enough.

Connie finally spotted *Control* and pulled it from the stacks. "Gotcha, Miss Jackson."

I watched the girls skulking down the posters aisle toward us like a pack of Valley Girls on the hunt. They stopped in front of us, and Sonia Carter regarded me derisively. "What're you doing over here, Luna? The devil-worshiper bands are on the other side of the store."

I feigned a yawn and rolled my eyes. "Must be a slow night if that's the best you can come up with. Real original."

She folded her arms across her generous chest, the attribute that made her popular with jocks and the envy of her coterie—that and her talent for intimidation and insolence. "Whatever," she said. "I just came over to remind Connie about the senior trip meeting after school Monday."

"What meeting?" I asked.

She unwrapped a piece of bubblegum and popped it into her mouth. "Don't worry about it. I figured you'd fly to Mexico on your broomstick."

"Only if I can borrow yours," I threw back.

She blew a bubble then popped it with her finger. "You're cute, for a mutant," she said.

The other girls laughed on cue—three replicas of each other, right down to their supercilious expressions and blue eye shadow. Two of them had been in my Brownie troop when I was eight. We'd roasted weenies and marshmallows on a bonfire in Grandma's backyard one Halloween night, Claudia drawing pumpkins on our cheeks, flushed from the flames and crisp October air. The other girl had sent me a Valentine's Day card when I had chickenpox in third grade and missed our class party. Even Sonia had been a childhood friend. But that was before Claudia died. Before I became *the other*, lurking like a dark orb in a lucent sky.

Connie gave me a shove. "Time to roll."

"Off to sacrifice a live chicken, huh, Luna?" More laughter.

"Careful," I said, giving her the devil horns hand gesture and an Ozzy Osbourne bug-eyed glare. "You might be next."

"You're a freak," she said, smacking her gum. "Just an ugly-ass Goth chick-wannabe freak."

Connie stepped between us. "Enough of this fuckery. Let's

go, Luna."

Sonia's eyes skated over me—large gold-flecked eyes ablaze with contempt. I recalled the day I'd caught her sobbing in the school bathroom after the news broke that her mother, who had abandoned her shortly after Claudia died to run off with her lover, had been killed in a car accident. Sonia was crouching by the sink, mascara streaked down her cheeks, her face an angry red. For a moment, something poignant and real passed between us, something rooted in the past. In that guileless moment we were little girls again, before I rejected the child I'd been, the friends I'd had, and the life I'd once known. I wondered for the first time if my rejection of her had precipitated her derision of me, if she needed me as much as her sycophants to retrieve what her mother had taken from her. I looked into her eyes and saw us both, more clearly than ever before—girls with missing parts, questions that deserved answers, faint possibilities that warranted exploration. The difference was I realized it and she didn't. I had a chance for salvation, an opportunity to be whole, to find out who I really was. If I didn't grab it now, I might wind up like Sonia—bitter, unreachable, lost. I broke our gaze, wishing I could save her, offer revelation that would give her hope. I couldn't, though. But I could save myself.

I reached around Sonia and plucked the *Outrider* poster from the bin, then looped my arm through Connie's.

"Now I'm ready," I said. "Let's go."

CHAPTER EIGHT

When Uncle Jack and Aunt Lorraine came home after my great-grandfather died, Uncle Jack hauled most of his belongings to the Salvation Army in his pickup truck and burned the rest in the field. The only things that remained in the shack were a battered trunk filled with old bibles, hymnals, and books by Billy Graham and the like, and a cane bentwood rocker that had belonged to my great-great-grandfather. We decided that when they returned to Full River for my graduation, Uncle Jack would raze the house, outhouse, and shed. All were in shambles, and Grandma worried some of the local miscreants would set them on fire on a lark.

My great-grandfather had built the shack in the fall of 1931, when his wife fell ill. He thought the austere quarters and propinquity to nature would be more conducive to healing than the rambling farmhouse, in which Grandma, only fourteen at the time, remained.

"Howcome you didn't go back home after Grandma Emily died?" I'd brazenly asked him once, sitting on Claudia's lap in the bentwood while she braided my hair.

"Sometimes people need to be near the place that caused them pain, Lunabelle," she said quietly, tying a blue ribbon around the tip of one of my braids. "Sometimes it's the only place where they can heal."

I twisted the other ribbon around my finger. "Howcome he couldn't heal her?"

He'd spat a wad of tobacco juice into an empty cup then cleared his throat crudely.

" 'Cause I came into the world cursed, girl. I just didn't know it 'til then."

One bleak Sunday morning not long after I'd purchased the *Outrider* poster, I sat in my great-grandfather's rocking chair and listened to *Led Zeppelin II* on cassette, the poster tacked to the wall by his cryptic fireplace. I'd purchased all of their albums on tape and listened to them incessantly, scrutinizing each track for evidence of a clandestine love affair between my mother and Jimmy Page. Was "Thank You," a song about eternal love, inspired by her? How about "What Is and What Should Never Be"? Or "Ramble On"?

I'd never thought of Claudia in a carnal way. I'd never seen her with a man. Sometimes she would disappear until late at night with those crystals she'd bought from a fortuneteller, usually right after one of her episodes. No note. No warning. When she'd return, she'd crawl under the covers next to me and coo in my ear like a dove until I awoke. *Where were you?* I'd ask. *With Mr. MacGregor,* she'd say. *In his garden?* I'd giggle. *No, baby. Down by the river.*

I'd made up a song about him. I'd sing it to her under the covers.

Mr. MacGregor, one, two, three
Mr. MacGregor, I can't see
Mr. MacGregor lives down by the river
Red roses and rabbits he does give her

When I read *Hammer of the Gods*, Stephen Davis' much-maligned biography of Led Zeppelin, I discovered that James MacGregor was an alias Jimmy Page often used at hotels to elude the press and rabid fans while on tour. I'd checked out the book from the library and read it in the shack by candlelight after Grandma went to bed, chain-smoking Marlboros and drinking beer. Night after night. Sordid detail after sordid detail—drugs, the occult, nubile groupies with their halter-tops and hot pants and wanton braggadocio. How could he have loved any of them? How could he have loved Claudia? Even if they had met. Even if they had fucked. That's all she would have been to him—a good fuck.

All it takes is one good fuck . . .

Or a bad one.

Intercourse, copulation, and banging work just as well.

I am the product of euphemism.

I am the product of Woodstock, the Manson Murders, Stonewall, Nixon, Chappaquiddick.

More than just owls and pines cried in the night the year I was born.

Man first walked on the moon in 1969.

Luna, Roman goddess of the moon, bright and beautiful and strong.

Jimmy Page could not possibly be my father.

I could not possibly be his daughter.

Preposterous—all of it.

But what if it wasn't?

What if my father was a god—a sainted sinner, reformed Augustine?

He was, or had been, a disciple of the occultist Aleister Crowley. He owned Crowley's house in the Scottish highlands.

On the first pressings of *Led Zeppelin III* he'd inscribed Crowley's edict on side one—*Do what thou wilt*. I'd asked Claudia what it meant. *Find your path, who you are, then forge ahead*, she'd said.

Who was I? My last name was the same as my mother's, my grandmother's, my grandfather's, who died before I was born—Kane.

Claudia, Margaret, Hyram, and Luna Kane.

The name remains the same.

Who was I?

If Grandma didn't know, maybe Jimmy did.

Between the check from Grandma, Aunt Lorraine, and Uncle Jack and the money I'd saved from work, I could afford a plane ticket to London. I had a passport. I'd read about Jimmy's houses in Kensington and Windsor in *Hammer of the Gods*. I knew from a magazine article I'd stumbled across in the Record Shack that he still owned both. I had to find him. I had to know who I was.

Mr. MacGregor, one, two, three

Mr. MacGregor, I can't see

Mr. MacGregor lives down by the river

Mr. MacGregor, a name he will give her

PART TWO:

"BABE I'M GONNA LEAVE YOU"

CHAPTER NINE

EXCRESCENCE: **a** growth, lump, swelling—*an excrescence on a plant*—an unattractive or superfluous addition or feature—*that hat is an excrescence*— a disfiguring, extraneous, or unwanted mark or part—*an excrescence in your breast.*

That's what the doctor called the lump my grandmother had kept secret for months.

Excrescence.

A lump by any other name . . .

There are over one hundred species of owls, all with different names. Most are solitary nocturnal birds of prey. They fly silently, stealthily. They eat their victims headfirst, whole, consuming all but bones and fur and teeth. Those unwanted parts they evacuate as pellets. Those unwanted parts they treat like shit.

The wise old owl, an emblem of luck.

Unless it flies inside your house.

Grandma set her purse on the kitchen table and sat down gingerly.

"Do you have pain in other places too?" I asked, twisting the string of my hoodie sweatshirt around my finger.

"I don't have pain anywhere. I'm just tired." I studied her eyes, as if they might augur health and healing. "Luna, old ladies don't plop into chairs like teenagers. They ease into them."

"So you feel okay, then?" She cut her eyes at me and began fussing with her windblown hair. When she'd had chemo after her mastectomy two years ago, all of it had fallen out and she'd worn a stiff gray wig a lady at her church whose mother had recently died of cancer had given her. I'd told her wearing a dead person's hair was macabre, but she'd dismissed the notion in favor of practicality and donned the synthetic mop until Dr. Hollis proclaimed her cured and sprigs of her own hair began to sprout. When I found the wig in a box in the attic I surreptitiously chucked it into a dumpster behind the Mini Mart. Had Claudia been alive then, she would have used her crystals to conduct one of her hippie healing ceremonies to expel any lingering malignant energy. *You have to go to the source of the pain, the place where it all began, if you want to get rid of it, or at least keep it at bay*, I remember her saying. My leg twitched underneath the table, as if she were nudging me, telling me I should have done the job myself. Now it might be too late.

"So the doctor wasn't worried?" I asked Grandma.

"He said it was probably nothing."

No, he said it was an excrescence.

I tried not to glance at her chest—her left breast, the one that was left. Endometriosis had claimed her uterus when I was a child. If she lost her remaining breast, would she still be a woman, technically speaking? Is a vagina all it takes to define the female sex?

I took an unsettled breath. "What do we do now?"

"Heat up some soup or order a pizza."

"I don't mean that."

"Luna, we're not gonna let this knock us off-kilter. I've got a biopsy scheduled for Friday. No need to worry unless there's something to worry about."

"Shouldn't you call Aunt Lorraine?"

Grandma reached for my hand. "You're gonna yank that string clean out if you don't stop, and they're the devil to re-thread."

Her hand was cold, chapped. The skin around her nails cracked every winter. From December to March she'd wear rubber gloves when she washed dishes to avert the sting of sudsy water. I'd offered to take over KP duty, but she preferred routine—she washed and dried, I dusted and vacuumed. Always had, always . . .

I thought of her mother, my great-grandmother Emily, how she must have suffered at the hands of her pious husband before the excrescence in her own breast consumed it, expelling nothing but her soul. That it left to Providence.

We were both motherless children, Grandma and me, and our fathers were at least partly to blame.

"Did you hate your dad for what he did to your mom?" I asked abruptly. The question was indelicate, tactless even, but I was angry. I wanted her to hate him. I wanted her to say it.

"Wasn't any point in hating him." She gave a sober smile. "Daddy wasn't always so . . . peculiar. He'd pack us up in the wagon on Sundays after church in the summer and we'd have a picnic at the river. And he used to play the banjo. Bet you didn't know that, did you?" I shrugged. There was a lot I didn't know. Too much I didn't know. "He smashed that banjo to pieces and used it for kindling after Mama died," she said. "And he wouldn't go anywhere near the river."

"Why not?"

"Oh honey, I don't know. Something about Revelation, rivers turning to blood. Mama's passing liked to have killed him. He was different after that. Lord knows he tried to save her. He took a mail-order class on faith healing some no-count traveling preacher told him about. He loved her. He'd have done anything for her."

Except take her to a doctor.

"You ever think of her?" I asked, wrestling my eyes from her chest.

"Sometimes," she said after a strained pause. "I don't remember her that well. She passed when I was young. I remember she used to braid my hair when I was little, and she'd sing to me before I went to sleep—'You Are My Sunshine'. And she was a great reader, like your mama and you."

I pressed my hands between my knees to keep from twisting my string again. I didn't want to hear any more. I wanted to go back to that morning before everything changed. I wanted to close my eyes and wake up ten, eleven, twelve years back to the smell of Pop Tarts in the toaster and the sound of Uncle Jack singing "Walk the Line" in his baritone while he puttered about outside and Claudia and Grandma in the kitchen doing whatever it was they did in those illusory moments before I was fully awake, when nothing was real and everything true—those sacred seconds when anything was possible.

"Doctor Hollis really said there's nothing to worry about?" I asked, my throat tightening.

Grandma rummaged through her purse for her Pizza Hut coupons. "That's what he said."

****

Claudia had once told me owls are a symbol of the moon, the feminine. Ancient Christians associated the owl with Lilith, Adam's first wife, a willful, lubricious, evil woman, they thought. Some Native Americans consider the owl a sign of protection and prophesy, others a sign of death. Most tribes believe it to be the animal totem for people born between November 23 and December 21.

I was born at 11:56 p.m. on Wednesday, November 26.

Wednesday's child is full of woe.

Thursday's child has far to go.

Four minutes made the difference between *woe* and *go*. Either way, I drifted into life on the wings of an owl, both of us crying in the night.

I'd brought my totem into my grandmother's house.

Did I offer death or protection?

Could I save her if I left?

Would I kill her if I stayed?

Was I an excrescence?

I watched her napping on the sofa after dinner, Mary Hart wrapping up the latest celebrity news on *Entertainment Tonight*. I knelt beside her, close enough to smell the pepperoni and garlic on her breath. How could I leave her now? Everyone else had already gone—her mother, father, husband, her favorite daughter. How could I possibly leave her now?

She stretched her arms and yawned. "Must've drifted off," she said sleepily.

I forced a laugh. "You've never made it all the way through a TV program yet."

"I doubt I missed much. I don't even know who half those people they were gossiping about on that show are." She tucked her stocking feet underneath one of the throw pillows. "Honey, run upstairs and get my slippers for me. My feet are freezing."

I draped the afghan over her. "Want me to turn up the heat?"

"No, just get my shoes for me."

I took the stairs two at a time. Her room was next to mine. Claudia's was across the hall. I stood there gazing at her door—that cold, sardonic door, the one I'd opened then slammed shut again. The other day I'd caught Grandma gazing at it too. I was sure she hadn't entered. Only Jimmy was inside—on her wall and, now, inside the sleeve of a record album on her floor, above and below, seeing everything all at once.

I clutched the banister.

I knew what I would do.

When the time was right, I would creep inside her room, breathe the revenant scent of lavender, kneel at her dusty turntable, commit needle to vinyl. I would listen to the owls cry, that portentous guitar, hear my mother's voice in my head.

Then I would leave Full River.

Not for long. I'd come back. And Grandma and I would both be healed.

CHAPTER TEN

THE LAST photograph of Claudia Grandma left in my room was taken by Uncle Jack in the hospital a few hours after I was born. She's sitting up in bed, her hair in a disheveled ponytail, watching with her new mother's bewildered gaze while Aunt Lorraine cradles me in her arms in the Naugahyde chair next to Claudia. I'm swaddled in a white and gray receiving blanket, Aunt Lorraine's lips pressed gently against my forehead, as if she, rather than her free-spirited little sister, were the one who'd labored throughout the evening to birth the child she'd always wanted but couldn't have. My newborn's eyes, unfocused in infancy, seeing only in black and white, are turned to Claudia. They were always turned to Claudia—even when I couldn't see her clearly.

With the picture, Grandma left a crude watercolor portrait of me Claudia had painted when I was a toddler. She'd taken up the hobby after learning Jimmy Page had once gone to art school. My hair is a mass of unruly sable curls, my face pastel pink, eyes dusky black. I'm naked, reaching out for Claudia with both arms, my mouth agape, as if I were beckoning her, desperate to touch her, hold her, possess her. I wondered if that was the pose I'd struck when I'd modeled for her that day, or if it was merely how she saw me in her mind's eye—needy and grasping.

I folded the paper and placed it in the box with her other photographs and trinkets. The crystals caught my eye. I gathered them and tiptoed into Grandma's room. She was downstairs patching a hole in my jeans, the radio tuned to the classic country station. Her room was smaller than mine. Like Claudia's, her walls were a buttery shade of yellow. She'd stitched white lace curtains for all three of us, but I'd taken mine down in favor of plain tan shades. The only photograph in her room was a faded snapshot of her with my grandfather Hyram shucking corn on the front porch, both of them stiff and stern, already old in their mid-thirties. Except for her dark hair, she looks the same. My grandfather's hair is blond, his face chiseled, chin square and determined, his shoulders broad. Grandma had unwittingly revealed their wedding had been a shotgun affair, one that preceded the arrival of Aunt Lorraine by seven months. My grandfather had been a field hand when they first met. After they married, he took over the management of the farm from my great-grandfather. I didn't know if she kept that picture on her dresser to remind her of her transgression or if she'd actually loved him. I'd never gotten more out of her than an elliptical account of their history. She always left out the middle eight, the melody that reveals far more truth than just the facts.

The radio clicked off near the end of "Wolverton Mountain," and I heard Grandma puttering toward the stairs. I brought the crystals to my lips and kissed them. I wanted to swallow them, feel their energy surge through me, taste their color. I wanted to stand over Grandma as she slept and exhale a burst of magic rays and she would be cured. Instead, I said a prayer I knew was futile, then slipped the crystals underneath her mattress and skulked back to my room. I had no talisman for my own bed. I'd left myself uncarapaced. Suddenly, I felt as naked as I was in Claudia's painting.

Why had she painted me naked?

I imagined her at the easel, a rainbow palette before her, her brush, steeped in color, stroking my body. Her little girl, craving her like forbidden fruit dangling from the Tree of Truth, Knowledge, and Light. She'd known what I wanted. She'd confessed it in pastel and black, yet she'd sacrificed me for Jimmy. She lit candles for him, but not me. She danced for him, but not me. If he'd reached for her, she would have painted herself in his arms. She would have crawled inside his chest and burrowed in his heart, his blood coursing through her like a Dali painting. He would have been enough to sustain her. She would have been happy. With him. Not me. I wasn't enough. I couldn't save her.

It seemed to me that more often than not, sex, or the desire thereof, brought nothing but exigency and grief, the pleasure ephemeral, or absent altogether. It had been the impetus of Aunt Lorraine's marriage, the price she'd been willing to pay for a child, someone to love her the most, an empty promise that left her bitter and begrudging. I'd never been the least bit interested in sex. I'd never had a boyfriend or even been kissed. I didn't want to touch anyone, and I didn't want to be touched. Except for the penetrating blade of a razor, I hadn't been. But my mother had. And she'd intimated that Jimmy had been with her. That image, dark and dangerous, evoked a feeling I couldn't quite name. Not desire. That was too intimate, too physical. Curiosity—that was it, an eagerness to get closer to them both, to feel the power of a single act. I was curious.

****

I ambushed Denzel in the school parking lot a few days later and propositioned him. It was more like a proclamation than a question, dispatched with the same impassivity as a doctor delivering a grim prognosis.

"You're crazy, girl," he said, his sorrel eyes wide and wary. "What makes you think I'd do the deed with you? You'd probably put some devil curse on me and my dick would fall off."

I plopped on the hood of his car, a souped-up Datsun with a broken sunroof, and fished a pack of cigarettes from my backpack. "I'll pay you," I said levelly. I'd been prepared to offer compensation. Even then, I wasn't sure he'd accept. He was still desperately pursuing Connie, who'd grown increasingly exasperated with his advances. Sleeping with her non-boyfriend would hardly be a betrayal. Besides, he was the only guy I knew whom I thought might consider the offer.

"Lemme get this straight," he said. "You gonna pay me to fuck you?" He sucked his teeth then sang a few bars of "Nasty Girl" by Vanity 6.

I hopped off the car and slung my backpack over my shoulder. "Never mind."

"Wait a minute now. Hold up." He tucked his hands beneath his armpits and swayed smugly from one foot to the other. "How much?"

"Ten bucks," I said.

"*Ten bucks!*"

I lit a cigarette and blew a plume of smoke in his face. "And a six-pack."

"You're a crazy bitch."

"And you're a horny motherfucker, aren't you?" He grimaced. "When's the last time you got laid, Denzel?"

He tossed his books inside the car and slammed the door. "None-of-your-goddamn-business-1988, that's when."

"That long?" I sniped.

He hocked up a loogie and spat on the ground. "You need to get outta my face."

I took a long, contemplative drag on my cigarette. "Look, just think about it, okay? It doesn't have to be a big thing. No strings attached. No one has to know."

He ogled me as if he were surveying the terrain, unsure if he wanted to cross the threshold. "Sure you won't talk?"

"Not to anyone. I swear." I crossed an X over my heart with my finger. "So we've got a deal?"

He shrugged. "What the hell. Free pussy's free pussy. Even if it is yours."

We met behind the gym that night. The parking lot back there was more secluded than the main one in front of the school. Denzel had offered to pick me up for another ten bucks, but I didn't want him anywhere near the farm. I didn't want my memories of home tarnished by the prurience of that night.

You can always back out, I'd thought when Grandma handed me the keys to her sedan. *Chalk it up to impulsive youth, a psychology project gone awry.* I'd hesitated at the back door, my heart racing. I could go back upstairs and finish writing Connie's essay on *Frankenstein*, then watch a movie on TV with Grandma—something old and black and white. We'd nuke a bag of popcorn and pretend she didn't have a biopsy the next morning. Everything could go on as is.

Except it couldn't. *Is* had already become *was.*

I opened the door.

A gyre of ashen air, cold and bitter, stung my face. I imagined Claudia watching me, what motherly advice she might offer, what I would say to her in that pivotal moment.

What happened to the rainbow, Claudia?

It ended, baby.

How?

With a bang.

Not with a bang but a whimper.

No, baby. With a bang and *a whimper.*

I shivered. *That's what I thought. Just the same, I'll go and see for myself.*

****

Denzel and I stood under an awning at the field house, our teeth chattering.

"We gonna do it here?" he asked dubiously, warming his gloveless hands between his thighs.

"Why not here?"

" 'Cause it's fucking cold as shit, that's why not."

"Not *out* here. Inside your car."

A frigid rain began to fall. The floodlight by the hulking double doors flickered and we both started.

"Let's go," he said. "I don't wanna be out here all night."

I handed him the beer and climbed into the back seat of his car, surprisingly clean and trash-free. Grandma's was littered with my crushed soda cans and empty junk food bags, petrified french fries lost in the cleft between the gearshift and front seats.

Christy Alexander Hallberg

"You got the money?" he asked, sliding in next to me.

I dug a wrinkled ten-dollar bill from my coat pocket and gave it to him. We sat there looking at each other, sizing each other up, the heater blowing a steady stream of warm air through the grille-less vents, the spicy scent of Denzel's cologne tickling my nose. He smelled like Uncle Jack on Christmas mornings after he splashed on the Brut Aunt Lorraine gave him every year.

"Okay if I have a cigarette first?" I asked, trying not to breathe.

"Not in the car."

"Can I at least have a beer?"

"Hell no. That's my beer." He looked at me askance. "You didn't get it from Connie, did you?"

"I bought it myself, asshole. From that old guy at the Mini Mart. He never cards me."

We wriggled out of our coats, then Denzel began fumbling with my KFC shirt buttons.

"I'll do it," I said, pushing his hands away. "You're gonna rip the buttons off."

"You working later?" he asked, pulling his sweater over his head.

"Maybe."

"With Connie?"

"Relax. I'm not working tonight. I told my grandma I had a shift so I could get out of the house without her giving me the third degree."

"Oh," he said, the relief in his voice unmistakable. "Remember, you swore you wouldn't tell anyone about this."

"I know," I said. "So did you."

I folded my shirt and placed it on the front seat. I'd covered the scars on my chest with Grandma's foundation and pressed powder. I figured between that and the dark, they'd be invisible.

Denzel cracked his knuckles then forced his hand underneath my bra. I felt my nipples harden at his cold touch and flinched.

"What's wrong?" he asked, his hand massaging my breast like one of those therapy balls neurotic people use to relieve stress.

"Nothing," I said. He clutched my wrist with his free hand and moved my arm toward his crotch. "Look," I said, "I'm not into foreplay. Let's just do it and get it over with."

He clucked his tongue. "Whatever."

He began tugging his t-shirt loose from his jeans, coffee-colored skin bulging over the waistband. The thought of bare skin—anyone's skin—touching mine unnerved me.

"No, leave it on." I gave a placating smile. "No offense."

He covered his pudgy midriff with his sweater. "You took yours off. What's your problem?"

"I don't wanna get it messed up. My grandma . . . Nothing personal." I tossed his sweater in the front seat with my shirt. "You've got something, right?" I asked. He gazed at me blankly. "You've got a rubber, don't you?"

"You're not on the pill?"

"What difference does that make? Does the word *AIDS* ring a bell?"

He looked at me sharply. "You think I'm a fruit or something?"

I jerked away from him. "I don't know what you are. Who woulda thought Rock Hudson was gay?"

"Well I'm not," he snapped.

"How do you know you don't have AIDS?" I persisted, incensed my experiment might be a wash.

"I just do."

"Somebody else you've been with might've given it to you and you don't even know it yet. Symptoms can take a while to show up."

He punched the back of the seat. "I *don't* have AIDS. There's no way."

"So you wore rubbers before?"

"Come on, man." He dropped his eyes and began to fidget. "I said I don't have that shit, and I don't."

A thought struck me, one I hadn't anticipated. "You've never done this before, have you?"

"Fuck you. I've done it hundreds of times."

"You're a virgin, aren't you?"

He grabbed his sweater and struggled to find the armholes. "Take your beer and shit and get the hell outta my car."

I touched his cheek. It was an impulse, an unmediated move that felt strangely natural. His skin was smooth, soft. He wasn't particularly handsome. He was too beefy for that, but he had potential—the thickness of his lashes, curve of his full mouth, serpentine white scar through his left brow, probably acquired from some childhood accident like the scar on my calf. Baby fat and a petulant façade were all that separated him from handsome. I'd always thought him unremarkable in every way.

"It's okay," I said, careful not to sound pitying or condescending. "I won't tell that either."

He gripped the door handle, as if he were weighing the

possibility of flight with the pleasure of fucking.

All it takes is one good fuck . . .

Or a bad one.

I thought of the painfully awkward sex talk Aunt Lorraine had given me when I first got my period. She covered basic anatomy and the logistics of intercourse (her word) with the help of the same blue booklet Grandma had given her in lieu of a sex talk when Aunt Lorraine was an adolescent. *Abstinence until marriage is what nice girls do*, she'd told me, a clear dig at Claudia. *But married people have several options if they don't want to conceive at a given moment—condoms, birth control pills, the withdrawal method. And then of course, some people are sterile*, she'd said tartly, a clear dig at herself. She'd gone on to unmercifully offer a detailed explanation of the withdrawal method before demonstrating on a green banana how to put on a condom so I could make sure my *husband* did it correctly.

I started to giggle. Denzel threw open the door. "Just get the fuck out."

"I'm sorry," I said, forcing the farcical memory from my thoughts. "I wasn't laughing at you. I was just thinking of some stupid thing my aunt did a long time ago. Really. I wouldn't laugh at you now." I reached over him and closed the door. "Just pull out, okay?" I said. "Before you . . . you know. Just pull out before then and it'll be okay."

His hostile expression gave way to diffidence. "So you've done it before?"

I wiggled out of my jeans and underwear. "Sure," I said. "Hundreds of times."

He closed his eyes and leaned toward me. We kissed mechanically, no tongue, no passion. We both knew the tryst was perfunctory. I felt a sharp pain between my legs when he heaved himself inside me, and I gasped.

"Sorry," he grunted.

He buried his face in my hair and pressed his full weight on me, his legs cramped against the door, the rattling heater muffling the sound of rain beating the windows. He began to thrust, so hard I knew I'd have bruises in the morning.

My mind began to wander. First, to the corny movies I'd seen of girls losing their virginity in the back seat of their high school boyfriend's car, sappy love songs playing in the background. Then to that Joyce Carol Oates story "Where Are You Going, Where Have You Been?" *My sweet little blue-eyed girl*, the cryptic stranger calls his sweet little brown-eyed girl, the one he seduces like the devil to come to him, barefoot and shiny like the day she was born, the girl he would drive into the violent sun-kissed hinterlands from where she might never return—not like she was before. She would never be like she was before.

Denzel was groaning, just like in the movies—sweating and groaning and grinding.

I don't feel anything, Claudia. Nothing but dead weight and that red-hot rip at the beginning.

Oh, baby . . . the river . . . the river . . .

Mr. MacGregor lives down by the river. Red roses and rabbits he does give her.

Just don't kill the rabbit, baby.

Denzel began thrusting faster. He was groaning in my ear. Louder, his breath ragged, the cologne that smelled like Brut strangling me. I couldn't speak. His body was rigid against mine.

One last thrust.

He came inside me.

Claudia . . .

"Jesus Christ," he murmured. "Jesus Christ." He was crying—just a little, quietly, hot tears on my neck.

I held him, told him everything was okay, not to worry. My body would keep our secret. I promised.

He rolled off me and pulled up his pants and wiped his eyes. Even in the dark I could see he was trembling. He leaned over the front seat and opened the glove box. "Here," he said, passing me a rag. "It's clean."

I wiped myself off, then slipped on my underwear and jeans.

"Want a beer now?" he asked. He sounded contrite, as if he'd just broken some cardinal rule and longed for dispensation—from me or God, I couldn't tell. Maybe both.

"No," I said, buttoning my shirt. "I gotta go."

"Yeah. That's cool."

I opened the door. Rain sprayed my face.

"I think I've got an umbrella in here somewhere," he said.

"That's okay. Thanks anyway." I draped my coat over my head and stepped back into the night.

"See you around," he called, not looking at me, not yearning for me, a hint of regret in his voice. I knew he would cry after I left, alone in the car, hidden from ridicule.

"Yeah," I said flatly. "See you around."

****

I lit a fire in my great-grandfather's hearth and curled up in the rocking chair close to the flames, *Led Zeppelin I* playing on the boombox. I'd called Grandma from a payphone at the Mini Mart and told her I was spending the night at Connie's, then I'd bought more beer and cigarettes and hiked to the shack from the dead-end past our house, where I'd hidden Grandma's car.

I could still smell sex on my body—musky, acrid. Nauseating. The rain hadn't washed it off. I was sure the old man at the store had smelled it—the way he looked at me when he rang up my contraband, like I'd just been ravaged by a pack of libidinous warlocks. But then, he always looked at me that way.

I drained my beer and cracked open another—my fourth. My head was buzzing.

Jimmy roared into a torrid Spanish guitar solo in "Babe I'm Gonna Leave You."

I tapped my cigarette ashes into one of the empty cans. I was freezing. I'd peeled off my wet clothes and bundled up in the quilt I kept in my great-grandfather's trunk with my cassette tapes and Led Zeppelin magazine articles and books, along with my great-grandfather's religious tracts and Bible. The irony amused me.

I dragged the chair closer to the hearth.

"Talk to me, Claudia." The cadence of my voice was foreign to me, like when you hear yourself on a tape recording and wince at the aberration.

"How was it, Claudia? With Jimmy, I mean. It was Jimmy, wasn't it? Backstage somewhere? Outside on the ground by the river? Was it more than once?" I blew my nose on the quilt. "What was it like? I hated it. I hated all of it—the feeling, the smells, the sounds. What was it like with him, someone you loved? It was Jimmy, wasn't it?"

I glanced at his face on the poster on the wall.

"You know he didn't love you, don't you? Deep down, you've got to have known he didn't love you. He wouldn't have left you if he did."

I was sobbing, wailing in chorus with Robert Plant. I flicked my cigarette butt into the flames then lit another.

"What about me, Claudia? Did you love me? Why'd you leave me?"

The floorboards creaked underneath the rocking chair. I used to wonder how my great-grandfather could stand living there. No electricity or indoor plumbing. Cold in the winter, boiling hot in the summer. A pinewood coffin stored in the shed less than twenty feet away. Death was closer than the outhouse.

Claudia used to spend hours with him. Most of the time she'd go alone, but sometimes she'd bring me with her. I'd cling to her, terrified he would grab me and try to throw me into the fire like the witch in *Hansel and Gretel*.

"He's creepy," I said to her after one visit. "Why do you go see him so much?"

"He's all alone. He doesn't have any friends. Just that cat, and she's on her last life."

I clasped her hand and swung her arm back and forth. "Howcome you don't have any friends, Claudia?"

"I don't know. I guess I don't need any. I've got you, and Mama. And Granddaddy Jesse has us." She swept her hair up and tied it into a bun. "You shouldn't look down on him just because he's not like you, Luna. He's not as creepy as you think."

I made a fish face and stomped through a mud puddle on the dirt path. "He is so."

"So, so, suck your toe. All the way to Mex-e-co," she sang.

"I think there's something wrong with him," I said. "Everyone thinks there's something wrong with him."

She sighed. "Look, baby, sometimes things happen that change a person."

"I think he's bonkers."

"He misses Grandma Emily."

"Missing someone doesn't make you bonkers."

She grasped my hands and dragged me through another mud puddle, turbid water splashing our clothes and legs.

"Now *that's* bonkers!" she said. I cackled and pelted her with fistfuls of mud.

"You're bonkers, I'm bonkers, the mud's bonkers, the sky's bonkers, the barn's bonkers . . ." Everything I saw until I went to bed that night was bonkers, including that black and white photograph of Jimmy in Claudia's room. Everything.

"Babe I'm Gonna Leave You" faded with Robert's mournful refrain, then Jimmy's emphatic final chord, like an exclamation point.

My mother had left me one breezy summer night in 1979, the sibylline Hermit with his lantern and Jimmy's violin bow guiding her flight. Heaven was a lonely mountaintop in the Scottish Highlands, hell, a clapboard farmhouse in the Southern pines.

I dropped the quilt and stood naked in front of the fire. One or two steps forward, I'd be in the flames. One or two steps back, I'd be in the cold. Both were calling me. Grandma was calling me. Jimmy. Claudia. I wanted them all. I was them all. And I knew I always would be, no matter what I found in London. I had to get there, though, and Connie held the key, literally and figuratively.

CHAPTER ELEVEN

CONNIE'S HOUSE was a two-story red brick Colonial in Rock Ridge, an upper-middle-class neighborhood near the high school, with manicured lawns and two-car garages and a community pool and golf course. Her parents schmoozed with clients on the green then pondered Reaganomics over cocktails at the club house, where they were the only African American members. Connie and her ten-year-old sister, Grace, had their own bathrooms and a playroom full of video games and Grace's massive collection of Barbie dolls. The living room boasted a big-screen TV and a leather sectional sofa big enough to seat a party of six and the family dog. The Stanleys had everything but a white picket fence. Theirs was a world as foreign to me as London. In some ways, it was foreign to Mr. and Mrs. Stanley too.

They'd grown up poor black kids in eastern North Carolina in the '50s and '60s, when the word *nigra* was bandied about as often as watermelon jokes, and Little Black Sambo figurines adorned tabletops next to bowls of Brazil nuts, which Grandma used to cavalierly call *nigger toes*. They'd attended segregated schools and worked menial jobs, including barning tobacco on our farm, to put themselves through college. Then, when Connie was twelve, they opened the first African American-owned CPA firm in Full River. They'd crossed the color line in a town that, by the late '80s, pretended there'd never been one. But there had, including the one that cut deep through the fields of my family's farm.

Connie had once alluded to a scuffle her dad had had with my Grandfather Hyram during the summer Mr. Stanley worked for him. The details were sketchy, but I gathered my grandfather had unleashed a torrent of racial slurs over a benign comment Connie's dad had made to Aunt Lorraine. My grandfather pushed him into the tire swing and Mr. Stanley got tangled in the rope and nearly choked to death before freeing himself. That was the last time he or Connie's mother set foot on the farm. They were amiable to Grandma and me, but I sensed a lingering resentment in them, and in Grandma, vestigial traces of her Jim Crow lineage.

The week after her biopsy Connie and I lounged on her sofa and watched a video of *Top Gun*. Her parents had gone out to dinner and reluctantly left Grace in our care. The Stanleys' neurotic Chihuahua sat beside me, growling every time I reached for the bowl of popcorn on the coffee table.

"Can't you toss that dog in the backyard for awhile?" I said, placing a pillow between the dog and me as a barricade.

"I wish. My mom would kill me."

"Your mom's not here. She'll never know."

"She will when she comes home and finds the little monster frozen at the deck door." Connie nudged the dog off the sofa. "What's with you tonight?"

"Nothing. Just trying to watch the movie."

"Bullshit."

"I heard that," Grace squealed. She was lurking in the hallway, hoping to overhear a tantalizing piece of gossip she could blackmail us with.

"Go play in the traffic, runt," Connie barked.

Grace skipped into the room and plunked down on Connie's lap, the dog yipping after her. "Can I watch the movie with you?"

"No."

"Can I have some popcorn?"

Connie shoved her off her lap. "I'll nuke you a bag, but you have to eat it in your room."

I fast-forwarded through the "You've Lost that Loving Feeling" scene while Connie microwaved the popcorn. Grace gyrated in front of me chanting, "Hammertime," the dog spinning in circles, violently chasing its tail.

"They should've drowned her at birth," Connie groused, collapsing beside me after she'd banished Grace and the dog to her room. "Now, you gonna tell me what's up or not?"

I picked a stray thread on my jeans where the patch Grandma had sewn was coming loose. The results of her biopsy had come back. So had her cancer. I'd seen the diagnosis coming. The moment she'd told me about that excrescence, I'd seen it coming like prophesy. I was still shocked when she delivered the news—shocked and stunned and every other synonym for *this is fucked up*.

"My grandma's sick again," I said faintly.

Connie tucked her legs underneath her, then promptly untucked them and set her feet on the floor, as if she wasn't sure how her body should react. "Is she gonna be okay?" she asked.

My insides felt heavy with premonition. "She's gonna die," I said starkly. Connie laced her fingers through mine and squeezed.

I glanced at the garish watercolor beach scenes on the wall. The first time I'd seen the ocean had been with Connie when we were sixteen. Her parents had let her drive us to Atlantic Beach for a day trip. Our friendship was full of firsts—from pedestrian milestones to sacred secrets, ties that bound us together like skin and bone.

"I have to tell you something, Connie," I said, untangling my fingers from hers.

"What?"

"I think I fucked up."

She cocked her head, like that annoying Chihuahua, and I wondered if that old saying about people taking on the characteristics of their pets over time might actually be true. "What are you talking about?" she said.

I took a deep breath then came out with it. "I sort of did it last week."

"Did what?"

"You know. *It.*"

Her eyes bulged. "Get outta here. You did *it?*"

"Keep your voice down," I hissed.

"You did *it*, and you didn't tell me?" She threw her head back and whooped. "Halleluiah, you finally got laid!"

"Connie—"

"I was afraid you'd wind up in a monastery with a shaved head, dressed in one of those brown thingys, like in *Kung Fu.*"

"Connie—"

"Not that there's anything wrong with that. You looked good with a shaved head back in the day."

"Connie, listen to me."

"I can't believe you didn't tell me sooner. I called you right after I did it the first time. And the second. Might've been a third if it hadn't been so . . . you know, mehh. Anyway, now I've decided to save myself for Prince." She ran to the hallway to make sure Grace wasn't listening then shimmied back to the sofa. "So who was he?"

I drained my glass of Pepsi* and felt it tingle all the way down my throat. "Denzel," I said. "I did it with Denzel."

Her face dropped.

"I wasn't gonna tell you, but—"

"Then why did you?"

The chill in her voice gave me pause. "It didn't seem right not to."

She punched the volume up and settled back on the sofa, feigning interest in a movie we'd seen so often we could recite the dialogue. I took the remote from her and turned off the TV.

"Connie, I don't know what to say."

"Then turn the goddamn movie back on."

"Am I missing something? I thought you couldn't stand Denzel." She crossed her arms in front of her and pursed her lips. "Do you like him?" I asked.

"No, I don't *like* him."

"Then what's the problem?"

She snorted derisively. "If you really don't know that, you wouldn't have said you fucked up."

I blanched. "I'm sorry. I'm really, really sorry, Connie. I mean it."

"Why'd you do it with him?"

"I don't know. I thought he wouldn't tell anybody."

She grabbed the popcorn bowl and marched to the kitchen.

"Connie, I would never have done it if I'd thought you liked him."

"I said I don't." She dumped the kernels into the trash can then scrounged a bottle of Coors from the refrigerator.

"Better not let your little sister see you," I said, trailing into the kitchen.

She retrieved another bottle and handed it to me. "Now we'll both get in trouble."

"Connie, I'm sorry."

"What exactly are you sorry for?"

"What exactly are you upset about?"

She took a pull on her beer. "Shit, I don't know. It just feels weird, like you took what was supposed to be mine."

"But you didn't want it."

"I know that, but I didn't say you could have it."

"*It* was never yours to give. And *it* has a name."

"Yeah—*asshat*."

I pictured Denzel in the back seat of his car, how awkward we were with each other, how his tears felt warm on my neck, how afraid he was I'd tell Connie about us, and I realized I'd just betrayed him. "He's not an asshat," I said. "He's actually a nice guy, and he's still crazy about you."

She pushed herself up on the counter and flexed her bare feet, examining her freshly polished toenails.

"So you like him?" she asked coolly.

"No. Not like that."

"Oh, I get it, you just used him. Sounds like you're the asshat."

I laughed tartly. "You just figured that out? Isn't that what everyone's been trying to tell you for years? *Stay away from*

Luna. Howcome you hang out with that freak? You could be one of us if you ditched that bitch."

"Don't pull that shit. Don't try to make me feel sorry for you."

"I don't want your goddamn pity," I spat.

"You don't know what you want, Luna. You don't know what you're doing or which way to go."

I pulled my plane ticket from my back pocket and waved it at her. "I know exactly where I'm going," I said.

She snatched the ticket and read it. "This is to London. You're going to London?"

I searched my pockets for cigarettes then remembered I'd vowed to quit once and for all after Grandma gave me the biopsy results. I'd thrown away my last pack and now I was kicking myself.

"Luna, you've never been on a plane. You've never even been out of North Carolina. You think you can just haul your ass all the way across the ocean and knock on some Rock star's door? First of all, you don't have a clue where he lives. Second of all, what the fuck you gonna say to him: *Hey, man, I think you're my daddy?*"

"I don't know what I'm gonna say to him. But I'll find him. I know where he lives."

She hopped off the counter and slapped my ticket in my hand. "What's the exchange rate? What's the difference between crisps and chips? What's a loo?"

"You think you're so smart 'cause you've been to England."

"I'm smart enough not to go hoofing off by myself to places I don't know a damn thing about."

Grace burst into the kitchen clutching a Barbie doll, her

face wide with concern. "What're y'all yelling for?"

Connie swept her up and perched her on her hip. "It's okay, Gracie. Nothing to worry about."

The little girl leered at me. "Did you do something bad?"

"No," Connie said. "We were just talking."

"Didn't sound like *just talking* to me. When's Mama coming home?"

Connie set her back down on the floor and held her at arms' length. "You wanna sleep in my bed tonight?" Grace wagged her head. "If you keep your trap shut when Mama and Daddy come home, I'll let you."

"Rex too?"

"No way. Keep that dog outta my room."

"Okay, but I'm bringing my Barbies."

Grace dashed back upstairs, her Michael Jackson t-shirt—an old one of Connie's—billowing around her. Connie chugged the last of her beer then popped a piece of gum in her mouth.

"Hurry up and finish that," she said. "My parents will be back soon."

I poured my beer down the sink. "I didn't want it in the first place."

"Luna, I just don't want you to get hurt, that's all. I know you're all mixed up and stuff, but . . . this doesn't make any sense. It's crazy."

"Look, I know what I'm doing. Maybe I haven't worked out all the details, but I know what I'm doing. And I need your help."

She threw up her hands. "Okay, yeah, uh-huh. I was waiting for that. Well, I'll tell you right now I don't want anything to do with this. And what about your grandma? You gonna just go off and leave her now that she's sick?"

"I'll only be gone a week. Nothing's gonna happen in a week's time—no treatments or operations or whatever. I'll be home in a week, then I'll take care of her."

"She'll worry herself half to death between now and then."

"I'll leave her a note."

Connie smacked her gum fervently. "So what do you need me for, then?"

"I need a ride to the bus station."

She looked at me with suspicion. "The bus station?"

"Yeah. My flight leaves from Atlanta. I'm not asking you to drive me all the way to Atlanta."

"That's good, 'cause that's not gonna happen."

"Will you at least drive me to the bus station in town?"

She paced the floor—white ceramic tile that, along with the white cabinets and appliances, made the room look more like a morgue than a kitchen. "Howcome you're not flying out of Raleigh?" she asked.

"I don't want any layovers. Atlanta's direct to Heathrow, plus it was the cheapest fare I could find, even with the bus fare."

"I still don't see how you could leave your grandma."

I slouched against the wall. "I can't explain it, Connie. It's like I'll never be whole if I don't go. Like if I find the missing piece, maybe I'll be okay. Then maybe we'll both be okay—Grandma and me. Even my mom."

"That's way too abstract for me, girl. And way too risky. Here's what I think—at the end of the day, you'll be out all your Mexico money, your grandma will be pissed as hell—not to mention hurt—and you won't know anything more about your dad than you do now."

I stalked back to the living room for my shoes. "You don't get it," I said stonily.

"No, *you* don't get it."

"I'll find him."

She sprinted around the sofa and grabbed my shoes. "Okay, so why don't you go later, after your grandma—you know—*after*."

" 'Cause then it'll be too late. I'm supposed to go now."

"Why?"

"Don't you see? Claudia met Jimmy Page in late February '69. She'd just turned eighteen a few days before. I'm eighteen. It's late February. I'm supposed to go *now*. Everything comes full circle *now*. It's goddamn Providence."

The garage door rattled open.

"I'm going no matter what, Connie. Please help me."

She handed me my sneakers and peeked over my shoulder at the back door, both of us anxious to settle the matter before her parents walked in. "Okay," she said quietly. "I still think you're wrong, but okay."

"I'll owe you big time."

"You got that right." She shook her head glumly. "What exactly am I supposed to do?"

CHAPTER TWELVE

CONNIE DROVE me to the dead-end near my house after her parents went to bed. I'd planned to stay the night at Connie's, but I felt a sudden urge to go to the shack after they got home. Part of me was afraid she would change her mind about taking me to the bus station if I stayed. Another part of me knew there was something I had to do before I left town, and time was running out.

I snapped open a plastic garbage bag and began filling it with cassette tapes from the trunk, *Physical Graffiti* playing on the boombox. I'd decided I liked that album best. "Kashmir," "Night Flight," and "Houses of the Holy" resonated with me in a way most of the band's other songs didn't. Claudia had rarely played them, or any of the albums after *Led Zeppelin IV*, for that matter. Maybe that's why *Physical Graffiti* appealed to me; it was mine alone.

I pitched *I'm With the Band,* Pamela Des Barres' salacious tell-all about her years as a 1960s groupie on the Sunset Strip, into the fire and watched the flames hungrily consume the pages. She'd written extensively about her fling with Jimmy during the summer of '69. I wondered if she thought he'd written songs for her too, if she still felt the rush of red river water in her soul, heard phantom owls crying in her head.

I also burned *Backward Masking Unmasked* by Jacob

Aranza, a farcical booklet on subliminal messages in Rock music I'd found in a 50-cent bin at a yard sale. Aranza devoted a whole chapter to Led Zeppelin, focusing his wrath primarily on Jimmy, whose interest in the occult he blamed for a series of tragedies that befell the members of the band. I assumed he was referring to the death of Robert Plant's six-year-old son, Karac, of a mysterious stomach virus in 1977, and drummer John Bonham's passing in 1980, after an alcohol binge at Jimmy's Windsor home, bringing an abrupt end to the group.

Aranza also perpetuated the myth of Satanic messages in "Stairway to Heaven." I'd read in *Hammer of the Gods* about a rumored deal the band had made with Satan in exchange for fame and fortune. Connie had recoiled when I'd read that part of the book to her. "Oh come on, it's horseshit," I'd said. "Like that old Blues legend about going down to the crossroads to hitch a ride with the devil."

Claudia had told me the apocryphal story of Bluesman Robert Johnson's pact with Satan at a desolate Mississippi crossroads long before I read about it in *Hammer of the Gods*. She'd dismissed it with a wave of her hand. *You know what a crossroads is, don't you, baby? Just a place where you have to decide which way to go. You have to think for yourself, and nothing scares people more than a freethinker.*

I'd gazed out the window of her room at the bare maple tree in our backyard. It reminded me of an arthritic old man, grizzled and grim, lonely in the bleak winter night. I imagined the devil and a cadre of sycophants dressed in ceremonial robes dancing around the tree to "Dazed and Confused" or "No Quarter," invoking tenebrous spirits, Jimmy Page ever vigilant from afar. *Are you a freethinker, Claudia?* I'd asked her. She'd stroked her brush across the canvas—a surreal self-portrait in black and white, one of her many paintings I'd destroyed after she died. *No,* she'd said vacantly, then streaked a big X across the canvas. *I'm not a free anything.*

I fished the last of the cassettes from the trunk and sealed the bag with a twist tie. All that remained were my great-grandfather's books, including a battered King James Bible. Grandma told me he'd burned her mother's beloved novels along with his banjo after she died. *Great Expectations, Jane Eyre, Wuthering Heights, Pride and Prejudice*—all of them, gone. He'd insisted the books were blasphemous, complicit in her suffering. I pictured him lurking by her bedside, reciting one Bible verse after another to her emaciated body. *The Good Book,* he'd called it. *The Word of God the Father.*

I placed it on the pyre, watched it crackle and char in a spate of angry flames. Then I flushed with fear—if there was a God, now would be the time He'd come calling. I waited for the thunderbolt. *No, that's Zeus,* I thought. The Lord is supposed to come like a thief in the night.

"You're the only thief that comes to me at night, Claudia," I said.

What have I taken from you, Lunabelle?

"What have you *not* taken from me?"

I ripped the *Outrider* poster from the wall and threw it into the blaze. Jimmy's face ignited then withered. I was the one rendering fire and fury. I was the Alpha and the Omega, the first and last, the beginning and the end.

I burst into tears and tried to save what was left of the poster. Glowing cinders stung my hand. I jerked back and

106   *Christy Alexander Hallberg*

tumbled to the floor, the poster disintegrating in front of me.

"I'm sorry," I gasped, snot running down my chin. "I tried to save you. I really tried. I'm so fucking sorry."

****

Aunt Lorraine had arrived unannounced by the time I trudged inside the mudroom around nine a.m. I'd surreptitiously called her the day before to give her the news about Grandma's cancer, hoping she'd come home so that Grandma wouldn't be alone when I skulked off to London. She stood steely by the door, still bundled in her coat and scarf, brown eyeliner caked in the creases around her eyes from squinting into the morning glare. Grandma bustled about in her bathrobe making coffee, her hair still in pin curls, canvas slippers clip-clipping on the floor.

"You're just getting home?" Aunt Lorraine said, shivering in the draft that blew in with me. "Where in the world have you been?"

"Calm down, Lorraine," Grandma said. "She spent the night with her friend Connie."

Aunt Lorraine peered through the window over the washing machine. "I didn't hear a car."

"She dropped me off a little ways back. I wanted to walk."

"You wanted to walk? It's twenty degrees outside." She pulled off her leather gloves and pressed her hands against my cheeks. "You're like ice. What were you thinking?"

"At least she's got sense enough not to drive clear across the state at four-thirty in the morning." Grandma cut her eyes at me. "But then, you wouldn't have done that had someone not been a busybody and made a phone call she didn't have permission to make." She set an iron skillet on the stove and culled a package of bacon from the refrigerator. "Jack couldn't get away?"

"He's meeting us in Durham in a few hours."

Grandma leered at her over her glasses. She only wore them in the mornings. It took her eyes at least one cup of coffee to wake up, she'd say. "He's meeting *who* in Durham in a few hours?"

Aunt Lorraine slipped off her coat and hung it on the back of the door. "Us, Mama," she said. "We're taking you to see a specialist at Duke. Jack's got an old friend who's an oncologist. He's squeezing you in first thing Monday morning. We'll leave today and stay in a hotel near the hospital. And that's all there is to that."

Grandma stirred a tablespoon of sugar in her coffee, then took a noisy sip. "I hope they don't charge you for canceling an appointment at the last minute," she said.

"For once, Mama, don't be so stubborn. It's for your own good."

"Don't talk to me like that. I'm still the parent in this house, and I'll make my own decisions about which doctor I see."

"I don't mean to be disrespectful. I just don't want to take any chances with your health." She lit a cigarette and sat down at the table. "This is your life we're talking about."

"I'm not going. And that's all there is to *that*."

Aunt Lorraine pointed at me, her cigarette pinched between her fingers. "Think of Luna. If you won't do it for me, do it for Luna."

My eyes darted from her to Grandma. I'd booked my flight

for Monday, the last day of February. Aunt Lorraine's timing was perfect. I'd be gone long before they returned. "I think you should go, Grandma," I said with a bent smile.

"Come on, Mama. I bet you can't think of one reason not to, can you?"

Grandma took off her glasses and massaged the bridge of her nose. "All right," she huffed, "I'll go. But I'm telling you both right now I'm not having surgery or taking chemo treatments again. I don't care what some so-called specialist says."

"Let's not put the cart before the horse," Aunt Lorraine said. "Why don't you go ahead and get packed. Luna and I'll fix breakfast."

"What for? It's only Saturday. Why do you want to leave today instead of tomorrow?"

" 'Cause I don't wanna give you a chance to change your mind."

Grandma glanced at the calendar above Aunt Lorraine's head. "Monday's February 29. It's a Leap Year. You made me an appointment for Leap Year Day?" she muttered.

Aunt Lorraine nodded buoyantly. "For good luck."

"Daddy always said that day was bad luck." She handed me the package of bacon then glanced at the floor. "Which one of you tracked in all that dirt?"

"Luna, sweetie, take off those muddy sneakers," Aunt Lorraine said.

Grandma reached for the broom by the refrigerator. "How'd you get your shoes so dirty?"

I stared at my feet. A ring of caked mud clung to my sneakers.

"Just take them off, Luna. We need to get a move on, Mama."

"You sure you'll be okay here while I'm gone, honey?"

My heart fluttered. "Sure I'm sure. Wouldn't you be okay if I was gone for a few days?"

Grandma looked at me incredulously.

"She'll be fine, Mama." Aunt Lorraine steered her toward the staircase. "Just like you'll be fine while she's in Mexico this spring. We'll all be fine, now go pack."

Grandma headed upstairs grudgingly. I kicked off my shoes, and Aunt Lorraine passed me the broom. "That dirt road's not muddy this morning. Where were you, Luna?"

The tune, like the rhythm of my childhood, chimed in my head:

Down by the river with Mr. MacGregor . . .

****

The Tar River is only a mile from our farm. Less in the sultry summer twilight, cicadas trilling in the woods, cottonmouths slithering through cattails, splashing into dark water, the smell of moss and witch grass pungent in the breeze. It's farther in the frost-laden dawn of February, the ground frozen and brown, blue-gray sky rippled with fiery shades of red, the air sleepy and sheer. I'd hauled the garbage bag filled with Led Zeppelin cassettes to the boggy riverbank and dropped it into the water. I'd had to use a dead tree branch to force it below the surface, but once I did, the river did the rest. When the bag was completely submerged, I pulled off my knit gloves with my teeth then scooped the charred remains of the *Outrider* poster from my pocket. All I could recover after the fire burned out and the ashes cooled was a handful of soot, most of which smeared my hands and the lining of my jeans. I dipped my hands into the biting water and opened them. The cold stung more than the smoldering cinders had.

I wanna be cremated when I die, I'd told Connie, *my ashes scattered in the river.* She'd told me that was a helluva morbid request to make right before my flight. *I don't believe in superstition*, I'd said. *What do you believe in, Luna?* I'd pictured Claudia, standing in the rain in our backyard, quoting that philosopher she liked, her face tilted upward, as if she were performing a holy ablution. *I believe in water*, I'd said to Connie—*water and moonlight and fire and flight.*

CHAPTER THIRTEEN

MY HIP was a mallet, my shoulder a cudgel. The wood unwary.

Violation is often violent. It's always profane, irreverent. Especially on hallowed ground.

Two violent shoves. A mournful creak—like a death rattle. Then the door gave way.

I stepped forward. A jagged crack marred the floorboard in the threshold.

Step on a crack, break your mama's back.

I stepped over the crack. Into the dark room. It gets dark early in February. The sky withers and dies by six—one half of twelve, the Witching Hour. I couldn't wait for the Witching Hour. Connie would arrive to take me to the bus station at seven.

I lit a candle, a tall white one I'd bought at the Mini Mart, along with a bag of incense and a razor. I would have bought a six-pack, but the old man wasn't there.

I was sober—in body and soul.

I closed my eyes.

"I'm here, Claudia."

Maybe I wasn't there. Maybe I wasn't real—just a zephyr sweeping through cracks in a facade, no body and nobody.

Can you hear the music?

"I *can't* hear it, Granddaddy. Not yet."

I opened my eyes.

So much dust. Like a shroud covering a corpse. The room looked dead, bloodless. The last time I'd been inside there had been blood. On the walls, the floor, the white lace curtains, Claudia, me. Blood spatter, the policemen had called it. Fresh blood is bright red. I'd worn it like a red herring until Grandma cleaned me up. I don't remember who cleaned up the room.

"The walls are yellow again, Claudia."

I glanced around, taking it all in. Wide-brimmed straw hat dangling from her closet door handle. Silver-plated tray covered with a plethora of perfume bottles on her white veneer dresser. Rose-colored beanbag chair in a corner. Her easel set up next to it. Pack of Tarot cards and a teak incense holder on top of the bookshelf by the window. Someone had taken down the bloody curtains. The window looked naked and grim.

I walked toward the bed.

"Jimmy's picture is still here. A little dusty, but it's here."

I lifted the candle to get a better look. He was still beautiful—arms outstretched, like a black and white sacrificial lamb. I'd sacrificed him to the flames. Not *this* him; the *Outrider* him. To kill the seraph would have been a damnable offense.

My hands were shaking. I set the candle on the nightstand. I couldn't breathe. The air smelled of mold and mothballs.

Light the incense, Luna.

I whipped around, startled, dazed.

Something crunched beneath my feet. I remembered the *Outrider* album I'd left on the floor. I dropped to my knees and held the shattered record to my chest. "I'm sorry, Claudia. I wanted to play it for you."

I know that, baby. You tried. That's what matters.

I dumped the pieces of vinyl on the floor. "I ruined it. I ruined everything."

Light the incense, Luna.

I placed a stick of incense on the holder then struck a match. The heady scent of lavender began to fill the room.

I lit the white candles on top of the bookshelf too. I'd forgotten they were there. I'd forgotten the beanbag chair and straw hat. She used to twirl it by the blue satin ribbons. I'd forgotten which books used to line her shelves. Most of them were gone. More victims of blood spatter. I wondered if Grandma had given them to my great-grandfather to burn.

The stereo beckoned.

Her records were neatly stacked in the cabinet underneath the turntable.

Go ahead, baby. You know what I want to hear. Play it.

"In a minute. I'm not ready yet."

I could see my reflection in the window; flickering candlelight framed my face.

"I'm on fire," I said.

No, you're the moon.

"There's not one out tonight—a moon, I mean."

Did I ever tell you a full moon makes owls more vocal?

"I don't remember."

What do you remember, Luna?

"The owls crying."

What else?

I clutched my stomach. "I think I'm gonna be sick."

Play the record, Luna. It's time.

I pulled *Led Zeppelin IV* from the cabinet and opened the cover. The Hermit stood solemnly at the top of a mountain, lantern and staff in hand. The inner sleeve bore the lyrics to "Stairway to Heaven." I set the record on the turntable. Side Two, Track Two—"Four Sticks." The disk began to spin. I placed the needle on the groove.

Jimmy's guitar was a juggernaut—savage, feral, carnal, like the Bacchae thrashing and fucking in ancient Thebes.

Bonzo's drums . . . like thunder. The hammer of the gods.

Then Robert's voice, that primeval wail.

The music surged over crests and valleys. I was transported with it, through the tribal fire, submerged in the river.

"Claudia . . ."

What do you remember, Luna?

****

The day of the leather-bound journal with gold-tipped pages. The day of the jangly anklet and the story of my name and the gust of wind that carries the pungent smell of tobacco from the field across the dirt road and the crew of high school boys whistling at you above the distant din of the tractor. The sound of you jangling upstairs to your room. Your door slamming, the lock clicking. The owls and red river and rainbow, arriving for the last time.

July 28, 1979. I am nine years old. You are twenty-eight.

You're not like me, Luna. Say it.

I'm not like you, Claudia.

I wait on the porch for you to come out of your room. You do once. I hear your door unlock, your light step cross the floor—to the bathroom, I assume, but I don't hear the toilet flush or the water run. In a minute you're back in your room.

Night falls. Grandma and I try to eat dinner. We're both distracted by the crying owls. I've got a headache. Grandma gives me a Tylenol and I trudge upstairs. Your door is closed. My door is open. Grandma's is closed. She and I always keep our doors open when we're not in our rooms.

The owls are crying.

Louder, louder.

I open Grandma's door and peek inside. A wooden box is on her bed. I've never seen it before. The lid is off.

The owls are crying.

I walk toward the box. The initials HK are carved into the lid. The only person I can think of with those initials is my grandfather—Hyram Kane. I approach the box. It's empty, except for the plush dark velvet lining. My pulse quickens. I know what was inside. I know what the impression of a gun looks like.

The box is empty.

I run to your door. I pound on it.

Let me in, Claudia!

Grandma calls my name from the kitchen. I don't answer.

Let me in, Claudia!

I shove my hip and shoulder against the door. I'm only sixty-five pounds, but I try to force my way inside. I still think your door is locked.

The music is throbbing through the walls, vibrating in my chest.

I reach for the doorknob—maybe, maybe, I think. It turns.

Candles flicker on the bookshelf. The window is open, white lace curtains stir in the breeze. They're so sheer I can see the moon through them.

You're sitting on the floor in front of the stereo with your back to me, the gun pointed at your temple. You don't hear me come in. The smell of lavender and fear fills the room.

You jolt at my little girl hands on your shoulders, jerk your body around to face me, a look of surprise in your eyes, then tenderness and pain, and something else—awareness. You love me, *I think in that pause before struggle. I can see it in your eyes.*

Mama, *I whimper.*

I grab the gun from you. You're too shocked to stop me. But then you reach for it.

Luna, no! *You shout.* It's loaded.

You're stronger than me. You pry my fingers from the barrel. I lurch forward to reclaim it. If I can jerk it upward, wrench it away from you, I can hurl it through the window, into the pines. I can save you.

You wrap your hands around the grip. Our fingers touch. I can't tell whose are whose. We have the same hands.

Let go, baby! *You plead.*

I can't. I have to save you.

My head is swimming in a lavender haze. Everything is in a lavender haze—you, me, the owls, Jimmy.

He's watching. I wonder if he sees in color or black and white.

My body tenses—present tense. I'm trapped in the present.

Grandma is bolting up the stairs. She's screaming. She startles us both.

I let go of the gun. It was reflex. I swear it was. I didn't mean to.

The explosion is demonic, a roar from the bowels of hell, glass shattering, guitar grinding—a contrapuntal nightmare.

You look at me, your mouth agape, eyes wide, glazed, your forehead awash in blood. I can't tell if you meant to do it or not, if it was reflex too. You reach for me. Luna. *I can barely hear you. Your voice is like mist—wet, ethereal, ephemeral.*

You slump against the stereo. The record skips—just a beat, one jungle beat.

Red is running down your face. Your hair is red. Your arms are red. Your tears are red.

Grandma clutches me, swings me around. She thinks I've been shot. Your blood covers me. Mine is still coursing through my veins. I'm not dead. I'm not like you.

Grandma scrambles over to you. She looks funny on her hands and knees, moving frantically, like the piglets when I chase them in the pen. I like to hold them like babies, kiss their pink snouts. I name them. You told me I shouldn't; it'll only bring pain.

Tell me the story of my name, Claudia.

I feel the floorboards beneath me. Below them the kitchen, then the earth. I'm neither grounded nor airborne. I'm nowhere. I'm nobody.

Tell me the story of my name, Claudia.

I'm wailing—animal, guttural sounds.

Your eyes are open. Fixed on me—my long dark hair and bare legs splotched with mosquito bites and the red heart you scrawled around the stitches on my calf, your blood staining my face and my clothes.

I am the image you take with you to the mountaintop.

Not Jimmy.

Me.

Your eyes are fixed on me.

PART THREE:
"NIGHT FLIGHT"

CHAPTER FOURTEEN

"HOLY SHIT, what have you done?" Connie exclaimed when she arrived to take me to the bus station, catching herself in the mudroom doorway. She gave a cartoonish headshake then tromped through the kitchen and squatted beside me on the floor. "What the hell have you done?"

I combed my fingers through the narrow strip of spiky hair in the center of my scalp. I'd shaved the sides of my head with the razor I'd bought at the Mini Mart earlier that evening. I hadn't owned a razor since I'd stopped cutting myself years ago. Despite Aunt Lorraine's badgering after wispy sprigs of hair began appearing on my legs and armpits when I hit puberty, I'd refused to shave, just as I'd refused to pluck my eyebrows or coat my eyelashes with mascara. I nurtured hair that defied the protocols of femininity and assaulted the long, dark tresses that acquiesced—with Grandma's scissors after Claudia died and with a razor now that she was reborn. Like Lady Macbeth, I'd unsexed myself, from crown to toe.

Connie waved her hand over my head, as if she were trying to make my hair magically reappear. "Are you drunk?"

"No," I said, my voice quaking. My eyes were achy and burning. I brushed away the tears clinging to my lashes and sniffled.

She tore a paper towel from the roll on the counter and

handed it to me. "What happened?"

"I can't talk about it right now."

"Why not?"

Because she's mine again, I thought. *My mother is mine. I remember it all. She's the red I see and the owls I hear and the lavender I smell. She's the moon and the river and the rainbow's end. All of it. I'd tried to save her. Then she'd tried to save me. She'd put her father's pistol to her head, then she'd held my face in her eyes. With Jimmy as our witness, she'd chosen me. She was mine. I was hers. And I would tell no one until I knew if Jimmy was ours.*

"I promise I'll tell you everything, Connie. Just not yet." I blew my nose then pitched the napkin into the trash can.

She leaned against the counter and tapped her foot on the floor. Her shoes were damp with the wintry mix of snow and sleet that had begun to fall that afternoon. At first, I'd worried the turn in the weather was portentous, that I'd miss my only chance to go to London. Then I decided it was a good omen, like synchronicity, in a Jungian sort of way—snow crystals dissolving on my grandmother's windowpane within five feet of the crystals I'd placed underneath her mattress, the note I'd written that explained it all resting on her pillow. The coincidence was meaningful. Or the meaning was coincidental. Either way, I knew I was going to London.

****

The Full River Greyhound station is like every other small town bus station in America: cheap linoleum floors with scuff marks and gravel residue that crunches underfoot; crinkled potato chip bags stashed like footnotes under metal chairs, wads of gum stuck to the bottoms; dingy white walls, reminders of the days when travelers chain-smoked over Styrofoam cups of stale coffee while they waited for a bus to Anywhere But Here, the smell of Camels and Winstons lingering in the building's brittle bones.

I dragged my duffel bag inside while a grizzled old man I vaguely recalled from my great-grandfather's funeral held the door open. Connie trudged in behind me, my backpack slung across her shoulder.

"Help you?" the clerk asked curtly. She didn't bother to look up from her crossword puzzle.

I dropped my bag by a row of chairs near a space heater and sat down. "Just waiting for the eight o'clock bus," I said. She gave me a trenchant glance and tapped her pencil on the laminate countertop—a relic of the '60s, no doubt, like everything else in the room, including her.

"Need a ticket?" I told her I'd already bought one, and with a disgruntled *humph* she returned to her puzzle.

"What's her problem?" I muttered to Connie.

"What do you think?" she said, pointing to my head. "What in the world made you think that was a good idea?"

"I wanna stand out, make Jimmy notice me."

She sucked her teeth. "I hate to tell you, but you're not gonna be the only person in London with a Mohawk."

"Yeah, well, maybe I wanted a change," I said, pulling my hoodie over my head. "New country, new hair." *Maybe even a new dad*, I thought.

Connie browsed the bus schedules tacked to the walls, reading aloud some of the more interesting destinations.

"Check this out. Takes four days to go from here to San Francisco. Imagine how tired your ass would be if you had to sit on a bus for four days." She snagged a brochure on package deals to Kings Dominion then sat next to me by the heater. "It's cold in here," she said with a shiver. "I hope the snow doesn't hold you up."

"It won't," I said.

"It could, you know. You could miss your flight, then you'd be stuck in Atlanta. Remember that guy who killed all those black kids there in the '70s? I wouldn't wanna get stuck in some nasty bus station in Atlanta. Sure you wanna go through with this?"

I eyed her indignantly.

"Seriously, all kinds of freaky people hang out in bus stations." She patted the top of my head. "Case in point."

I swatted her hand away. "You were all for it that day at the Record Shack when I told you I was thinking about getting a Mohawk."

"Well, it's one thing to have weird hair in your own country; it's another thing to have it in somebody else's. But whatever. It's your hair."

We sat there, not talking, not looking at each other, listening to the old lady harangue somebody named Walter over the phone for leaving dirty dishes in the sink. I thought of Grandma. She'd sense I wasn't home the moment she walked into the kitchen and saw the mess I'd left. She and Aunt Lorraine would search the house for me, wondering if I was at work or at Connie's, then Grandma would read my note and notice Claudia's open door, and for the first time in nearly ten years, she'd look inside. Then she'd remember, just like me. It would all come back to her—in fits and starts or all at once, I couldn't say. But it would all come back, in full color, full volume. And she'd understand why I'd left the door open. She'd know we could never close it again.

"I'm sorry about Denzel," I said to Connie. The apology was a non sequitur, but her feelings about the incident had been troubling me since my confession.

She flicked her wrist indifferently. "I'm not mad about that anymore."

"It didn't have anything to do with you—or even with him and me. We both knew the score."

"I know, Luna." She pulled a butterfly comb from her afro—the mate to the one she'd given me at the Record Shack the day I'd bought the *Outrider* poster. "I was gonna give this to you, for good luck, but now you don't have any hair."

I took the comb from her. "It'll be good luck whether I wear it or not. Thanks, Connie."

"Now it's my turn to tell you a secret," she said, twisting the back of her silver hoop earring, a nervous tick of hers. "UNC sent me an early acceptance letter. I'm all set for fall semester."

I dropped my eyes. I hadn't thought about next month, let alone next fall since my great-grandfather died. It finally dawned on me that after summer break, Connie and I wouldn't be together anymore. I didn't know where I'd be, especially now that Grandma was sick, but it wouldn't be Chapel Hill. Connie would make new friends. Her life would be different from mine. *She* would be different. How could we not drift apart? Except for Grandma, I'd be alone.

"That's great," I said dryly. "I'm happy for you."

"Liar."

"No, really. I'm happy for you. Chapel Hill—that's fantastic. It's what you always wanted."

She shifted her attention from her earring to her fingernails, meticulously pushing back her cuticles, another nervous tick. "You could still apply," she said, a hint of melancholy in her voice, as if she was just as apprehensive about leaving me as I was about being left.

I unzipped my backpack and dropped the comb inside. "Girls with Mohawks don't exactly mix with a school like Chapel Hill. Too buttoned down. Besides, I don't think I'm college material. Hell, no one in my family's ever gone to college, unless you count that secretarial school Aunt Lorraine went to."

"What are you talking about? You're smart enough to get in. You stink at math, but you rock at literature and history and all that stuff, and you're a kickass writer."

"I don't need a college degree to be a writer. Maya Angelou didn't go to college. Neither did Truman Capote. Jack Kerouac went, but he didn't graduate. Formal education is just another opportunity for white dudes in suits to make kids like me think they've got a shot at the American Dream. It's all bullshit."

"Get real, Luna. I know you're gonna be rich and famous one day, but you need something to fall back on until you are."

"You sound like Aunt Lorraine."

Her mouth turned down in an exasperated frown. "You won't get anywhere waiting tables. First person who stiffs you on a tip you'd tell to fuck off."

"I'm not gonna be a waitress, for chrissake."

"What are you gonna do next year?"

"I don't know. A lot could happen between now and next

fall. A lot could happen between now and next week," I said sullenly, wishing the coffee machine on the ticket counter was brewing a pot of Coors instead of Folgers. "Besides, when I finally do leave home I'm *really* leaving home—North Carolina, the South. Maybe I'll beat you to New York. We could be roomies in the Village."

She leaned down and held her hands in front of the heater. "I'm not living in the Village," she said gruffly.

"After I win the Pulitzer I'll spring for a cool apartment in Soho."

"After I win CEO of the Year we're moving to Park Avenue."

The hulking bus roared into the parking lot and stopped with a snort in front of the station.

"Your bus is here," the old lady announced, as if we couldn't see it through the plate glass door.

The driver barreled inside and headed for the restroom. I stared at the three or four people gathering their bags outside. One of them, a young woman with a down jacket and long blonde hair, threw her arms around the middle-aged lady waiting for her under the awning—her mother, I imagined. The two of them rocked back and forth, as if they hadn't seen each other for a lifetime, then collected the girl's skis and disappeared around the side of the bus. A tightness gripped my chest.

I glanced at Connie. Her caramel eyes glistened in the pewter glow from the streetlight drifting through the window blinds.

"Guess this is it," I said.

She took a labored breath then threw her shoulders back. "When does your bus get to Atlanta?"

"Early afternoon. My plane leaves at six."

"What do you want me to tell your grandma? You know she'll call."

"I don't think she will. She won't need to."

The driver shuffled back into the waiting room and nodded at us, his rust-colored comb-over flapping in the rush of air from the ceiling vent. "You coming on the eight o'clock?"

I swallowed hard. "Yeah."

"Well, come on out and let's get your stuff loaded."

We followed him to the mud-splashed bus, and I handed him my duffel bag. A gray wind blew the smell of body odor and pungent cologne in my face. I wondered how long he'd been on duty and hoped he had a case of energy drinks stashed underneath his seat.

"Remember what I told you about changing your money when you get to the airport," Connie said. "And ask someone at the information desk how to get to your hotel. Might be a little tricky, what with the tube lines and all, but you'll figure it out."

"I know, I know. Geez, Connie, you're gonna be the biggest pain-in-the-ass mama who ever lived."

She forced a smile. "You're really and truly sure you wanna do this?"

The driver tapped the horn and scowled at me. "Another minute and we're leaving without you. I got a schedule to keep."

I gave her a quick hug then mounted the bus steps.

"Hey," she called. "Good luck with Jimmy."

The door whooshed shut and I hesitated, looking at her standing in the snow, my hands pressed against the glass. I wanted to tell her I loved her, that she was the best friend

I'd ever had, that she could have my stuffed Snoopy and my journals if the plane crashed, and I was sorry my grandfather Hyram had treated her dad like an antebellum field hand, and I was already jealous of anyone she would love more than me in the coming years. Instead, I waved goodbye and watched her vanish in a plume of exhaust fumes, like a smoky fade-out in a Hitchcock film, and tried to ignore the hollow feeling in my gut and the rush of tears welling in my eyes.

CHAPTER FIFTEEN

THERE ARE some images that don't leave you, no matter how much the picture fades and crinkles in your memory: an obese drunk redneck whistling "Ring of Fire" while he pisses on the floor in the Raleigh bus station is one of them. I sat by the vending machines watching him, hoping he wasn't waiting for my connection. He lurked in a corner, whistling and pissing and staring at me, probably hoping the skinny Goth girl would sell him a dime bag.

It was after eleven p.m., and the last two hours had been a phantasmagoria of bawdy characters and bizarre behavior and a blur of winter-washed scenery through a frosty bus window. On the ride from Full River to Raleigh, I'd sat across the aisle from a loquacious elderly woman who was on her way to see her son in Dallas. A couple with a toddler sat behind me, the little boy kicking the back of my seat, the man explaining to his wife in graphic detail why he prefers doggie style to the missionary position. Two African American twenty-something women huddled together in the back of the bus, speaking in staid whispers.

Lesbians, Connie would have said with a wink.

I remembered a conversation we'd had about two young women we'd noticed covertly holding hands in the KFC dining room once.

"How do you know they're lesbians?" I'd asked, after she'd made the same declaration about them.

"Look how cozy they are with each other."

I studied the way one of them stroked the other's hand with her thumb, how their thighs were touching, how careful they were not to meet each other's eyes. "We're cozy sometimes," I said. "Not like that, but we're cozy sometimes."

"That's different. We're not lesbians," Connie said. She clasped her hands behind her back. "At least, I'm not. If you are . . . that's cool. I'll love you just the same."

"I'm not gay, Connie," I said.

"There's nothing wrong with it if you are."

I leaned against the fry station, feeling the heat against my back. "You think I'm gay?"

She shrugged. "I just said there's nothing wrong with it."

"You're trying to get me to say I'm gay."

She took my shoulders and forced me to meet her gaze, like an erstwhile counselor in a teen angst movie. "Are you?" she asked.

I shook away from her and straightened my shirt. "No, I'm not gay," I said in a sort of growl.

"So you're straight?"

"Maybe I don't know what I am," I said softly. I popped a fry in my mouth then wiped my hands on my shirt front. "Maybe I'm trying to figure that out."

Connie had jostled behind the counter, making a show of restocking the cups, a bemused expression on her face. "Doesn't matter," she'd said. "If androgyny is good enough for Prince, it's good enough for me."

She'd never broached the subject again, and she'd defended

me from anyone who called me a dyke. I thought of her while I eavesdropped on the girls on the bus and wondered who would defend me now.

The whistling man in the Raleigh station bought a Snickers bar from the vending machine and sat down next to me.

"Going to Atlanta?" he asked, alcohol oozing from his pores.

I shifted as far away from him as I could. "Maybe," I said.

He took a bite of his Snickers and chewed greedily. My stomach growled. I hadn't eaten since breakfast. "Hungry?" he asked, his mouth full of chocolate.

"I'm fine," I said.

"There's a burger joint nearby. I'll buy you something to eat if you want." I stiffened. I wished the elderly lady who'd befriended me was still there, but her connection to Dallas had arrived half an hour ago. I scanned the room for any familiar faces. Everyone on the bus from Full River was gone.

The whistler placed his beefy hand on my thigh. "What *can* I buy you?" he said with a smirk, oblivious to the security guard lingering by the ticket counter, chatting up a janitor.

My face flushed. I felt naked, as if my clothes had disintegrated, leaving the body that had perplexed me since early adolescence exposed and fragile.

"I'd have to tell you if I was a cop, you know. It's the law. I promise I'm not a cop."

"Yeah, well, I'm pretty sure the guy across the room with the gun is," I said.

His eyes swiveled from me to the guard, who was now watching us.

"My mistake," he said, then waddled to the men's room, the cop following close behind. I fished my journal and pen from

Christy Alexander Hallberg

my backpack and recorded the whole nefarious scene, the plot of a short story already taking shape in my mind. I imagined Connie's reaction when I'd relay the incident to her next week: *I told you that Mohawk was a dumb idea.*

I had a four-hour layover in Raleigh. The bus to Atlanta wasn't scheduled to depart until three-thirty in the morning. I wandered around the dreary waiting room, careful to avoid the whistler and the steely-eyed indigents loitering near the door, scoping out road-weary travelers they could take for a few bucks, stealthily slipping outside whenever the cop drew near. An emaciated girl with a pasty complexion and mousy brown hair that smelled like cigarettes and beer cornered me in the bathroom and asked for money. I gazed at her, nonplussed.

"I don't have any cash," I lied.

"Anything at all would be great," she said, her North Carolina accent smoky and languid.

A woman with two little girls clad in matching Hello Kitty dresses breezed past us. She paused long enough to catch my eye, as if to convey a tacit warning to keep our degenerate hands off her children. I wanted to tell her I wasn't like the panhandler, that we came from different planets, she and I, our soundtracks were different, our genres were different—mine was Roman Mythology, hers Southern Gothic. *A Mohawk and black lipstick do not a Faulkner novel make, lady.* She ushered her little girls inside a stall and stood outside the swinging door, guarding them from whatever tawdriness we exuded.

I pulled a five-dollar bill from my pocket and thrust it at the bedraggled girl, hoping she'd take it and go. "That's all I've got," I said.

She snatched the money then staggered off. Ten minutes

later I saw her huddled with a group of equally emaciated girls outside, knocking back a brown bag special of something. They shimmied about under a callous sky, passing each other the bottle, laughing at jokes I couldn't hear, snow flurries swirling around them. There was something unnerving about them—cynical, joyless, like the photograph of a vacant Jimmy Page backstage at Live Aid I'd seen in a magazine. The three surviving members of Led Zeppelin are sitting together against a gray backdrop before their much-ballyhooed reunion, Robert and John Paul Jones staring clear-eyed into the camera, both alert and present. Jimmy is slumped in a wooden straight-back chair, glassy-eyed, lids so heavy he can barely keep them open. He's holding a cup of something that probably smells like Jack Daniels, a cheeky smile on his face, as though he were ensconced in his own private alcohol-soaked world, amused by the chaos around him.

I pressed my hand against the cold glass door and let the chill sweep through me. "To tell you the truth," I whispered to the distant image of the girl, "I come from a long line of Faulkner novels. And I bet you're an ancient epic all by yourself."

"Coming or going?" a harsh voice behind me said.

I turned around. The security guard loomed over me, his hand patting his holstered gun in a deliberate manner.

"Neither," I said. "I'm waiting for my bus."

"You need to go in the waiting area, then."

"I'm just standing here."

The veins in his neck bulged. "Look," he said, "I don't care where you stand, but you're not hanging around here."

I grabbed my bags and ambled toward the waiting area, where there were no empty seats. Travelers sprawled on the unforgiving chairs, trying to sleep and keep an eye on their belongings simultaneously. The TV bolted to the wall blasted the latest news on the Jimmy Swaggart sex scandal and the Tawana Brawley rape allegations. Little kids toddled around carrying blankets and bottles, tormenting exhausted adults.

I set my stuff down and sat on the floor, draping my coat over my backpack to use as a pillow. I was too tired to care that the floor was grimy and hard. I drew my knees to my chest, propped my head on my backpack, and shut my eyes. *Just for a minute*, I thought. Long enough to forget I was stranded inside a squalid building that smelled like stagnant creek water, with a ramshackle crew of the loneliest-looking people I'd ever seen in one setting. I was teetering on the edge of sleep when the guard's brusque voice roused me.

"No sleeping on the floor."

I squinted up at him, the stark overhead light stinging my eyes. "There's no place to sit." I gestured to the chairs, teeming with weary bodies.

"I'm not gonna tell you again." He perched his large hands on his hips and spread his legs, as if he were playing a caricature of a cop in a *Saturday Night Live* skit.

I forced myself to my feet, and he swaggered off to hassle the other somnolent people on the floor.

I bought a prepackaged turkey sandwich from the vending machine and ate it sitting on the toilet in the ladies' room, the sibilant sound of running water and hot air from the hand dryers my dinner music. I dozed in the stall, waiting for the man at the information counter to announce the arrival of my bus. I'd left Full River five hours ago, but I was less than one hundred miles from home. I could've hitchhiked and been halfway to Atlanta by now. I could've flagged down an itinerant preacher and bartered my soul for a ride. He'd meet his quota, and I'd be somewhere past Charlotte, listening to contemporary Christian music on his car radio, watching the desolate landscape flash by on I-85. Claudia had wanted to travel. We'd sit in her idling VW on the outskirts of town and she'd wax poetic about freedom, as if it lay on the other side of the county line, like Oz sparkling in a poppy field. *Where is freedom?* I'd ask her. *Anywhere but here*, she'd say, her voice dense with longing.

"This isn't freedom, Claudia," I murmured. "A shithouse in Raleigh isn't freedom."

You have to go farther, I thought. *All the way to a loo in London.*

****

At three-thirty, my bus to Atlanta arrived. I gathered my backpack and headed outside, along with the obese redneck, whistling "Ring of Fire" again. The driver stood by the bus door twirling his keychain on his finger. He was a brawny man, like a bouncer at one of those strip joints we drove past on the way to the station.

"Only got room for one more," he said, shifting from one foot to the other.

"But I've got a ticket," I said.

He looked at me impassively.

"I can't wait for another bus. I've got to get to Atlanta by early tomorrow afternoon."

The whistler let loose an insolent laugh. "I gotta get

somewhere, too. We all gotta get somewhere."

He was sober now. Stone cold, hung-over sober. And he was still pissed that I'd blown him off in the waiting room rather than sucked him off in a dark alley behind some greasy spoon.

"I'll pay you," I blurted. His bloodshot eyes flickered. I dug through my pockets and found a twenty-dollar bill. The rest of my cash was hidden in the sleeves of my sweatshirt in my backpack. "I know it's not much, but . . . " I peered pleadingly at the bus driver. "He can use his ticket for a later bus, right?"

"Yeah," he said. "There's another one coming in a couple hours."

I waved the bill at the whistler. "So this will be enough for a burger, or something, to tide you over." I held my breath and waited. Finally, he grasped the money and folded it inside his jeans pocket.

"Strange thing, ain't it," he said. "Just a little while ago, it coulda been me giving *you* money." He let his eyes roam unbridled over my body. "Reckon I'd have asked for a refund, though." He spat on the cement then lumbered back toward the building, clutching a translucent plastic trash bag bulging with clothes.

The driver twirled his keys restively. "If you're coming, climb aboard."

It was dark in the bus, except for the glaring terminal lights streaming through the windows. I searched the rows of seats for the coveted empty one. A sea of faces stared back at me—bleary-eyed, spiritless. I spotted the empty seat in the back, right in front of the toilet, and trudged down the narrow aisle, careful not to bonk anyone with my backpack. A man with an

American flag tattooed on his forearm dozed in the seat next to mine. I heaved my backpack onto the luggage rack and sat down while the driver climbed on board and started the engine. We'd already merged onto the interstate by the time I realized I'd left my duffel bag in the bus station.

Keening terror seized me. I stormed up the aisle to the driver.

"We have to go back," I gasped.

"You're not supposed to be up here. See that sign? No passengers near the driver when the bus is in motion."

I clenched the metal bar by his seat. "I left my bag at the station. We have to go back."

He gaped at me in the rearview mirror. "If you don't sit down I'll put you out at the next stop."

"What about my bag?"

"You can call the Raleigh station when we get to Charlotte."

"But I'll never get it in time for my flight in Atlanta."

"Sorry, kid." He sounded conciliatory now. "That's the best I can do. We're not going back, so you might as well sit down and try to get some sleep. We'll be in Charlotte at six-thirty."

I plodded back to my seat and took a mental inventory of the contents of my backpack: passport, cash, journal, sweatshirt, Connie's butterfly comb, Claudia's anklet, itinerary. I could get by with that. Clean underwear, socks, shirts, jeans, toiletries, and a Polaroid camera were luxuries I'd have to sacrifice. At least I had the essentials. The trip was still a go. I leaned my head against my seatback and let the rhythm of the road lull me to sleep.

CHAPTER SIXTEEN

W~RITE~, ~MY~ mother once insisted. *Tell me a story.* I put pen to paper and scribbled the words as we taxied down the runway in Atlanta. Poetic snippets. Mawkish teenage reverie:

The moment of takeoff—when the rubber leaves the road. When the bird is on the wing and flight meets night.

Time to fly now.

Time to fly now, baby.

To the stars and the moon, cradled in my mother's eyes.

Nothing here for you now.

Nothing here for you now, baby.

Not home, not memory. The Hermit was abroad—truth and knowledge and light in one hand, power and presage in the other.

Climbing, climbing. Ten thousand feet. Twenty thousand feet. Thirty thousand feet. Like magic. Like mystery.

Like Freedom.

I'd be there at dawn.

PART FOUR: "HOUSES OF THE HOLY"

CHAPTER SEVENTEEN

I PASSED through customs in a fugue, dazed from exhaustion, adrenaline pulsing through me like a strobe light. The whole airport was pulsing—people rushing by, dragging suitcases and children, speaking languages as varied as their dress; a woman's sterile voice announcing arrivals and departures through the loudspeaker; capricious carts motoring the elderly and infirm through the terminal, staccato horn blasts parting the herd. The Atlanta airport had been much less chaotic, less intimidating, but then, a mere bus ride had been all that separated me from home. Now over four thousand miles and an entire ocean lay between us. No one tells you distance doesn't always mean freedom. Sometimes it just means separation, a temporary loss of baggage, both literal and metaphorical. Sometimes it just means lost.

I clutched my backpack and bumbled through a maze of fast-food restaurants and duty-free shops until I found a currency exchange kiosk, where an Indian man swapped my money for a stack of bills with Queen Elizabeth's face printed on the front, then directed me to an information desk near the escalators leading down to the Underground stations, where he said I could get help navigating the tube system.

"My hotel is supposed to be near Paddington Station," I told the lady at the desk.

She sat on the edge of her stool and smiled genially, her starched white blouse crisp and clean beneath her purple blazer.

"Take the Piccadilly line to Earls Court, then switch to the District line to Paddington Station," she said in a posh British accent that reminded me of a flinty dowager in one of those old movies Grandma and I used to watch. I felt a pang of wistfulness. She'd be home by now, back from her appointment with the specialist, who'd no doubt confirmed her diagnosis. He'd probably used the word *terminal*—much more insidious than *excrescence*—but still suggested surgery and chemo, which she'd already refused. I'd read enough books about tragic characters who succumb to cancer, or some other pernicious disease, to know recurrence meant death. She would have asked him how long she had left, and ever the stoic, begun planning for the inevitable and how to tell me the prognosis I instinctively knew.

The information lady looked at me solicitously, as if I were an orphan in a Dickens novel, destitute and drifting. "Are you all right, love?" she asked, her eyes soft and warm.

In that bewildered moment, the word *love* listing toward me like a silver tray of crumpets and scones, I exhaled. I'd made it. I was standing on foreign soil, in the land of Pip and Oliver Twist, the Brontë sisters and William Blake and John Keats. And somewhere in the same land, looming larger than a misty mountain on a moonlit night, stood Jimmy Page.

****

I wandered the choked streets around Paddington Station

for an hour looking for the converted Victorian house on Queensborough Terrace, where I'd booked a room through a travel agent in Full River. The frenetic energy of the city was palpable—locals, nursing cups of Costa coffee, dodging tourists in Union Jack sweatshirts purchased from tawdry souvenir stores near Hyde Park; jackhammers reverberating on chaotic construction sites; tinny music trickling from a plethora of Middle Eastern restaurants; car horns honking at oblivious tourists like me who'd forgotten to look right *then* left before crossing the street. I was overwhelmed by all of it—*gobsmacked*, as I'd overheard a man on the tube say, right after a disembodied voice implored *Mind the gap*. Even the air smelled English—like a cup of warm Earl Grey tea and starched white linen.

"Bayswater Station is only one stop on the Circle line from Paddington," the hotel clerk informed me after I'd finally found the place. "That station's much closer to the hotel."

"Yeah, well I didn't know that," I said abjectly.

He was a young guy, a little older than me, but not by much, coltish and surefooted, with thick reddish hair and a heavily moussed cowlick he kept swatting from his forehead, as if it were a nagging fly. There was a hole in his right earlobe, where the faux diamond stud he'd probably left on his nightstand before going on duty fit. The nametag on his white oxford said Peter. Peter, the conservative Boy Friday by day, earring-wearing club kid by night. He could have been a member of a New Wave band posing as a hotel clerk in a music video.

I handed him my passport and he looked up my reservation in a register. His hands were small and smooth. Uncle Jack would have called him an *inside boy*—the sort who shuns sports and calls AAA to change a flat tire. If there was one thing Uncle Jack couldn't abide it was an *inside boy*.

"How will you be paying?" Peter asked.

"Cash," I said. He gave me the invoice, and I fished a wad of bills from my jeans pocket and counted out the amount.

"Right, then," he said with a jovial nod. "Check–in is at half-past two."

I felt the blood drain from my face, chapped and raw from the biting wind. "But it's only ten," I said, the urgency in my voice obvious. His eyes skittered over me, his thin lips parted, as if he were about to summon a bobby to remove me from the premises. "Look," I said wearily. "I don't care if the room's dirty."

He chewed his bottom lip, then sighed and ducked into an office adjacent to the desk and returned with a key. "Don't say anything to my boss when he comes in. I'm not supposed to do this." He slid the key across the counter.

I slipped it inside my pocket quickly, in case he changed his mind. "Thanks," I said.

He shrugged. "He's a wanker, my boss. Bollocks to him." He flicked his hair from his eyes—large and dark, like mine. "Welcome to London, mate."

****

The room was small but neat and relatively clean. The previous occupants had apparently been fastidious. I surveyed the white walls, black scuff marks on white baseboards, black smudges on the white closet door. Everything was black and white, right down to the frayed bedspread and photographs of Princess Di and St. Paul's Cathedral on the walls. I'd always lived in the gray areas, the chasm between knowing and not knowing, and the ash pit of not wanting to know. Now I did want to know. Black *or* white—either one was preferable to gray.

I flopped on the twin-size bed and opened my backpack. I'd bought a toothbrush, toothpaste, and deodorant at the airport. I figured I could make do with my jeans and sweatshirt, but the thought of meeting Jimmy Page wearing dirty underwear seemed like blasphemy.

I pulled out my journal and reviewed the notes I'd made for the trip, based largely on what I'd gleaned from *Hammer of the Gods*. I'd felt brazen jotting down the information from the security of my great-grandfather's shack, Led Zeppelin roaring in the background, Jimmy guiding my hand from the *Outrider* poster like a cicerone. I'd felt fearless—an intrepid traveler of time and space, of whom Robert Plant sang in "Kashmir." Now I just felt fear, mocking laughter howling inside me. Who was I to think this journey would be anything but quixotic?

The elevator—lift, Peter had called it—creaked open and two voices speaking Spanish emerged then faded as the couple traipsed down the hall. I wondered how many guests were traveling solo, on a quest they could only make alone, one that would irrevocably alter the trajectory of their lives, no matter what they found at the rainbow's end, or the other side of a Rock star's front door. But which front door? Jimmy owned three houses—Tower House in London, Old Mill House in Windsor, and Aleister Crowley's former home, Boleskine, on a hill above Loch Ness in Scotland.

Mr. MacGregor lives down by the river . . .

I'd written him a letter on the plane and tucked it inside a manila envelope with pictures of Claudia and me—one of her when she was my age, another of the two of us on Grandma's front porch the summer before Claudia died, and a Polaroid I'd asked Connie to take of me at the bus station. I figured I could leave the envelope in his mailbox or slip it underneath a gate where someone would find it. I'd included my hotel address and phone number. One way or another he'd know who I was, and if he'd ever met Claudia, he'd remember her, then he'd contact me. He'd want to meet me. He'd want to make sure.

I lay down on the bed and stared at the water stain on the ceiling. I wished I could call Grandma, let her know I'd arrived safely, but I knew if I heard her voice I'd catch the next plane home, and I couldn't do that. I had six days to solve a riddle. I dropped my journal and envelope with my letter and photographs back inside my backpack, then grabbed my coat and started out.

****

"Can you tell me how to get to this address?" I asked Peter. I pulled a neatly folded piece of notebook paper from my pocket and gave it to him.

"29 Melbury Road in Kensington and Chelsea," he said, squinting at my small script, as if he were near-sighted but too cool to wear glasses. He opened a map and studied it earnestly. "Looks like High Street Kensington is the closest station. You can take the Circle line from Bayswater straight there. If you take the Central line from Queensway—that's the station near the corner of Bayswater Road; Bayswater Station's a couple blocks farther down—you'll need to change to the Circle after a stop or two."

The lines and stations and directions were a blur in my head. Peter must have seen the addled look on my face.

"Just stick with Bayswater," he said. "Circle line."

He straightened his tie and offered a curt greeting to a portly man walking through the door, dressed in the same white oxford and khaki trousers as Peter—his wanker boss, I gathered. The man hung his coat and scarf on a rack behind the desk, then stepped inside the office and shut the door without acknowledging me.

"What you looking for on Melbury Road?" Peter asked, smoothing his rumpled shirt.

I almost told him to mind his own business. Instead I came out with it. What the hell, I decided. "Somebody's house."

"Posh neighborhood. You know someone there?"

I flashed on Claudia that night at the drive-in when she took me to see *The Song Remains the Same: There are lots of ways to know someone, Luna. You can be face to face with a person and not know them at all. Or you can hear their voice in your head and know their soul.*

"I'm looking for Jimmy Page's house," I said sheepishly. "You know, the Led Zeppelin guitarist."

"What you want with that bloke?" He eyeballed my Mohawk. "I figured you were more of a Psychedelic Furs or Cure bird."

"I've got my reasons," I said.

He scratched his chin, clean-shaven and pale, like the rest of his face, save for the splattering of freckles on his nose and cheeks. "You're not some sort of mad stalker, are you?" He gave a waggish smile. "Aww, I'm just taking the piss." He offered me a brochure of Hop on Hop Off Bus routes and the street map he'd just consulted. "The bus is a good way to see the sites. Don't take the tourist boat, though. You'll freeze your bum off in this weather."

I bundled up in my coat and covered my head with my hoodie. "I doubt there's any way around freezing my bum off," I said.

"So you'll hit the shops or pop into a pub for a pint later. That'll warm you up."

"Bayswater, off at Kensington, right?"

"Brilliant. You're practically there already."

Not exactly. When I got to Bayswater Road at the end of the block, I headed in the opposite direction of the station and had to backtrack. By the time I reached the turnstile I'd forgotten how to operate the ticket machine and had to ask an attendant for help. I hadn't figured out the coin currency, so I dropped a fistful of change into her hand and let her feed the machine.

A horde of locals, most with earphones strapped to their heads, CD players in hand, breezed past me, their faces blank, like a moving piece of invisible art, sophisticated and inscrutable. I'd abandoned all pretense of urbanity at Heathrow. Naked vulnerability had proven far more profitable.

The attendant steered me through the turnstile and pointed to two flights of stairs that led to the train platforms. I hesitated, then chose the stairs on the left. Every destination since I'd arrived in London seemed like a fork in the road. One wrong turn led to another. Or rather, one missed stop led to Westminster Abbey.

"We're heading for High Street Kensington Station, right?"

I asked the old man sitting across from me reading *The Guardian*.

"No, no," he said stiffly. "That's the other direction."

"I'm on the Circle line, right? I thought it went straight to High Street Kensington."

He peered at me over his glasses. "It does. Where did you get on?"

"Bayswater."

He pointed to a map above his head. I hadn't noticed it until then. "Well then, you missed your stop."

I clutched the edge of my seat. "How do I get on the right train?"

The doors flew open, and the old man tucked his paper underneath his arm and hobbled off. I shoved my way through boarding passengers and sprinted up to the crowded street, where Big Ben stood erect and formidable, chiming the noon hour. Before I could get my bearings to ask someone how to find the right train, I got tangled up in a tour group and wound up standing in front of Westminster Abbey. I'd seen photographs before—iconic images interpolated between chapters on the Norman Conquest and the Magna Carta in history textbooks, and mimeographed on a handout on Chaucer from Mrs. Neville's class. But Westminster Abbey on a gray winter's day in the year of our Lord 1988 was majestic, a spectacle of medieval lore. I searched my mind for the words to the Prologue of *The Canterbury Tales*. I'd memorized the first part in Middle English at the beginning of the year for a class project, but now all I could remember was the photograph on the handout and how it seemed like a lie in the presence of the sandstone flesh. I moved with the tour group to the front of the line, paid the entry fee, then stepped inside.

I felt like an apostate come back to the fold, except the only divine inspiration I garnered derived from grandeur, not God—the ornate stained glass windows, coruscating in the feeble lamplight; the elegiac beauty of sepulchral chambers of kings and queens; Gothic arches, swooping upward like hands in prayer; Chaucer's tomb and the stone slabs lodged in the floor of the Poets' Corner memorializing writers I revered, and the sense of trepidation I felt at treading over them.

At the back of the Cathedral nave, near the coronation chair, were votive candle stands—racks of white prayer candles flickering in the sable silence. I thought of Claudia's room—the candles and incense, Tarot cards and crystals—a convergence of the profane and the holy.

A woman with a toddler clinging to her hip dropped a coin into the offering slot and lit a candle. Head bowed, eyes closed, she whispered something inaudible to all but God, then crossed herself and slipped back into the crowd. The ritual had a Voodoo quality about it, like she could just as easily have been summoning Damballa as Yahweh, or one of those deities in Aleister Crowley's Thelemic pantheon.

I felt awkward, unsure what to do. To pray or not to pray? That was the question and the answer.

I approached the stand and slipped a coin into the slot. A prayer for holy intercession couldn't hurt.

I lit a candle for Claudia, and another for me, and a third one for Jimmy.

The Holy Spirit and the Daughter and the Father, who art in England, hallowed be thy name.

I lit one more candle, for Grandma, and placed it in the last empty space in the rack.

Forgive us our trespasses as we forgive those who trespass against us.

I wandered back to the Poets' Corner and squatted on the stone tablet commemorating the Brontë sisters, writing in my journal a fable made true in my mind's eye in that moment of knowledge and light: I'm wearing a white granny dress and a jangly anklet and my long, black hair is woven delicately into braids with blue satin ribbons tied at the ends. I'm nine years old, hiding in a garden, chortling a song about a mystery man with rabbits and roses. Jimmy is searching for me. The tune—*my* tune—comes to him at last, pealing from a pagan hedgerow. He parts the bush with his violin bow. His eyes are glowing red.

I see you, Lunabelle.

I see you, Mr. MacGregor. I see your black and white face and your arms, outstretched for me, ready and waiting, and your wild hair like mine and your hands, long, slender fingers, skin like porcelain. Give me your hand. Give me your name. Say it, say it. Take me to the river and duck me under and say it and say it until I come up for air, until I take my first breath, floating beside you and the swans and my mother by the banks of the Thames.

Say my name.

****

An attendant at the church gave me directions to Kensington High Street Station. I walked through the expansive building, past the eateries and fancy shops to the exit, and up and down

Kensington High Street until I found Melbury Road, then, just around the bend, number 29: Tower House.

There was no mistaking it, looming like a giant Gothic sore thumb in the midst of a host of Queen Anne houses. I'd read that William Burges had designed it in the late nineteenth century in the French Gothic Revival style, with a medieval interior that includes a hall with astrological signs painted on the ceiling. The red brick façade boasts a cylindrical tower and conical roof that evoke visions of Bram Stoker and Mary Shelley furiously scribbling their macabre tales by a raging fire with a mad scullery maid shackled in the turret.

Jimmy had purchased the house in 1972 from actor Richard Harris, who swore it was haunted. Maybe it was—or is. Burges, an opium addict, had died in one of the bedrooms. In the mid-'70s, Jimmy loaned the basement film editing facilities to director, writer, and Crowley aficionado Kenneth Anger, with whom Jimmy was working on Anger's movie *Lucifer Rising*. The two had a falling out, and Anger claimed to have put a curse on Jimmy. Maybe that's why he never found his way back to the pines, back to the owls, back to us. Kenneth Anger had put a curse on him.

I held Connie's butterfly comb in my hand and sat on the curb across the street, watching his house, as if it were a sentient being on the verge of betraying its secrets.

My whole body wanted a cigarette. I wanted to smell like the fecund tobacco fields I'd left behind, the numinous fire in my great-grandfather's shack. I wanted to smell like home. I wanted Jimmy to remember the rich fragrance of North Carolina winter woods. Isn't smell the most likely of the five senses to trigger memory?

A young woman in heels and a tight skirt switched across the street and got into the Austin Mini parked beside Jimmy's house. She pulled away from the curb, and the wrought iron gate in front of his garage opened, as if her car were a magnet, a force of immutable attraction. I wondered if he knew her, if she occupied space in his life more intimate than the side of his road.

A black Jaguar rolled toward the gate and came to a stop at the end of the driveway.

I stood up, my breath caught in my throat. I watched the car turn onto Melbury and head in my direction. The windows were tinted. I couldn't see the occupants. But they could see me. If Jimmy was in that car, lounging in the back seat with a fine crystal shot glass filled with Jack Daniels, he could see me.

I brushed my hoodie from my head.

Roll down the goddamn window. Don't you know who I am? Where I come from?

The car inched along.

We were parallel with each other for a second, maybe two.

Roll down the goddamn window.

I could have darted into the road. I could have touched the glass. Shattered it with my backpack. Reached inside. I could have thrust the envelope with my letter and photographs at him.

Here, motherfucker. This is what you left behind. You're not who you think you are. Your life isn't what it seems. It's wider and deeper, with currents and tributaries that stretch for miles and miles, far beyond what the I and the you can see.

But I didn't. I stood on the sidewalk and watched him go. I would find him again. This was only the beginning. I still had five days left. Tomorrow—my second day; my second chance; Wednesday, March the second.

I would find him again.

****

A misty rain began to fall late in the day. I ducked inside a boisterous pub in Earls Court and stood in the doorway while my eyes adjusted to the muted light. The décor was Dickensian, with dark wood paneling and Tudor ceiling beams. Electric lanterns cast shadows on the walls that could just as easily have been of David Copperfield as the mob of thirty-somethings bustling about ordering drinks or chattering above the din at wooden tables. I wended my way to the bar and signaled to the bartender.

"Cheers," she said. "What can I get you?"

I scanned the shelves of wine and liquor bottles behind her and the row of beer tap handles in front of her. I'd never ordered a drink in a bar before. The legal drinking age in England was eighteen, but in America I was underage. I'd never even been inside a bar, and I was hardly a beer aficionado. I didn't know the difference between an ale and a lager or a stout and a porter. All I could think of right then was Budweiser and Coors, and neither seemed to be on tap.

"I'll take a pint," I said timorously.

She passed a corkscrew to her harried cohort then looked at me, her jaw set. "A pint of what?"

I pointed to the handle labeled London Pride. "That one, I guess."

Raucous laughter erupted from a gaggle of young women

huddled at the end of the bar. A group of rowdy men in khakis and oxfords were playing darts by the bathrooms. Everyone seemed oblivious to the American interloper who'd breezed in on a waterlogged whim.

"I changed my mind," I said to the bartender. "I don't want anything. Sorry."

I began elbowing my way to the door. A man in a Polo sweater and jeans rose from his chair and swept his hand in front of me. He gave a debonair smile and clasped an empty mug in one hand and the top of his chair with the other. The invitation seemed clear, so I sat down.

"I was letting you pass by," he said in a genteel *my name is Bond, James Bond* voice. "I wasn't offering you my seat."

Blistering heat crawled up my face and burrowed in my damp hairline. I hoped he mistook it for some sort of fever—the romantic kind that consumed Cathy in *Wuthering Heights*—or assumed I'd downed one pint too many.

"Sorry," I murmured, then fumbled to the door.

A memory from grammar school surfaced like jetsam while I searched for the nearest tube station. A little white mouse had found its way into my third-grade classroom from the patch of woods behind the playground. My teacher, a grim-faced lady named Mrs. Carter, chased it around the room with a wooden paddle. Finally, the mouse darted underneath a desk in a corner and sat there cowering while Mrs. Carter crept toward it like Nosferatu. Suddenly, she dove under the desk and began beating it to a bloody pulp, while a horde of nine-year-olds watched in horror.

"Why'd you kill it?" I bellowed after Mrs. Carter was finally satisfied that the smear of guts, fur, and blood on the carpet was dead. "You didn't have to kill it!"

She rocked back on her heels, her face flushed from exertion. "The only good mouse," she wheezed, "is a dead mouse."

A mouse is a mouse is a mouse . . .

And mingling where it's unwanted doesn't bode well.

CHAPTER EIGHTEEN

THE GRAYNESS of a London dawn—like mystery, enigma. Connie had once asked me if I were a season, what would I be? *Autumn* I'd said. *It's neither hot nor cold. I don't wanna be defined.* She'd smirked. *Figures. Aren't you gonna ask me what color I'd be?* I'd said. *Oh I already know that—something dark and depressing, midnight blue maybe.* I'd shaken my head. *I'd be gray. That's not a color*, she'd insisted. *Yeah, it is. It's a color without color.*

It's the color of a London dawn.

I yawned and rolled out of bed. I'd slept fitfully. The mattress was hard and lumpy, and the people in the next room had argued loudly in a language I didn't recognize.

Peter had said there would be tea and toast in the lobby for breakfast, but I wasn't hungry. The kabobs and chips I'd scarfed down at a Turkish street stall on the way back to the hotel after the pub fiasco had apparently not agreed with me.

What to do today? Where to go? Back to Tower House? I hadn't left the envelope there. The rain would have ruined it. I could try again this morning then wait in case Jimmy emerged. Or I could drop off the envelope then head to Windsor and leave another one at Old Mill House. Scotland was a last resort. The trip would take hours by train and require an overnight stay. Windsor was only thirty minutes from London.

I showered, then crawled back into my clothes, still damp from the day before, and headed down to the lobby. Peter's wanker boss reluctantly Xeroxed my letter and photographs and sold me some envelopes for a couple pounds. I dropped them into my backpack then meandered back to Melbury Road.

I stood outside the gate and wrapped my fingers around the bars. Any closer and I'd be inside—an *inside girl*, wandering through his garden, peeking in the windows, pounding on the front door.

I didn't get lost this time. I'd gotten off the tube at the right stop and found the house easily. Like I was coming over for a cuppa tea, to borrow some sugar, lend him a trowel and shears to trim the hedge.

I pressed my face against the wrought iron, cold against my skin. Another sardonic door to open.

I slid an envelope underneath the gate—a record of my existence—then headed for the train station.

****

It was still early when I arrived in Windsor—around 9:30—but hordes of people were already queuing up to tour the castle, hoping to catch a glimpse of the queen or, better yet, Di and Charles, strolling the lavish grounds with their two little princes, like the perfect happy family they would turn out not to be. The sun had come out before I left London and taken the chill off the air. I unbuttoned my coat and plodded off to catch the bus an attendant at the train station had said would take me near Old Mill House.

The estate was on a cul-de-sac at the end of Mill Lane, tucked behind a large white brick wall and another wrought iron gate. John Bonham had already been drunk when he arrived the night of September 24, 1980—another Wednesday, another Leap Year, the Harvest Moon burning through the clouds like a caution light. He'd kept drinking—quadruple shots of vodka, I'd read—then died in an upstairs bedroom in the wee hours of Thursday morning.

A few hours separated woe from go.

I stared at the main house. There were others on the estate, by the banks of the Thames, the river's edge, swans floating in the freezing water. Swan song for a drummer.

What about the owls? Had there been owls crying in the night when Bonzo died, hovering at the window, watching him, waiting? Where had Jimmy been? Upstairs? Downstairs? My eyes scanned the white facade, commonplace compared to Tower House. Which room was Jimmy's? Had he heard the crying? Had he heard the rumors that came in the days and weeks that followed? *Black smoke billowing from the chimney, black magic brewing in a white house. The Little Wizard conjuring the Beast.*

I sat down in front of the gate and hugged my knees to my chest. Death had invaded that house, just like mine. I could sense it—that white brick a pretext, an apparition, shielded by a veritable forest of trees, naked in the winter wind.

The sun shimmered on the water. Spring would come soon. Then summer. How hot does it get in England in the summer? What smells fill the air? Not Southern smells. Here is not there. I tilted my head toward the sky, felt the warmth on my face.

I don't wanna be autumn anymore, Connie. I wanna be summer.

I fished an envelope from my backpack and was just about to slide it underneath the gate when the front door of the house opened. I scrambled to my feet and hid behind the wall, my heart pounding.

I heard a woman's voice, a Southern accent. Familiar but foreign, not like the voices from home—a Louisiana backwater cadence, a fusion of patrician and plebeian.

Why was a Southern woman standing in Jimmy Page's doorway?

You've got the wrong woman, I thought. *The one you want is scattered in another river. You can't put the pieces back together. You can't conjure dust and ash. I'm what's left, flesh and blood. Everything is made of water—and of her and of you. I'm what's left.*

I craned my neck to see around the wall. She was standing by a black car, a Jaguar with tinted windows. Her hair was long and blonde, her belly swollen, huge, a zeppelin about to burst.

She was pregnant.

Another woman's voice—British, servile—called from inside the house.

"Telephone for you, Mrs. Page. It's your husband."

Your husband. Mrs. Page. He was married. I didn't know he was married. And now he was about to have a family—a perfect happy family. I knew he and a longtime-girlfriend had had a daughter in the '70s. I'd read about the baby in *Hammer of the Gods*. He'd never married her mother, though. He'd never made that kind of commitment, and that had made it easy for me to dismiss the union. He'd never taken vows, worn a ring, given a woman his name. He'd kept that most defining possession for himself.

Your husband. Mrs. Page.

He was married.

He had a wife, who was carrying his child and living in his house.

Mr. and Mrs. MacGregor live down by the river . . .

"Cain't I call him back?"

Cain't—she said *cain't.* Claudia had never said *cain't.* Her accent had been smooth, like butterscotch, her grammar perfect—the queen's English. She spoke Jimmy's language, not some sort of mongrel Southern slang.

The British woman stepped outside. A maid? Secretary?

"He says he needs to talk to you now," she said.

The blonde turned sharply, clearly miffed, and stalked back inside the house.

Claudia was prettier, I thought, her features far more striking and luminous, as if she were swathed in a golden nimbus, like a goddess, an angel.

I slid the envelope underneath the gate. Maybe the maid would see it, or the chauffeur. Maybe they disdained the lady of the house and would relish the thought of delivering such a message to their lord and master. If she—*Mrs. Page*—found it first, she'd destroy it, rip it to shreds, toss the contents into the trash, or burn them in the fireplace. She'd stand guard and witness the cremation then force a servant to sweep up the ashes and scatter them in the river.

I dropped to my knees and jerked my arm through the iron bars, stretched my fingers toward the envelope. I couldn't reach it. I'd thrown it too far. I scurried over to the riverbank and found a stick that had fallen from one of the barren trees. I poked it through the bars and dragged the envelope close enough to grab. Then I ran—away from Old Mill House and Mrs. Page. She'd never touch my letter, my mother's photographs, her sepia smile seared in resin and polyethylene. I ran—until I was out of breath and my legs were like licorice.

She'd never touch any part of me.

****

In the Burning Times, a woman's touch could condemn her to the flames. Not just any woman—the eccentric, ethereal. A woman who gave birth out of wedlock. A woman with a birthmark.

It's a sin to suffer a witch to live.

Bind her to a stake and set her ablaze.

Or throw her in the river and see if she floats. If she drowns, she's innocent. If she doesn't, she meets the tinder. Either way, she's fucked.

I sat at a scarred wooden table in a pub on Mill Lane and nursed a cup of tea. I'd forgotten my way back to the bus stop, so I'd returned to Jimmy's street.

The pub was called The Swan, the most haunted pub on Mill Lane, the barkeep boasted when he poured my tea. He said until the nineteenth century, the place was used as a coroner's court, with a mortuary conveniently located in the back.

"You're not afraid of ghosts, are you?" he asked me, nonchalantly polishing his eyeglasses with his apron.

"No," I said, "especially ghosts who like a pint every now and then."

He threw his head back and let loose a guffaw. "Good on ya." He reminded me of Uncle Jack, with his beard and broad shoulders and that mischievous sparkle in his eyes that always irked Aunt Lorraine. *What are you up to, Jack? Stop it, Jack. That's not funny, Jack.*

I sat by the fireplace, glowing embers spitting and popping in the grate. I wondered if ghosts blew in through the chimney at night and hobnobbed with the patrons, sharing ale and incantations and secrets from beyond the grave. I opened my journal and stared at the blank page. No words came. Just the hum of discursive thoughts, like a snowy TV screen that hypnotizes you if you don't look away.

Mrs. Page . . .

Two syllables doth a lady make, a lady in gold, all that glitters is gold, the touch, the feel of gold around her finger, a talisman, a symbol, marking her, binding her to another in a land not of milk and honey but lords and ladies and castles by a river and—

"Did you tour the castle yet?" the barkeep asked.

The clarity of a human voice, almost tangible, cleared the fuzz in my head. "What?" I said.

"Windsor Castle. Have you joined the legions of tourists mucking about the place yet?" There was no one else in the pub and he was obviously feeling chatty.

"I'm not really here to see the sites," I said.

"That so?" He set a plate of scones in front of me and topped off my tea. "All the same, you should see the castle. Lots of history. Got its own ghosts, too."

"I came to see something else."

"What's that?"

I took a bite of a scone and chewed mechanically. I didn't feel like talking about my misadventures right then, and definitely not with a stranger who'd probably deliver a glib remark and write me off as a foolhardy groupie.

"Do you know Old Mill House?" I asked grudgingly.

He gave a more subdued guffaw. "So you're here to see Pagey. Led Zeppelin fan, are you?"

"You know Jimmy Page?"

"Sure I do. He pops round every now and then for a bit of sauce—sometimes with the missus, sometimes not. Nice chap, Pagey."

I tapped my pen on the table. The man behind the bar unloading beer glasses from a dishwasher less than ten feet away from me knew Jimmy Page, served him beer and stale scones and whatever else he wanted and cleaned up behind him like a kitchen wench. That man, who reminded me of my burly uncle, knew Jimmy well enough to call him *Pagey*. I was sitting in the same pub Jimmy frequented, maybe even the same seat. I pictured him warming himself by the fire, downing *a bit of sauce* with the locals, talking of . . .

In the room the Rock stars come and go, talking of Michelangelo.

Actually, I couldn't picture him here. The place was far too quaint for him, its haunted history more benign than brooding. Besides, his house had its own haunted history. He needn't go out for that sort of ambiance. And what would he talk about with the locals? Aleister Crowley? The meaning of his cryptic symbol, Zoso? Where to purchase a Gibson doubleneck guitar?

The barkeep poured himself a glass of sparkling water and sprinkled a pinch of cinnamon in it. "Good for the sinuses," he said with a wink.

I nodded indifferently. "You think he'll come in today?"

"Sorry, love. He was in last night and said he'd be off in the morning—I forget where. Publicity for his new record. You know he's got a new record coming out, right? And Robert— Plant, that is—has a new one just come out the other day. Interesting timing, innit?"

I knew about Robert's album, *Now and Zen*. One of the music magazines I'd bought at the Record Shack had an article about it. Apparently, Jimmy had played on a track or two and Robert had returned the favor by performing on *Outrider*.

"You sure you don't know where he went?" I asked. The barkeep looked at me cautiously. "I'm not a stalker," I said. "I swear I'm not. I just want to meet him. It's important."

He drained his glass then poured another. "Where are your parents?"

"They're at the hotel. They know where I am."

"Hmm. On holiday, I 'spose. Off from school."

"We're on a break," I said, amazed by my talent for mendacity. "My mom's a huge Zeppelin fan. She'd freak out at the chance to meet Jimmy."

"Well, I doubt there's much chance of that, but if you're a mind to go to London, he'll be there in a couple of days. Said he was judging a guitar contest with Brian May of Queen and some other bloke."

I scampered to the bar. "Where's the contest?"

"Don't know. I should think it would be easy to find out. A mate of mine works at a record store on Denmark Street. In London," he added. "Roger's his name. Actually, he's a mate of a mate. He's a nutter, that one, a real rounder, but he'll know the latest scuttlebutt on Jimmy. Band managers keep record stores in the know." He scribbled something on a napkin and gave it to me. "Show him this and tell him Clive's friend William sent you."

"You're sure Jimmy said the contest was in a couple of days?"

"That's what he said, love."

A woman with two flaxen-haired little girls came swinging through the door. William hustled around the bar and scooped both girls in his arms, kissing their cheeks and foreheads gleefully. The woman's face was closed, absent any trace of affection. She handed William a pink suitcase, told the girls she'd pick them up on Sunday, then left without a word to William.

"Go on in the kitchen and have some biscuits," he said, shooing the girls with a dishrag. "Soon as Melinda takes over here, we'll be off to the park."

The elder of the girls pulled a fish face. "Melinda's always late, Daddy," she sniped.

William nudged his wire-rims low on his nose and crossed his eyes. "Off with you before I scale you and throw you in a frying pan with today's special." They squealed and skipped into the kitchen, their Mary Janes clomping on the hardwood floor.

I left a few pounds on the bar and collected my backpack and coat. "Thanks for the tea and scones."

"Don't forget about Roger," he said, pointing to the napkin. "Denmark Street, near Tottenham Court Station. Tell him William sent you." He held the door open, sending me off to the hunt, fed and watered and armed with magic runes. "By the way," he said. "Tell your *mum* Jimmy's about to be a dad again. He's already got a daughter, you know—must be about your age by now."

My face burned. "Maybe he'll have another one soon."

"I reckon he'll be wanting a son this time."

"Doesn't much matter what he wants," I said tersely. "He'll have to take what he gets."

****

I purchased a bottle of screw-top wine at a market near my hotel and went to Kensington Gardens to watch the sunset. Other than the sip of Champagne I'd had at Aunt Lorraine and Uncle Jack's twenty-fifth wedding anniversary party, I'd never tasted wine. But I was celebrating, so I decided to broaden my alcoholic horizons and give Chardonnay a try.

William's record store mate, Roger, had proved to be a priceless commodity. *Pricey* is a more apt word. *Do I know about Jimmy Page and a guitar contest? Yeah, yeah. Saturday the fifth, Hammersmith Palais. You need a ticket, though. Unfortunately, we're sold out. Pity, innit? Reckon there might be a few floating round somewhere, though,* he said, a cheeky look in his eyes.

"Uh-huh," I said coolly. "You wouldn't just happen to have one, would you?"

"Maybe, maybe not."

I followed him from the t-shirt display to the cash register, where he rang up a Pet Shop Boys CD for another kid with a Mohawk.

"Why don't you ever play anything good in here, Roger?" the girl said. "Every time I come in you've got that bloody blues shite on."

"What shite would you prefer we play?"

"You know what I like."

"How 'bout a little Gary Glitter? The Bay City Rollers?" he said tartly.

She snatched the bag and pocketed her change. "Bollocks to you, Roger. Your problem is you're getting old. You're a gaffer, you are. You don't know what's what anymore." She glanced at me. "You American or Canadian? I never can tell the difference."

"Run along, Evie," Roger said. "We've got business, the American and me."

He steered me towards a back room that smelled like sweaty gym socks and closed the door. "I've got a ticket if you want it," he said, leaning against a row of lockers, his arms crossed insolently in front of him. He couldn't have been more than twenty-five, hardly an old man, but his James Dean slouch was ill-fitting, like an outdated coat he refused to relinquish.

I began mentally calculating the money I had left. "How much?" I asked.

"Thirty pounds."

"Like hell," I brayed.

"I thought you wanted to go to the show," he said.

I studied Roger's face, dissecting his sharp features, noting his idiosyncrasies—the speck of green stuck between his teeth, as if he'd eaten spinach for lunch and forgotten to floss afterward, the downward turn of his mouth, even when he smiled, the comical twitch of his left eyebrow, like a gangster in a Bogart film. I couldn't trust him, I decided, but I'd thought I could trust William. What if he and Roger were in cahoots to fleece me out of what was left of my trip funds? Maybe he'd already known Roger was a scalper and figured I was gullible and desperate enough to pay top dollar for a ticket. Maybe he'd phoned Roger after I left to give him a heads up.

"Did William call you?" I asked.

"William? What for? I barely even know the bloke. Do you want the ticket or not?"

It occurred to me I might not even need a ticket. Roger had given me the day and location of the contest, the crucial clues. I could get there early, catch Jimmy as he arrived, confront him right there on the sidewalk. If I missed him, I could probably bluff my way inside. Connie and I had become masters at weaseling into R-rated movies by ninth grade.

"Tell you what," Roger said. "I'll let you have it for twenty-five quid."

"Forget it," I said, my hand on the doorknob.

"Fine. I always fancied a backstage chat with Jimmy Page."

I dropped my hand. "What do you mean backstage?"

"His manager gave the store a few VIP tickets to raffle off." He shrugged his bony shoulders, savoring the moment. "What's it to anyone if I kept one for myself?"

I moved clumsily toward Roger. "So I'd be able to talk to Jimmy, without security or someone hovering around?"

"You'll be able to talk to him. Don't know about security and such."

"How do I know you're not lying?"

Roger opened a locker and rummaged through a wallet inside. He pulled out a ticket and waved it at me. "Says *VIP* doesn't it?"

"What's the catch?"

"No catch. Thirty pounds."

"You said twenty-five."

He gave a droll smile. "Price just went back up."

The door opened and the other clerk on duty stuck his head inside. "What you doing in here, Roger? We got customers. Stop messing about."

"Coming in a minute."

The clerk eyed me then mugged at Roger. "You know, mate, if you're on the pull, do it on your own time."

"Fuck off," Roger snapped. "I said I'll be there in a minute."

"You just see that you do," the clerk said, then slammed the door.

"Well," Roger said, "You got the money or not?"

I emptied my jeans pockets and counted out fifteen pounds. "That's all I've got," I said.

He raised his twitching eyebrow. "You've got to have more than that. What about your hotel? They letting you stay there for free, are they?"

"I had to pay the hotel up front. I've got fifteen pounds left."

He cursed under his breath then gave a mirthless laugh.

"Come on," I said. "Don't be an asshole."

He plucked the money from my hand and thrust the ticket at me.

I opened the door and stepped into the hallway.

"I would've taken twelve," he said triumphantly.

I reached into a side pocket of my backpack and brought out a wad of cash. "Yeah well I could've paid thirty." I flipped him the bird, then closed the door in his face.

****

Christy Alexander Hallberg

Kensington Gardens at dusk . . . The raw breeze had chased off all but a cadre of homeless people huddled together in the tall grass and a tenacious jogger or two near the spot I'd staked out by a bush strung with flashing colored lights, sparkling like a psychedelic Christmas tree, "Fur Elise" chiming from a nearby food stall. I sat on a bath towel I'd nicked from my hotel room with my backpack, wine, and a copy of Crowley's *The Book of the Law*, and drank the Chardonnay straight out of the bottle. I'd found the book in Atlantis, an occult bookshop in Bloomsbury, when I was wandering around looking for a place to buy underwear and couldn't resist splurging on it.

I'd roamed through London for hours after leaving the record store—Piccadilly Circus, where tour buses crawled along beside boxy black taxi cabs, passing money exchange kiosks and red telephone booths and people of more ethnicities than I knew existed and a swarm of tourists perusing maps, cameras dangling from their necks; Trafalgar Square, where street performers vied for tips and a group of bumptious boys pitched coins into the fountain; Regent Street, with its wide sidewalks, cafes, boulangeries, and glut of designer clothing stores I didn't bother entering. The city was rabid with humanity and sounds and machines. I stood on Waterloo Bridge and watched a couple kissing on a tourist boat. It was just a glimpse, really—two blurry figures in a Monet painting drifting in the dappled sunlight. I couldn't tell if they were young or old; if they loved each other or had just met; what, if anything, they whispered to each other when they broke their embrace.

A gust of loneliness blew through me.

Everything could change for me in three days—the ground

beneath my feet, the color of the sky. Everything. In three days. The city could be mine.

Kensington Gardens at dusk . . . The sun was on fire. I was swimming in a feverish lake of wine, Crowley by my side:

I am the blue-lidded daughter of Sunset;

I am the naked brilliance of the voluptuous night-sky.

To me! To me!

In three days. Everything could belong to me.

CHAPTER NINETEEN

I AWOKE in the morning with a thundering headache—not my first hangover, and hardly my worst. I was nine years old the first time I got drunk, alone in my dugout the night of my mother's funeral.

After the service, the Ladies Auxiliary from Grandma's church brought food to the farm and waited for Grandma and me to return from the river. They stayed late into the evening, washing dishes, tidying up the house, doing their Christian duty for a fellow parishioner, in spite of the *shameful* way her daughter had died.

Aunt Lorraine and two of her friends had spent the evening packing my mother's photographs and clothes and trinkets in cardboard boxes and plastic trash bags. *Luna doesn't need to see all this,* I heard Aunt Lorraine mutter to them in the living room. *Out of sight, out of mind. She's young. She'll forget in time.* I watched them from behind the drapes—how stealthily they emptied closets and cleared tabletops, excised the tumor with rigor and skill. *How could Claudia do this to that child, Lorraine? I don't wanna talk about it,* she'd retorted. The anger in her voice was monstrous, an entity all its own. *I don't ever wanna talk about it again. I don't wanna hear her name again. And I don't want Luna to hear it either. Y'all understand?*

Grandma had sat dazed and silent at the kitchen table,

pious women fawning over her, offering her fried chicken and homemade pies and cakes, a panacea for calamity and infirmity alike. Dr. Hollis had given her a bottle of sedatives—*For Luna,* he'd told her. *Won't hurt the child to give her half a pill as needed for a few days.* We'd both taken one before the funeral, and I was still foggy that night. When Aunt Lorraine led her coterie upstairs, I staggered out the front door and headed to the barn, where Uncle Jack and some of the men had absconded with a quart of moonshine in a Mason jar. I curled up in the cool grass near the open doors and eavesdropped on their drunken banter, the stories they swapped about everything *but* Claudia. *Y'all hear about Roy Gillikan? Hornworms got his tobacco.* The Farmer's Almanac *says we're in for a warm winter this year. Did you hear the one about the preacher with a boner who walks into a bar and says* gimme anything that goes down easy? And the laughter, on and on, knee-slapping, grotesque laughter, on and on—Uncle Jack with his smoker's throaty cackle, Mr. Adams' subdued *tee-hee-hee*, Mr. Johnson's unbridled crow, the church deacon whose name I didn't know with his air-gulping chuckles—on and on. How easy it was for them, I'd thought. All of them. So very, very easy to forget, to start anew, as if what was never was, as if it had never had a face or a voice or a name. The laughter, on and on. I'd pressed my hands over my ears and curled my body tighter, into a ball, a fetus with hair ribbons and doleful black dress Aunt Lorraine had bought for me the day before. I wanted to forget too, to block out *that* night and everything that had come before. I hadn't spoken since Claudia died. No one but me knew what really happened in her room.

Make it go away, please, please, make it go away.

The men lumbered out of the barn and back to the house.

Make it go away, please, please, I won't say her name ever again.

I unfurled myself and crawled inside the dark barn, the car shed floodlight glinting on the iron tools mounted like weapons on the walls. They'd left at least a fourth of moonshine in the Mason jar. I held it gingerly in my hands and ambled by moonlight through the brush to my dugout. I'd ambled through the woods the night she died, too. I'd sneaked off to my great-grandfather's shack, peeked through the window, watched Grandma deliver the news, listened to him snarl the word— *abomination*—followed him into the copse of trees near the footpath and witnessed the ceremony, heard him chant her name, conjuring her, imploring her: *ClaudiaClaudiaClaudia*

Make it go away, please, please, I won't say her name ever again.

I unscrewed the top and breathed in the turpentine smell, gasping, coughing. I closed my eyes and poured the searing liquid down my throat. One gulp, two, three, dry heaving, eyes watering. The price we pay for erasure.

I'd awakened in Grandma's bed in the morning, blind with pain, sick from my own stench, Uncle Jack lurking in the doorway like a contrite child, Aunt Lorraine scowling at him. *Don't ever forget how you feel right now, Luna,* Grandma had said grimly. *Don't ever forget.* But I did. I forgot everything— Claudia's gait, her hair, her eyes, her laugh, like wind chimes in a gale. Her name. It had taken time, months of silence, homeschooling until Dr. Hollis said I was ready to return to class, then the cutting and gutting—first the razor then the bottle. The face of a phantom staring blankly at me from the cover of a record album all it had taken to bring it back. As it was then, the evening forgetting began, it is now, in the British morning light—the bottle again, the pain again. I couldn't forget this time. Even if I tried.

****

I rolled over on my back on the lumpy hotel bed and moaned. I'd unpeeled my clothes and passed out naked, tangled in the covers. This is how John Bonham died, I thought. Drunk, alone, in someone else's bed. He had a daughter, and a son. He'd left them behind with their mother, the wife he supposedly adored. They'd buried his cremated remains in a bucolic cemetery in a village in Worcestershire—Rushock, it's called, just outside Kidderminster. A three-hour train ride away. I hadn't planned on going. Scotland had seemed inevitable, but now there was no point in making such an arduous journey; I'd already tracked down Jimmy. Anyway, I didn't have enough money for an overnight trip. I could afford Rushock, though, and maybe a jaunt to Headley Grange, the manor house where Led Zeppelin recorded their fourth album, the one with "Four Sticks."

I eased out of bed and shuffled to the bathroom. The eyes squinting back at me in the mirror were bloodshot and weak, the face ashen, like a death mask. A shower and tea and toast, that's what I needed. And Advil. I'd seen half a dozen McDonald's and a few Pizza Huts and Subways in the city; surely they had Advil.

The phone on the nightstand rang and I lurched against the lavatory.

"I think you left a notebook in the lobby," Peter said, his

voice crackling through the receiver, as if he were calling from one of those ubiquitous red phone booths on the other side of town instead of the lobby on the ground floor.

I grabbed my backpack. The top was open. Crowley was still there, the empty wine bottle, the towel and bag of underwear I'd bought at a thrift shop in Camden, everything except my journal. It must have fallen out when I stumbled through the lobby last night.

"Still there?" Peter asked.

"I'll be right down." I threw on my clothes and bolted for the stairs.

My journal was on the countertop, the cover open, my name scrawled at the top of the page. I glanced at Peter, sitting on a stool behind the desk, an inculpable expression on his face.

"Did you read it?" I asked sharply.

He brushed his cowlick from his forehead. "Well, I had to find out who it belonged to, didn't I?"

"That's obvious from the first page."

He leaned over and glimpsed the red script. "So it is. Not very clear, is it—the handwriting, that is. A bit squiggly."

"Not any squigglier than the rest of it."

"That's why it took so long to figure out who it belonged to."

"Just how long did it take?"

"The last page gave you away. The bit about the wine and knickers." He cracked a puckish smile.

I felt what was left of the color in my face drain. "That's a shitty thing to do, read someone else's journal. In fact, it's a little creepy."

"Oh come on, I didn't read much. I promise. I was just curious if you'd found Jimmy Page's house."

"All you had to do is ask."

He chewed his bottom lip, another tick of his I'd noticed the morning we met. "You really think Jimmy's your dad?"

"Jesus Christ. You read the whole thing, didn't you?" My voice was charged with anger and humiliation. "You're the wanker, not your boss."

His dark eyes grew serious, the remnants of blue eyeliner underneath his lashes a droll contradiction. "I'm sorry about your mum," he said softly. "My mum's dead, too."

I traced the rose-colored letters of my name with my fingertip. "How'd she die?"

"Car crash, 'bout a year ago. My dad's remarried now." He smirked and folded his arms across his chest contemptuously. "Fancy that, not even a year and he's already taken up with another bird."

A group of middle-aged American women with garish makeup and poufy hair filed out of the elevator, gabbing about what time Harrods opens and the pronunciation of Trafalgar Square. *I'm telling you it's Traffle-gar.*

Peter looked at me and rolled his eyes.

The ladies dropped pieces of bread into the toaster then slathered them with strawberry jam and carried them on paper plates back to the elevator.

"Where you off to today?" Peter asked me.

I massaged my throbbing temples. "Nowhere until I get rid of my headache."

"Rough night, aye. Too much drink?"

I glanced at my sock feet, cold on the white tile floor. In

my rush I'd forgotten to put on my sneakers. "You wouldn't happen to have some Advil or aspirin or something, would you?"

"No aspirin, but . . . " He swiveled on the stool and surveyed the room.

"There's no one here," I said. "What've you got?"

"Something I was saving for my girlfriend and me for tonight," he said, his voice low, conspiratorial. "I can get more, though. A mate owes me a favor."

A litany of illegal substances ran through my mind, some of which I'd tried, others I feared too much to touch. "What is it?" I asked haltingly.

"Nothing hard. Just a bit of whacky backy. Great for all kinds of pain. It's yours if you want it."

"No thanks," I said. "I'm on a pretty tight budget."

He eyed my journal. "Consider it a gift from one mum-less mug to another." He brought out a wrinkled joint and pack of matches from a satchel underneath the desk and gave them to me. "So what you going to do about Jimmy Page?"

"You must've skipped that part in my journal."

"I told you I only read a couple of pages."

"Well if you must know, there's a guitar contest he's judging Saturday night," I said. "I'll see him there."

Another group of tourists entered the lobby. A man in a turban asked Peter in broken English for directions to the National Gallery. His companions—another turbaned man and two women with headscarves—poured steaming tea into paper cups and admired the black and white photographs of Buckingham Palace and other London sites hanging on the walls. More hotel guests emerged from the elevator, then

Peter's boss arrived, so I poured a cup of tea and headed back to my room, a piece of plain toast in hand, to smoke the joint and plot a trip to Rushock.

****

I'd only been high once—the summer before tenth grade. A farmhand I'd caught toking up behind the barn had bribed me with a joint from his stash not to tell Mr. Lewis, the man Grandma had rented our fields to after Uncle Jack and Aunt Lorraine moved to Morganton. Connie and I had smoked it at the river one humid night, bullfrogs grunting in the marsh, mosquitoes assaulting our bare arms and legs, the red tip of the joint glowing in the dark. *I don't feel a thing*, Connie had said, then flopped on the mucky riverbank in a fit of giggles. I marveled at the floaty sensation in my head, so different from the heaviness of alcohol, like I could fly away with one more hit, touch the sky then the stars, the heavens, only I didn't believe in heaven. There was only the abyss, nothingness. I sat down beside Connie and clasped her hand. *Don't let me fly away*, I begged her. *If I do, I'll never come back.* Connie had stared at me quizzically, her eyes glassy, then flicked the joint into the water and held me in her arms until the paranoia passed. We'd never smoked again. This time was different, though. I'd already flown away. As soon as I touched a star, I'd be going home.

I lit Peter's joint and took an eager toke, holding the smoke in my lungs until a dry, cloudy cough forced its way out. When the hazy, lazy feeling came, I crawled into bed. I'd sleep off my hangover, then figure out how to get to Rushock.

I used to record my dreams in my journal. They were nightmares mostly—elusive figures stalking me in shadow worlds where the laws of gravity and logic don't apply. I preserved them like corpses before burial, for what I don't know. In time, the need to archive them vanished and I stopped. On the train to Kidderminster, the closest station to Rushock, I scribbled in my journal all I could remember of the trippy dream I'd had while I slept in my hotel room that morning. My great-grandfather had been sitting in his rocker beside his own headstone in his shack, his face hidden behind a veil, his old tabby cat purring in his lap. A hungry fire blazed around him, flames licking his body. I was standing in the doorway, one foot inside the shack, the other on the muddy bank of a snake-filled swamp. *Come on in and shut the door, girl*, he said. I looked behind me; water moccasins were coiled at my feet. *Don't be scared*, he said. I couldn't breathe. The heat from the fire was suffocating. *Come on in and get some nourishment*, he said. *You're skin and bones, girl. Emily fixed a right good supper for you.* I glanced around the room for my great-grandmother, but there was no one else there, just my great-grandfather, talking to me through the flames. *Ain't nothing to be afraid of, girl*, he said. *Liar, liar, pants on fire*, I bellowed. He shooed the cat then pushed himself up from the rocking chair with his cane and tottered toward me. *You gonna feed them snakes, or you gonna come inside?* he said. *Where's Grandma Emily?* I asked. *She'll be along directly.* He was moving slowly, a walking inferno, the veil still covering his face. *Where're you going?* I asked. *Don't rightly know*, he said. I pointed to his headstone. *You forgot that.* He shook his head. *That ain't nothing but a name on a rock*, he said. *A mark that don't mean nothing.* He kept coming toward me. The cat hissed then skittered past me through the door. *Come on give us hug, girl. Ain't seen you in a long time.* He reached out for me. His arms were like charred kindling. I stepped back, closer to the snakes. *Careful now*, he said. *Them snakes is demons. Come on now, girl, give us a hug.* He opened his arms wide. *But you're on fire*, I said. *Don't be scared*, he said. I let him envelop me in his arms, heat pulsing through me, my skin melting with his, my blood flowing through his veins like warm, crimson tides beguiled to shore by the sun and the moon. I stepped away from him. He lifted his veil. My Great-grandmother Emily's face looked back at me. I couldn't see her features clearly, but I could tell she was smiling. *Go on inside, honey*, she said. Her voice sounded familiar, like homemade chocolate chip cookies and sweet potato pie. *I know you*, I said. *'Course you do, honey.* A flock of owls fluttered by us into the house. They perched on the mantle and hooted, their bodies gleaming in the flames. *Owl in the house means death's coming*, I said frantically. My great-grandmother took my hands and led me across the threshold. *Don't be scared, honey*, she said. She dropped my hands and stepped outside then closed the door behind her, leaving me alone with the owls and the flames and a blazing tombstone with my name on it.

I closed my journal and sank into the seat. That was all I remembered of the dream—an old woman I'd only seen in crinkled photographs who'd died in agony over half a century ago sending me to my own agonizing death. I thought of the Death card I'd drawn once when I was playing with Claudia's Tarot deck. *Does that mean I'm gonna die?* I'd whimpered.

She'd knelt beside me on the floor and kissed the top of my head. *It's upright,* she'd said. *That means transformation, beginnings, change.* The next card was even more disturbing—flames shooting from a lonely tower on a craggy mountaintop, ghastly bodies falling to their deaths. *That one's upright too,* she'd said. *It means something you thought was true is really false.* I'd wiggled around and buried my face in her chest. *Which is worse?* I'd asked. She'd stroked my hair, then whispered in my ear—*Depends on if you know truth from fantasy.*

The train screeched into the Kidderminster station around three o'clock that afternoon. I rubbed my eyes then floundered up the aisle. The pot had cured my headache, but I couldn't shake the whirligig feeling that remained.

I wasn't sure how to get to the cemetery, or even how far away it was, and I couldn't find an attendant to ask. I wandered to the front of the crude station building to look for a bus stop. The rain and gray and cold had returned, and with it a sense of foreboding. I stood under an awning and shivered. I'd worn another hole in the knee of my pant leg, and my coat, a fleece-lined denim jacket Grandma had given me for Christmas when I was in eighth grade, was becoming frayed and thin. She and Aunt Lorraine had both bought me new clothes through the years, but for some reason I'd always thought this particular pair of jeans and my jacket brought good luck, so I'd refused to let Grandma trash them.

I rubbed my hands together then blew on them. I wished Peter had slipped me a cigarette with the joint. I wished I were standing behind a cash register waiting on customers at KFC with Connie, pitting crispy and original recipe against each other like chickens in a cockfight. I wished I were home, on the farm in the summertime, sunshine streaming through the dew-streaked kitchen windows, Grandma, her hair in pin curls, frying eggs in an iron skillet that had once belonged to her mother, the smell of freshly-brewed coffee and smoky bacon wafting in the air, Joan Lunden and Charlie Gibson chirping *Good morning, America* on the TV in the living room.

I hate this town, I'd blustered to Grandma once. We'd been walking along the riverbank after a Saturday in the Park carnival on the Town Common. *I know you do*, she'd said, leading me through the thicket back to the car. *But you won't always.* She stopped walking when we reached the clearing and gazed into the twilight sky, the horizon awash in brilliant shades of red and gold. *Then again*, she'd said flatly, *maybe you will.*

A taxi pulled up in front of me, and the driver rolled down the passenger-side window. "Need a ride?" she asked.

I wasn't sure I had enough money for a taxi—not if I wanted to go to Headley Grange and eat for another four days. "I was sort of hoping to catch a bus," I said.

"Right, then." She readjusted the rearview mirror then shifted the car into gear.

"Hang on a sec," I called. "Is there a bus that goes anywhere near St Michael's Church in Rushock?"

"Not on Thursdays," she said. "The one-thirty-three only runs on Mondays, Wednesdays, and Fridays."

I stubbed the sidewalk with the toe of my shoe. "Well, how far is the church from here?"

"About a fifteen-minute drive."

I unzipped the side pocket of my backpack and counted what was left of my cash. "I don't know," I said.

"Going to John Bonham's grave, are you?" She lit a cigarette then trained her eyes on the spiky strip of hair bisecting my head. "You look a bit knackered," she said. She took a long drag on her cigarette then blew a stream of smoke through her nostrils, a trick I'd tried to master but never could. "My daughter went roaming all over creation by herself when she was your age, too," she said. "Full of beans, she was. I used to pray some nice lady would take her in and look after her." She sighed and shook her head. "Get in. I'll only charge you for one way."

I leaned over to get a better look at her. She seemed harmless enough—cropped salt-and-pepper hair that accentuated her prominent jaw, slight frame with a generous bust not even her sweater and MacKintosh could hide, and a wrinkled pucker Grandma warned me I'd sport one day if I didn't quit smoking. She looked both maternal and hard, a West Midlands working-class mum, resilient and resourceful.

"How'd you know I'm going to John Bonham's grave?" I asked.

She smiled knowingly. "What else would you be wanting with Rushock?"

A gust of wind sprayed rain in my face. I didn't have an umbrella. I'd get soaked if I walked.

She tapped her cigarette ashes out the window then turned on the meter. "Come on, love. It's brass monkeys out. Get in."

****

The highway to Rushock was narrow and lush, or it would be in the spring. Willows and oak trees skirted the road.

Hawthorns and jasmine bordered the occasional house. Rain pattered the taxi windshield. The BBC on the radio announced the coming of a penumbral lunar eclipse that evening.

"You won't be able to see it," the driver said, negotiating the road with one hand, gripping her cigarette with the other. "Sky's a bit dodgy with the rain and clouds. Besides, it'd just look like the full moon. I know," she insisted. "My daughter's a Sixth Form science teacher now."

I stared through the window at the pallid sky. "You mean there's a full moon tonight?"

"They say people go barking mad on a full moon." She glanced at me in the rearview mirror, her eyes wide and dour. "Proper silly superstition, innit?"

Proper silly, I thought, rubbish, bullshit. But what truth lay beneath the fiction and poetry, like the storied land I was roaming?

I knew I was pregnant with you the night of the March full moon, Claudia had said the winter before she died. *I could feel it, sitting on the tire swing in the yard, the moon lighting up the sky. I didn't know your name yet. But I knew I was pregnant that night.* She'd tucked me into bed then pattered to the door in her bare feet, her white nightgown brushing the floor. *Right from the start, Lunabelle, you've been guided by the moon,* she'd said, switching off the light. *And you always will be.*

The driver rounded a bend, and a small stone Anglican church in the midst of a pastoral meadow came into view like Brigadoon. "There you are," she said, rolling to a stop in the gravel parking lot. She reached over the front seat and handed me an umbrella. "Have a go. I'll wait. Be nice to rest my eyes a bit. Been up since the crack of dawn tending to the old ball and chain. You'd think he was down with the scurvy instead of a wee cold."

I got out of the car and opened the umbrella. "Which direction is his grave?"

She lolled her head against the back of her seat and rubbed her eyes. "Other side of the church. You can't miss it."

I rambled through the churchyard, weaving between old headstones and markers shaped like Celtic crosses, most with engravings as faded as the memory of the souls they honored, until I spotted a large stone with drumsticks and cymbals and whiskey bottles in front of it. Someone had laid a bouquet of artificial flowers across the top. I crouched down to read the epitaph:

Cherished memories of a loving husband and father
John Henry Bonham
Who died September 25th 1980
Aged 32 years
He will always be remembered in our hearts
Goodnight my love, God bless

What a waste, I thought. Only thirty-two—four years older than Claudia when she died. What a goddamn, fucking waste.

I sat back on my heels, my knees pressed against the cold, damp ground, and wept.

How peaceful it was there among the dead, so quiet, except for the rain and wind and the muffled sound of my sobs. No footfalls or train whistles or car horns. No one was watching or listening, no one but the dead, and everyone knows dead men tell no tales. They become tales, fodder for family lore, swapped like photographs over dinner, the context forgotten, the story only half true, the image unclear, until even that's forgotten and all that's left is a blighted name on a rotting marker—my great-grandparents, my grandfather, and soon, Grandma.

I didn't know why I'd come to Rushock. I had nothing to say to the ashes buried beneath the stone. I couldn't even say goodbye because we'd never said hello. Jimmy had never told him about me. He couldn't have. He didn't know about me himself. Maybe he'd told him about Claudia, though— the angel with the broken wing who'd somehow flown away. Maybe the whole band knew about her. I could have grown up in the wings of a concert hall, playing tag with Bonzo's two kids, smearing stage makeup all over our faces, sneaking sips of Jack Daniels left unfinished before a show, Peter Grant— Led Zeppelin's ferocious manager—banishing us like naughty sprites to our fathers' dressing rooms until the concert's end. But another little girl had wandered those corridors instead of me—the daughter Jimmy claimed, born on March 24, 1971, another Wednesday's child, Scarlet Lilith Eleida Page. It's her name John Bonham knew, not mine.

I collected the whiskey bottles and zipped them in my backpack. The time had passed for the hair of the dog that bit him to do him any good. To tease him seemed cruel. I propped a photograph of Claudia and me against the front of his headstone, by the drumsticks, all four of them. The rain would destroy the picture by nightfall, but I left it anyway.

"Now you've seen us," I said aloud. "We've met." I kissed the tips of my fingers and pressed them against his name. "Goodnight," I whispered.

****

Christy Alexander Hallberg

The driver dropped me at the Kidderminster station in time for me to catch the four-thirty train back to London. The rain had slackened to a haunting drizzle, but she insisted I keep her umbrella anyway.

"You won't need it if you take it," she said. "Sure as you don't, it'll rain to beat bollocks."

I thanked her and fished a ten-pound note from my backpack and gave it to her. "Will this be enough?" I asked.

"I reckon five quid will do," she said.

"Oh I couldn't let you do that. Five isn't even as much as what the meter read just to get to the church."

She reached over the seat, grabbed my wrist, and dropped five coins in my palm. "Listen, love, never turn down a good deed. It's bad luck for the good-deeder." She patted my hand. "You put that in your pocket and run along. Tell your folks a nice English lady looked after you one dreary afternoon when you were out gadding about." She nodded to the group of young men in ripped jeans and black leather jackets approaching the taxi. "Gawd blimey," she grumbled. "Reckon I'm off to that graveyard again."

I crawled out of the back seat and one of the ruffians slid inside. "How much to Rushock and back?" he asked the driver in an accent that reminded me of Colonel Klink in *Hogan's Heroes*.

"For the lot of you?" she said, clicking the meter on. "Twenty pounds, give or take."

I stifled a laugh and scurried inside the station.

****

I had a thirty-minute layover at the Birmingham New Street Station—long enough to go to the loo, double-check the train schedule, and lose my ticket and every bit of my money except the five pounds I had in my pocket.

Lose is not the right word for what happened. A thief made off with my backpack while his mate peppered me with questions about America. *Lovely accent you've got. Where're you from? Really? Where 'bouts? North Carolina, aye? Never heard of it. Is it near New York? Big country, innit? Cheers now, I'm off to catch my train.*

I turned around. My backpack was gone.

The air seeped from my lungs.

I stood there gawking at the empty space on the floor where my bag had been not two minutes ago.

The impossibility . . . a sleight of hand, an optical illusion, a temporary leave of my senses—the full moon had driven me barking mad.

It had to be there.

But it wasn't.

I whipped back around. The inquisitor had vanished, sucked into the maelstrom of travelers.

The loudspeaker announced the arrival of my train.

I dropped to my knees and began wildly scouring the floor beneath the row of chairs where I'd been sitting. One row after another, scrambling on my hands and knees amongst the plethora of feet and suitcases and purses and crumpled soda cans and empty bags of crisps.

At the end of the last row I glimpsed it, bulging from the top of a trash can, the side pocket open like a gaping wound. I

Christy Alexander Hallberg

knew it was empty before I saw the evidence. The culprit hadn't bothered with the other pockets. He must have discovered the cash immediately and left well enough alone.

My legs buckled, and I tumbled against the trash can, both of us crashing to the floor. An attendant helped me up and righted the bin. A menagerie of pre-teens pointed at me and giggled until a lady—more than likely somebody's mother—swatted one of them across the head.

"Are you all right, Miss?" the attendant asked, still holding onto my arm. "Do you need a doctor?"

I shook my head no. I couldn't afford a doctor. I couldn't even afford a train ticket. The culprit had made off with that too. I was nearly three hours away from the hotel room I'd already paid for, with no way to pay for another one here.

"Can I help you to your platform?" the attendant asked.

I didn't know what to say. My money was gone. Long gone by now. Telling him I'd just been robbed wouldn't make any difference.

"Miss?"

"I'm fine," I said. "Thanks for your help."

He gave me a dubious look. "If you're sure," he said, releasing my arm.

Suddenly, a thought struck me. Maybe I could buy a bus ticket to London. Buses were cheaper than trains. How much cheaper, I didn't know, but they were definitely cheaper.

"Do you know how much a bus ticket to London Paddington costs?"

He shrugged. "Sorry, Miss. Haven't a clue. The coach station is about a mile away if you'd like to ask someone there."

I tore a sheet of paper from my journal, and he sketched

a route to the bus station, adding details about landmarks to look for along the way, then I ventured back out into the rain and cold, bumbling my way in the dark through another unfamiliar town until I found the station. I darted inside and approached the woman at the ticket counter. The next bus to London would depart in an hour. Tickets were ten pounds.

I stared at the board above her head, reading it over and over, hoping I'd missed something—a discount, reduced fare for people traveling alone, special rates for Thursdays after six o'clock, anything.

"No discounts," she said impatiently. "Price is ten pounds."

"Which terminal is the bus for London?" I asked.

"Terminal six, but you need a ticket first."

"I've already got one," I lied. "I was asking for my friend. She's a little short on funds."

"No discounts," the lady barked, then motioned for me to step aside.

I snaked through the station, watching people coming and going, making my way to terminal six, biding my time, gathering the verve to do what had to be done.

While the driver loaded the baggage, I sneaked on board the bus and took a seat in the back. My insides knotted. I began to sweat. The driver climbed aboard. He stood menacingly at the front of the bus and surveyed his cargo, counting heads, weeding out the stowaways from the paying passengers, searching for the girl with the Mohawk who'd lied to the ticket lady and committed the egregious sin of self-preservation.

He began walking down the aisle, slowly, making eye contact with everyone he passed, asking to see their tickets. I pulled my hoodie over my head and slumped in my seat, squeezing my eyes shut, pretending to be asleep, my head resting against the frigid window.

He was coming closer. I could hear his heavy footsteps.

I tried to make snoring sounds, like Connie when she falls asleep after a bender.

He was right beside me.

My stomach rumbled violently.

"Is she all right?" I heard him ask my seatmate, a young woman with an infant sleeping on her lap.

"I don't know," she said. "Seems a bit under the weather to me."

"You've got a ticket?" he asked her.

"In my bag, in the rack above." She jostled in her seat, as if she were about to get up to retrieve it.

"No, no," he said. "Don't bother."

He stood there a moment longer. I could feel his eyes on me.

"If she seems unwell, let me know," he said.

"Yes, of course," she said.

He trudged back up the aisle and started the engine.

I barely moved the whole journey. I barely breathed. Not until we pulled into Victoria Coach Station and the baby began to cry. The mother cradled the little boy while the man sitting across from us brought her bag down for her.

"Come on, darling," she murmured to the child. "We're home."

Yes, I thought, we're home—safe and sound and broke. But not completely broke. I had five pounds, two bottles of whiskey, and clean underwear. Better yet, I had a ticket to meet Jimmy Page the day after tomorrow. I'd left that in my hotel room, thank goodness. I slinked off the bus, bleary-eyed, my head swimming, and went searching for the tube that would carry me back to the lumpy hotel bed awaiting me.

****

Peter was standing in the shadow of a streetlight outside the hotel when I turned onto Queensborough Terrace, his arm draped over a girl's shoulder, hers wrapped around his narrow waist. She was tall and thin, her long, crimped hair pulled up in a side ponytail, baggy jeans rolled above her slouchy white socks and loafers, oversize sweatshirt ripped at the collar like Jennifer Beals in *Flashdance*. Peter stepped away from her when I approached and tipped his turquoise fedora comically.

"Back from the chase, aye? Any luck this time?"

"A big fat fucking no," I grumbled.

He emerged from the shadows. His hair looked bright orange in the glare of the streetlight. "What happened?" he asked.

"Some asshat stole my money when I was in Birmingham."

The girl perched her hands on her hips. "Wanker," she said.

"You're having me on," Peter said. "*All* of your money?"

"Damn close." The cold was numbing my ears. The rain had stopped, but the night air was penetrating. "What are you doing out here?" I said, my teeth chattering. "It's freezing."

"We're—Anna and me, that is—we're off to the club," he said, twirling his hat on his finger. "I just came by to pick up my check while the old man's out. I bunked off work today. Told him I was sick and left early. He's a bit thick, the old duffer." Peter gave a wolfish smile. "Oh, Luna, this is Anna, my girlfriend. Anna's reading Literature at university. You two should get on well."

"Pleased to meet you," she said blithely, untangling the strands of crucifix necklaces around her neck from the *Frankie Says Relax* pin on her coat.

"How'd you get back to London if you didn't have any money?" Peter asked.

"I hopped a bus when the driver wasn't looking."

He snorted. "Fucking brilliant!"

"Oh bollocks," Anna said. "Let's go sit in the car before we freeze our arses off."

I followed them across the street to a battered green Austin Metro. Anna unlocked the doors and we piled inside—Peter and Anna in the front, me in the back. She cranked the engine and "Venus" by Bananarama blared through the speakers. She lowered the volume, and Peter tilted the air vents toward the back seat and switched on the heat.

"So what you going to do?" he asked me. I noted the small gold hoop in his earlobe. I'd pictured him with a kitschy faux diamond stud instead. The gold clashed with his hair.

"Don't know," I muttered. I nudged my hoodie off and combed my fingers through my Mohawk. "I've still got three days left before I head back to the States. I was hoping to go to Headley Grange tomorrow, but I guess that's out."

He lit a joint, took a toke, then offered it to me. I shook my head no and yawned. I hadn't realized how tired I was until I caught a whiff of the marijuana.

Peter exhaled and passed the joint to Anna. "What's at Headley Grange?" he asked.

"I know that place," she said. "It's not too far from here."

Peter shrugged. "So?"

"It's where Led Zeppelin recorded their fourth album—you know, 'Stairway to Heaven' and such," she said. "My brother used to play that record over and over. He's a big fan."

"You mean George?" Peter said, retouching his eyeliner in the rearview mirror. "The prat."

Anna sucked her teeth. "Not George. My other brother, James."

"An even bigger prat." Peter caught my eye in the mirror. "Stay away from King's Cross, Luna. Nothing but slags and lags there." He tossed the eyeliner into the glove box. "True, innit, Anna? He spends all his time round there in a council flat with that bird he picked up on a street corner, pissed all the time, selling the junk, or putting her back out on the corner for a few bob."

"Peter—"

"He's bent as a nine bob note. And the other one, George, he's one of those fascist National Front twats. Falls in lock stock and barrel every year when they march on Remembrance Day." He shook his head pugnaciously. "Nationalism at its finest. Maggie Thatcher my arse."

"Oh don't start, Peter." Anna pressed the joint between his lips. "What do you want with Headley Grange, Luna?" she asked. Peter gave her a subtle wink I could barely see in the murky light. "Oh," she said. "Right." I knew then he'd told her about Jimmy and me, and probably my journal too, and I blanched. She fast-forwarded the tape to a song by Morrissey. "Why don't you bunk off tomorrow too," she said casually to Peter. "Tell the old man you've got the flu. We could all go."

"Go where?" he said.

"Headley Grange."

"I thought you had a do tomorrow."

"Just some boring thing with my mum and dad. I can get out of it."

My eyes darted fervently from Peter to Anna. I slid my hands underneath my thighs and crossed my fingers.

"It's not anywhere near King's Cross, is it?" he asked Anna in between tokes. "Or Brixton or Shoreditch. I'm not going there either."

"No, Peter. It's not in the city. And you're one to talk about King's Cross and Brixton and Shoreditch. Finsbury Park is no better."

"Yeah well, I don't live there anymore, do I."

She stretched her legs across his lap and grinned coquettishly. "Come on. I'll drive. I think it's off the A3. Shouldn't take that long. Be a bit of a laugh, really."

"I'd owe you big-time," I said.

"All piss and wind, you are," Peter said. "You can't return any favors now."

"Sod off, Peter," Anna carped.

"I'm only messing about." He passed me the joint. I accepted this time and took a puff. "Well, you are on a mission," he said. "Be a shame if it all went tits-up." He pushed Anna's legs from his lap and sighed. "All right then. Let's go to Headley-wherever."

"Grange," I wheezed.

Anna cupped Peter's face in her hands and gave him a kiss. "I'll pick you up at eleven, then we'll pop by the hotel for Luna."

"You know I don't get up before noon when I've got the flu," he quipped.

She smiled indulgently at him. "Noon then."

"Want to come to the club with us, Luna?" Peter asked. "You might find it . . . illuminating." Anna elbowed him in the ribs and he chortled mischievously. "Well, it's called Heaven for a reason."

I took a last toke then handed him the joint. "No thanks," I said. "I'm hitting the hay." I hopped out of the car and stood in the road, a little wobbly, drowsy. Anna tapped the horn and they pulled away from the curb.

Peter rolled down the window and waved. "Noon tomorrow, then?"

I breathed in the exhaust fumes, that sulfur smell, the smell of movement and energy, the smell of possibility. "Noon tomorrow," I called after them.

CHAPTER TWENTY

I HELD the money in my palm, as if I were receiving the Blessed Sacrament. Three crisp new bills. Thirty pounds, glinting in the afternoon light blinking through the trees. We were standing outside a Liphook taxi office, where we'd stopped to ask for directions to Headley Grange. The drive had taken longer than we'd expected, but we'd finally reached the little village in East Hampshire near where the manor was located.

"What's this?" I asked Peter, transfixed by the money he'd placed in my hand.

"Thirty quid," he said insouciantly.

"Quite right," Anna said, affecting a posh accent. "Three tenners. Lizzie's mug on every one. Thirty quid indeed."

"Yeah, but what *is* it?"

Peter flicked his wrist, as if he were swatting my question into the gold-speckled sky. "A small donation from my stepmummy."

"Won't she know you took it?" I asked.

"I doubt that since we've never even met. Like I told you, I don't live in Finsbury Park anymore," he said tensely. "But sometimes I go round when I know she and my dad aren't home. The old man never changed the locks and she doesn't fancy banks. Keeps a wad of cash in my mum's jewelry box on the dresser."

"Daft cow," Anna minced.

"Look, take it," Peter said. "Bugger all if I'm giving it back."

He closed my fist around the money. The bills felt stiff against my skin. What had the taxi driver in Kidderminster said—*Never turn down a good deed*? Maybe his stepmother *was* a daft cow. Maybe the money was her ill-gotten gains from some lascivious affair that Peter had discovered. I didn't care. Ethics was something else I couldn't afford right then. I could get by on thirty pounds for the next few days if I was frugal. I could finish what I started without starving.

"Go on," Peter said. "Take it."

I nodded. "I 'spose it's bad luck if I don't, huh."

Anna giggled. "Bad luck for the old bat either way."

I gave a weak laugh. "Guess I can spring for something besides tea and toast for lunch now."

"Nah," Peter said. He darted to the car and slid across the hood. "I nicked another tenner for that."

Anna and I dodged a taxi pulling into the parking lot and jogged across the road to her car. "You navigate, I'll drive," Peter said, ducking behind the wheel.

"You can't drive for shite, Peter."

"Yeah well, I'm a worse navigator."

"Fucking hell," Anna grumbled. We crawled inside and Peter plucked the keys from her purse. "The bloke in the office said the place is off Liphook Road," she said. "Not far from here." She opened a tube of Toffo and handed Peter a chocolate. "We can't go inside, you know," she said. "Someone lives there. There's a gate and all."

Peter licked the chocolate from his fingers. "Still want to

go?" he asked me.

"Of course she does. We can at least have a look." Anna offered me the tube and I took a banana piece. "You didn't think you could just knock on the door and ask some strange chap for a cuppa tea in his parlor, did you?"

She reminded me of Connie the night I showed her my plane ticket to London. *You think you can just haul your ass all the way across the ocean and knock on some Rock star's door?*

I broke the seal of one of the whiskey bottles I'd taken from Bonzo's grave and took a pull. "A house has more than just one door," I said, wiping my mouth on the sleeve of my coat. "Fuck every last one of 'em."

****

Peter nosed the car into a gravel driveway and stopped at the gate. Hedgerows blocked any sight of the house from the road, but from the end of the driveway, where we sat idling next to a security keypad and Beware of Dog sign, we could see it—a three-story ivy-choked stone monument to British Victorian life.

"Cheery little hovel," Peter said. "Who lives here? The Ghost of Christmas Past?"

"I think it used to be a workhouse for the poor and insane," Anna said. "It's supposed to be haunted."

Peter drummed his fingertips on the dashboard. "How do you know that?"

"I told you my brother was a big Led Zeppelin fan."

"Oh right, James, the King's Cross prat. Well, if he said it, it's *got* to be true."

I crouched down in my seat to get a better look. "It's perfect," I said. "Even better than I imagined. The only thing missing is a howling snowstorm." I took a sip of whiskey.

Anna grabbed the bottle from me, sloshing amber liquid on the seat. "Are you drunk?"

"No," I said, "I'm emboldened."

"Well you smell drunk." She scrabbled through her purse and brought out a small bottle of perfume. "Open your mouth."

"I'm not drinking perfume, Anna."

She aimed the bottle at my face. "Close your eyes. I'll just give you a squirt. You can spit it out."

Peter snickered. "Anna always does."

"Piss off or you're next." She spritzed perfume in my mouth before I could close it, and I gagged.

"Well done, Anna," Peter said, lowering the window. "Now she smells like an old bird's powdered arse."

The taste of florid alcohol stung my tongue. I opened the door and spit until my mouth was dry.

Peter cut the engine and took a slug of whiskey. "What now?"

I flopped back on the seat, my legs dangling out the door, the fresh air diluting the sickening smell of gardenias in the car. "Buzz the intercom," I said.

Anna clucked her tongue. "And say *what*?"

"I don't know. Get creative. Tell 'em you're delivering a package, or something. You can distract the owners long enough for me to look around. Just pretend you got the wrong address."

"That's rubbish," Peter said. "First off, we'd never get in. And even if we did, what exactly do you plan to do, aye? What if they've got watchdogs? Or alarms or security cameras?"

"Maybe we should just go," Anna said.

I sat up clumsily. "We can't leave yet. I know I can get in."

"Come on, Luna. He's not in there—Jimmy, I mean. You said yourself he lives in London. What do you think you'll find inside this old place?" Peter's voice softened. "You've seen it. You did it. You're here. Isn't that enough?"

I thought of Claudia, locked in her room with her lavender incense and black and white photo of Jimmy, a Rock 'N Roll dirge penetrating her walls. On the other side of that gate the owls first began to cry. I could hear the echo—four drumsticks pulsing through the heart of a house beyond the hedgerows. It haunted me, like a ghost creeping down dusty corridors, drifting up stairways, lingering in the place of its birth. The stories those walls could tell.

"I'm going inside," I said, my voice quivering.

Anna crawled into the back seat and wrapped her arm around my shoulder. The gesture startled me and I flinched. "Look, don't be mad, but Peter told me about your mum," she said. "I'm sorry, Luna. I thought we were doing a good thing, bringing you here. Now I don't know."

"I'm not mad, and I appreciate all your help, but . . ." Peter handed me the whiskey. I screwed the lid on and set the bottle on the floor. "I have to get inside that house. You don't have to wait for me. I can walk to the station and take a train back to London."

"We're not leaving you here," Anna insisted.

"Then will you wait? Just for a bit?"

"What about the gate?" Peter brayed.

"Don't worry about it. I'll climb over. It's not very high."

"What about watchdogs and such?"

"I can run fast, Peter. It'll be okay."

He hunched over the steering wheel and grunted.

"Just be quick about it," Anna said. "*Really* quick."

They watched me scale the fence and drop over to the other side, then Peter backed the car out and pulled up beside the hedgerow, out of sight from the house.

I trudged up the arched driveway. One scuffed black Converse sneaker in front of the other, gravel crunching underfoot. The sound was deafening. Surely the people inside could hear it. Any second, they'd barge through the front door and release the hounds and I'd be torn to bits, devoured by a pack of black dogs, jungle drums and necromantic guitar wailing in the background.

My feet pressed into the earth. One set of dusty footprints. *Don't let nobody take up your footprints, girl,* my great-grandfather used to say. *Lose your soul if you do.* I kept moving, toward the protruding A-frame sheltering the large double doors that looked like portals to an ancient city. A light burned in the bay window. I crouched behind the hydrangeas in front of the house. All I could hear was the rustling of the trees in the spectral breeze and my heart thumping in my ears.

I could try the door. Maybe it was unlocked. I could swoop inside, like those birds in my dream, and roost in a corner, wait for nightfall, midnight, when whoever lived there was asleep, wait for the fickle silence, then prowl the nooks and crannies of the house, take in what was mine, leave behind a vestige of myself—my touch imprinted on a wall, the smell of my skin mingling with rose-scented candles, my reflection seared in a mirror.

Christy Alexander Hallberg

Peter and Anna were waiting. There wasn't time for stealth.

I walked to the door. My hands were trembling. I knocked lightly then stepped back onto the gravel.

A lock clicked and the door opened. A distinguished-looking gentleman with sprigs of gray hair around his temples stood staring at me, his taut face circumspect, as if I were a Jehovah's Witness peddling unwanted salvation. He was a tall, reedy man, tidy and austere, his navy cardigan buttoned to the neck, his khaki trousers smartly pressed. I must have looked to him like I'd come to clip the hedgerow, or worse, slit his throat in broad daylight.

"Yes?" he said impatiently.

"I'm sorry to bother you, sir."

"How did you get in here? The gate is locked." I glanced over my shoulder, as if the gate were a figment of his imagination. "This is private property," he continued.

"Yes sir. I don't mean to bother you." My voice was childlike, squeaky and meek. "It's a long story that won't mean anything to you, but I . . . "

I didn't know what to say next. It was one thing to take a pull of whiskey and climb a fence; it was another thing altogether to look into a country squire's eyes and beg for entry to his home.

"Never mind," I murmured, backing away from him. "I'm sorry I wasted your time."

"Just a minute, young lady." He slipped his hands in his sweater pockets. "You've come to see the stairway, haven't you?"

A scratchy lump rose in my throat.

"American?" he asked.

I nodded timidly. "I'm only in England a few days. I just wanted to . . ." I steeled myself. "Yes sir, I've come to see the stairway."

"The Holy Grail of Led Zeppelin sites," he said, surprisingly genial. "You're not the first to show up unannounced. They come from all over the world. My mother always turns them away." He gave a breathy laugh. "This long story of yours, I suppose it's a melancholy one." I dropped my eyes. "I see." He held the door open and stepped aside. "You'd better come in, then."

****

The smells struck me first—the smoky smell of a fire crackling in the wood-burning stove to my left, the cinnamon smell of freshly-baked scones wafting from another room.

The stairway was to my right—a brutish dark wood structure angling upward for three stories, holding court in a captive house. I could see all the way to the top landing, where light poured in through the windows like the resplendent glow of paradise.

The stairway to heaven.

"It's quite something, isn't it," the man said. "The star of the house." He was standing behind me, admiring the icon that drew hordes of trespassers to his private property every year as if it were Mecca.

I craned my neck to study every twist and turn of the staircase. "Amazing," I gushed, unable to subdue my amazement.

"Indeed," he said. "The band strung microphones from the

banisters to capture the acoustics." He clapped his hands twice. The sound barreled through the room. "You can hear why they recorded the drum tracks in here." He was acting more like a tour guide with a vetted script than a disgruntled homeowner now. "I presume you know the fourth album, the song 'When the Levee Breaks'? And what's the other one? 'Four Sticks', I think it's called."

A tickling sensation skittered down my back. "This is where they recorded that song?"

He made a grand sweep of his arm. "This very spot. Well, more or less."

A log shifted in the stove and I jolted. He opened the heavy iron door and stoked the fire with an iron poker from a basket by the window.

"The house has been in my family, on my mother's side, for decades. She owned it when the band stayed here."

"Really? Was she living here at the time?"

"No, no. The house was a bit rundown then, drafty and damp. She'd fallen on hard times. That's why she began renting it out." He pointed toward the ceiling. "They bunked upstairs," he said. "I don't know which floor, perhaps both."

I followed his arm upward with my eyes. I wished I'd brought my journal with me. I wanted to log everything he said, record every inflection and gesture, every detail about Jimmy's time in the space I now occupied. I felt heady. I didn't trust myself to remember it all—the sound of the clock on the wall tick-tick-ticking, the chandelier that hung from the thick wooden beam jutting like an offshoot from the first landing, the dusky green runner that crawled up the length of the stairs. I tried to picture them here in the early '70s—Jimmy, Robert,

John Paul Jones, John Bonham. The four of them, young, at the peak of their creative lives, Robert and Bonzo spooked by ghosts in the attic, Jones perturbed by damp bedsheets, Jimmy reveling in the Dickensian aura. There was an energy about the place. I could sense it even from inside the car. I ran my hand along one of the balusters. The wood was cool and smooth. I climbed the first step, waiting for the man to admonish me. He pushed his glasses up on his nose and gave a proud smile. I took another step.

Was Claudia watching? Was she listening? Could she hear the tunes—"Stairway" and "Four Sticks," the former an airy lullaby of hope and salvation, the latter a desperate imprecation, a plea and a puzzle she thought she'd solved. John Bonham had sat at a drum kit three feet away from me and hammered out the beat. Jimmy may have stood where I did, holding one of those microphones he'd strung from the banisters to capture the sound he was searching for, the sound he would later press into a vinyl disc that would find its way to my mother's hands, my mother's stereo, my mother's soul, and now mine.

Was she here? Was she the lady bathed in white light, singing in the bedroom where Jimmy had slept? Did she show him that everything always turns to gold?

I felt the sting of tears.

"Are you all right, Miss?" He was looking at me queerly, as if he'd begun to second-guess his decision to let me inside his home.

I sauntered down the stairs, grasping the railing to steady myself. "I can't thank you enough," I said.

"Not a'tall. I let a Chinese couple in a few weeks ago. I'd left the gate open and they waltzed right in. It's the eyes that get me every time, that and the stories they tell." He opened the door and we stepped into the slanted afternoon light. "Well then," he said brightly. He took my hand and gave it a polite shake. "I hope you found what you were looking for."

I swept my eyes over the house, committing it to memory as best I could. "Yeah," I said. "I think I did."

CHAPTER TWENTY-ONE

I SAT on a curb across from the Hammersmith Palais the evening after Headley Grange, waiting for the doors to open, my teeth chattering in the cold. Peter and Anna had offered to drive me, but I'd said no. This part of the journey I had to make alone.

I slipped Connie's butterfly comb in my jeans pocket then clasped Claudia's chain around my ankle for good luck. I'd shown Peter and Anna a photograph of Claudia when they'd dropped me off at the hotel the night before. Anna had scrutinized the black and white image intently. "You look like her," she'd said.

"No," I'd said, taken aback. "She was blonde, for one thing. And beautiful. We don't look anything alike."

Peter squinted over Anna's shoulder to get a closer look. "I don't know, Luna. I think there's a resemblance. You both have this sort of otherworldly look about you."

Anna nodded. "It's in the eyes."

"No, not the eyes," Peter had said staunchly. "I can't put my finger on it, but there's definitely a resemblance."

The proposition had shaken me. I wondered if Grandma had ever seen any speck of Claudia in my face. If she had, she'd never let on. Connie had said I looked like Jimmy on the cover of *Outrider*, but then, his picture is blurry. *You're not like me,*

Claudia had demanded I say that summer's day mere hours before she died. I'd reluctantly repeated the words, but I hadn't meant them. Now, the notion of looking like my mother gave me pause. But it also captivated me.

A line was forming at the doors, mostly middle-aged couples in conservative dress, but a few rebels brought up the rear: Punk Rockers, come to ogle the third judge of the contest, Pete Shelley of the Buzzcocks; and Glam Rock groupie types in spandex bodysuits, who probably hoped Freddie Mercury had tagged along with Brian May.

I slung my backpack over my shoulder and hustled across the street as a massive black man in a dark suit propped open the doors. He lumbered down the line checking tickets, forcing eye contact with everyone, like the menacing bus driver in Birmingham. The groupies in front of me batted their sparkly shadowed eyes at him and promised they'd make it worth his while to introduce them to Brian May.

"Keep the line moving," he barked.

"How do you like that," one of the girls said in a thick Cockney accent once he'd passed by. She reeked of stale alcohol and cigarette smoke.

"He's a bender, that one," the other girl said. She jutted out her bony hip and perched her hand on her waist. "A proper twat."

"I bet he *has* a twat."

The couple in front of them turned around and scowled. "Oh, *excuse* me," Cigarette Girl said unctuously, then erupted into mordant laughter.

The lobby palpitated with restive fans eager to clear security and stake out a spot near the stage, or the backstage

Gods from the temporal world, unseen and unsullied, like mighty warriors en route to Valhalla.

He was less than four feet away.

He dropped a piece of paper and bent down to pick it up. I could see the top of his head, the crown, where his black hair was just beginning to thin.

He rose, and for a second I caught his eye.

One second is but a flash—a swirling, whirling flash. One thousand *milliseconds* take time. They tick by like heartbeats—

One millisecond

Two milliseconds

Three milliseconds

—like pulses of memory coursing through your veins—

A concert movie at a dusty drive-in

The ashes of an incinerated poster

A cunning stare from the cover of a record album

You can live a lifetime in the space they occupy. You can see it all in two vitreous orbs.

I opened my mouth. No sound came out, like in a nightmare when you want to scream but your voice is just a burst of tinny babel.

He was looking at me.

Nine hundred milliseconds

Nine hundred and one milliseconds

Nine hundred and two milliseconds

Two brooding bodyguards in black suits that matched Jimmy's negotiated the clogged vestibule and urged him down the hall. And then he was gone, ensconced in the VIP room with his exquisite wife and her bulging belly.

But he'd seen me—the skinny, pale teenage girl with a

door in the case of the Cockney Sisters.

I handed the woman at the security checkpoint my ticket and backpack. She poked through my belongings then slid the bag across the table toward me.

"Lovely," she said. "Thank you very much."

I gestured to my ticket. "It's a VIP," I said.

She grinned. "Yes, I see that."

"I'll have access to restricted areas, right?"

"You'll be able to get near backstage."

"But will I get to *meet* Jimmy Page?"

"There's no guarantee, but you'll definitely be in proximity, so you've got a good chance."

I ignored the impatient grumblings of the people behind me and leaned over the table toward the lady. "How good?" I uttered.

"I should be surprised if you *didn't* meet him," she said, then stamped my ticket and handed it to me. "Enjoy your evening."

I was about to ask her if she had any sway with the VIP room doorman when a woman brushed past me, blonde hair tumbling down her back, her gait nonchalant in a long black velvet skirt, silver bangles tinkling beneath the flared sleeves of her white peasant blouse, a hefty esoteric charm hanging from a silver chain around her neck. Except for the obvious baby bump, she was petite, like a heavily pregnant Stevie Nicks. I stared at her. She looked oddly familiar, like a relative at a family reunion whose face you recognize but name escapes you. Then it hit me: she was the woman at Old Mill House. Mrs. Jimmy Page. Up close, she was stunning, much more beautiful than I'd thought in Windsor. She could have been someone's hip older sister, a swinging Londoner who shops on Carnaby Street and goes clubbing in Soho and offers her adoring little sisters surreptitious sips of the eighteen-year-old single malt Scotch she swiped from their parents' liquor cabinet.

She was a whole different species from me.

I could disappear and no one here would notice. I could become violently ill on the tube and someone could pilfer my backpack with all of my identification and I'd wind up a comatose Jane Doe in the charity ward of a hospital. Or I could bury my passport with my past and begin a new life, one divested of cigarette cravings and crying owls and memories of razor blades and smoking guns. No one here would be the wiser. No one here would care, least of all Mrs. Page.

She bustled down the hall toward the auditorium, ignoring her husband's zealous fans armed with Led Zeppelin posters and crinkled concert ticket stubs they hoped he would sign.

The bouncer shoved through the small crowd blocking the entry from the security line. "Clear the way," he demanded.

The energy in the building shifted. Everyone stopped and gaped at the entry.

Jimmy Page walked into the room.

I could feel my breath—warm pulses of air rushing in and out, in and out, fluttering in my ears like white noise.

A group of women waved autograph pads at him. "Jimmy, would you sign this?"

"Clear! Off!" the bouncer roared, his arms outstretched in a profane pastiche of Claudia's sacred Jimmy photo.

Jimmy was less than five feet away.

I hadn't expected him to enter through the lobby. Surely there was some secret portal that whisked venerable Rock

Mohawk and ratty jeans and slight resemblance to a woman who'd believed with every fiber of her being that pensive child was his.

Jimmy Page could not possibly be my father.

I could not possibly be his daughter.

Preposterous—all of it.

But what if it wasn't?

In that second, the one after the thousandth millisecond, I believed it too—with every fiber of my being.

****

The auditorium was smaller than I'd expected. It was more like a dance hall, with a large stage at the front, spacious dance floor, tables scattered along the perimeter, and a long hallway snaking from the vestibule to the VIP room. An area was roped off in the middle of the room, with a table and chairs occupying the bulk of the space—the judges' table, I figured. I made a beeline for it, claiming a spot as close to the rope as I could get.

People were milling about—some nursing beers or glasses of wine; contestants lugging guitar cases heading backstage; a cabal of Punk Rockers queuing up outside the men's room, waiting to sneak a snort or toke up, I assumed. As expected, the Cockney Sisters were loitering by the VIP room, like ancillary stage props. Their doggedness paid off when Brian May stepped out. They pounced on him, heaving pen and paper in his hands in an epileptic frenzy. He autographed the paper, then one of the girls presented her bare back for his signature. I couldn't hear what he said, but I hoped, for the sake of his wife, he told them they'd have better luck with the bouncer.

Brian took a seat at the judges' table and shuffled through a stack of papers. My eyes darted around the dimly-lit room, looking for Jimmy. The man standing next to me whipped out a camera and pressed the shutter button just in time to catch Jimmy walk into the frame.

He sat next to Brian and Pete Shelley and slipped on a pair of reading glasses. I stared at him, deconstructing him like a Victorian novel. The juxtaposition between a bespectacled, thinning-haired Jimmy Page and the twenty-nine-year-old version confined in a frame over my dead mother's bed seemed like a warped reversal of *The Picture of Dorian Gray*. And yet, it humanized him. It made him more accessible. I'd never thought of him as mortal. In the abstract, yes—the way you know we're all just a cluster of cells and atoms powered by faulty wiring—but to me, he'd always been more of a mirage than a man. You can touch a man. You can feel his heartbeat, the rise and fall of his chest, the stubble on his chin, the calluses on his fingertips. You can feel his heat. I pressed my body against the rope. I couldn't reach him. But I was getting closer.

The first of the contestants, backed up by a house band, kicked off the contest with "Ace of Spades" by Motorhead. The guy had the classic Rock God look down pat—black leather jacket, saturnine pout, skeins of long dark hair framing pallid skin. He could have been standing next to Lemmy on the cover of a Motorhead album. I hated that song and Motorhead, but he was good. I watched Jimmy and Brian wagging their heads to the music, exchanging ready grins and the occasional note, which Jimmy would slip on his glasses to read. In the middle of the guitar solo one of the Punk Rockers yelled, "Pete Shelley is God!" then plowed into me, sloshing his beer on my feet.

"Sorry, mate," he shouted in my ear, as best I could tell from his slurred accent. He rummaged through his pockets then handed me a damp wad of toilet paper. "Cheers," he said, then staggered toward the stage.

Myriad scenarios involving damp toilet paper, all of them disgusting, raced through my head. I'd seen him emerge from the men's room moments before, zipping his fly as he dithered through the crowd. I dropped the paper and wiped my hands on the rope.

"I've got some baby wipes in my purse if you'd like one," the lady next to me said over the roar of the music. She was a frumpy woman in her early thirties, dressed in a plaid knee-length skirt and knit sweater, a look more befitting a 1950s housewife than a young woman of the '80s.

"Thanks," I said. "That'd be great."

She handed me a wipe then dropped the package back into her purse. "Do you know someone in the contest?"

"No," I said. "Do you?"

"Our nephew." She gestured to the man beside her, an equally frumpy anachronism clutching a bulky camera. "What's he playing, love?"

" 'Rock 'N Roll'—the Led Zeppelin tune," he said.

"I think we're more nervous than he is," the lady said, swelling with familial pride. "I reckon he was more nervous about meeting Jimmy Page than about playing."

I stifled a gasp. "Did he meet him yet?"

"I imagine so. He was backstage with him earlier."

The man elbowed me. "He promised to introduce us to Jimmy if he wins."

She pulled a face. "You can go with him, then. I'll not

mix with that lot over there," she said, jerking her head at the Cockney Sisters, still parked outside the VIP room door. "Disgraceful, if you ask me."

The song mercifully ended and the next contestant took the stage. I twisted my hoodie string around my finger and feigned interest in the guy massacring "More Than a Feeling" by Boston. "You think your nephew would be willing to introduce me to Jimmy too?" I asked.

The man gave a laugh. "I'll be lucky if he can get *me* backstage. But you might be able to get closer to Jimmy on the other side of the room. He'll walk right past you when they head backstage to choose the winners."

I glanced across the room. I'd be farther away from Jimmy on that side of the rope, and there were eight more guitarists to go before the end of the contest. "I don't know," I said. Then it occurred to me that a lot of people would probably start heading that way and I'd get lost in the shuffle. "Maybe you're right," I said briskly, recharged and eager to maneuver. I waited for the song to end then meandered to the other side of the room. The same bouncer from the lobby guarded the backstage door, his massive hands clasped in front of him, exposed and ready, like the lethal weapons they probably were. He stared vacantly at the ten-year-old boy on stage head banging his way through Free's "Wishing Well." I wondered if he even cared if Jimmy and Brian and Pete were mobbed by their fans, or if he'd much rather be at home, having a cuddle with his wife on the sofa, watching *Dr. Who* on the telly. Maybe he had a daughter—a moony teenage girl who'd covered her bedroom walls with posters of her idols, some for whom he'd worked. Maybe she'd sweet-talked him into introducing her to Boy George or sneaking her backstage at a Spandau Ballet concert. Maybe he wasn't as intractable as he seemed.

I inched my way toward him amidst thunderous applause for the child prodigy who'd wowed the crowd. He bristled when he saw me.

"Can I go in?" I asked, nodding at the door. "I've got a pass."

The Cockney Sisters glared at me. "Why don't you let us all in, aye?" one of them sniped at the bouncer.

He shook his head. "Sorry."

"But I've got a VIP pass," I said. I fished my ticket from my pocket and held it out to him. "See?"

"Sorry," he said. He was anything but tractable, I decided, and he certainly wasn't sorry. If he had a daughter, fortune had hardly favored her.

The next contestant cued the drummer and the room exploded into "Rock 'N Roll." I glanced at Jimmy, sitting in the dark in his black trousers, shirt, and jacket. He tapped his pen on the table and bobbed back and forth to his own music. I wondered how he felt watching a cocky kid in combat boots play a song he'd made famous when the kid was barely out of nappies. A group of girls about my age rushed the stage, dancing wildly, pumping their arms in the air, their skirts so tight I could tell even from a distance they'd gone commando for the occasion. I watched Jimmy watching the scene, training my eyes on the tilt of his head, trying to follow the path of his stare. Was he looking at them? Those girls were young enough to be his daughters. My stomach clenched. Was the one he claimed among us? I wondered if he worried what she might one day promise a surly backstage bouncer. Maybe he'd vanquished the thought. Maybe he clung to a fixed vision of her, one frozen in a time of satin ribbons and first words. Maybe he saw what he wanted to see, what he needed to see. Maybe he didn't want to know the truth.

The door opened and the bouncer stepped aside to let Jimmy's wife out. She whispered something to him then ducked back inside the room.

"Mrs. Page!" I blurted, loudly enough for her to hear. The words tasted sour, as if I were gagging on a mouthful of curdled milk. She turned and looked at me, a supercilious expression on her face. I swallowed hard. "I came all the way from America just to meet Jimmy," I stammered.

She recoiled, like a repulsed spectator at a freak show. I slouched toward her. The bouncer blocked me with his arm. *Don't make me beg*, I thought then realized I'd said the words out loud.

She cupped her hands underneath her belly. I wasn't sure if the motion meant *fuck off, groupie, I'm having his baby*, or if she'd been stricken by a sudden pang of maternal concern for me.

"You'll have to wait, like everybody else," she said in her Louisiana twang, then closed the door in my face.

So I waited, in the bowels of a crowded London theater, for the competition to end and for him to head my way.

When he did, he walked right past me. No stopping. No eye contact. Right past me. I pushed the Cockney Sisters out of my way. They pushed me out of their way when Brian came near. In the chaos of the moment I accidentally stepped on Brian's foot and he shot me a warning glance.

"Brian needs space," the bouncer snapped. With his back turned, he was oblivious to the Cockney Sisters, who slipped inside the VIP room behind Brian. They were in there all of twenty seconds before another bouncer booted them out.

"They've got Champagne in there!" Cigarette Girl squealed.

"Must be somebody's birthday," her pal said.

Cigarette Girl chortled. "Don't be a mug. They're rich. They have Champagne all the time."

A woman with a small spiral-bound notebook tugged her arm. "Did you get anyone's autograph?" she asked.

Cigarette Girl bobbed her head. "Well, not then, we didn't," she conceded. "But Brian signed one for us earlier." The other girl giggled and flaunted her autographed back.

The woman with the notebook flashed a greeting card at the bouncer. "I brought this for Jimmy," she said. "It's a congratulations card. He's having a baby, you see. His wife is, I mean." He folded his arms across his barrel chest and rocked on his heels. "I'd like to give it to him," she said tightly.

"You'll have to wait."

The door swung open and the three Rock guitarists traipsed out. A ruckus ensued—fans clamoring for contact, the bouncer struggling to reclaim order. Jimmy, Brian, and Pete hewed their way to the stage to announce the winner of the contest. I floundered across the room, tunneling my own path, as close to the microphone stand as I could muscle. The "Wishing Well" little boy won first place, and Jimmy handed the beaming kid a 1957 Gibson Les Paul guitar. I barged to the lip of the stage and stretched my arm toward him. He shifted his stance, moving a hair closer to me. I catapulted my upper body onto the stage, my lower torso dangling off the edge, and touched the toe of his shoe. He reeled back. One of the bodyguards pushed me down into the crowd, like a rancid piece of trash he'd kicked into the gutter.

Jimmy retreated to the VIP room, a horde of people in pursuit. I shook back into myself then joined the hunt, and once again, stood guard with the bouncer and the Cockney Sisters outside the door, our quarry trapped inside. This was my last chance. He'd have to come out to leave the building, and he'd have to get past me to do it.

****

I'd once read that all obsessions are protean. I was eighteen years old, standing outside a door, the other side of which was the object of my mother's obsession, and now mine. As it was in the beginning is *right now*. The *now* that would soon be *then*. It's the *now* that's protean. Like my own thoughts—of girls with glitter eye shadow and cheesy bodysuits and women with baby wipes and Punk Rockers who see God in the guise of a Rock star and closed doors I wanted to open. My head swam. I was drunk with desperation—for the door to open, to see clearly what was inside.

"I can get you in." A man—a boy, really—in ripped jeans with "Never mind the bollocks, here's the Sex Pistols" scrawled in black Magic Marker on one leg threw his arms around the Cockney Sisters. They squirmed free. "You want to meet Brian May, right?"

"You know Brian?" Cigarette Girl asked dubiously.

"What a load of codswallop," the other girl said. At some point during the night she'd smeared her eye shadow and she looked like a dazed Siamese cat, her indigo eyes on the prowl for prey.

"Do you want to meet him or not?" They both nodded coyly. "What's your names?"

The one with the cat eyes jerked her thumb at Cigarette Girl. "She's Keira. I'm Gemma."

"Keira and Gemma," he said, letting the words roll around in his mouth, as if he were savoring them before spitting them out. "What'll you do for me, aye?"

"Ha!" Keira scoffed. "What'll you do for *me, aye?*"

"Come outside and I'll show you."

"What a tosser," Gemma said. "He don't know Brian."

I listened to them prattle on until the bouncer pushed the girls aside and Jimmy crept out. He stood beside me. I was at his elbow. My arm brushed against his. He tried to move forward, but fans shoved pictures and posters and albums and autograph books at him en masse. *Jimmy, sign this, Jimmy, can I have your autograph, Jimmy, you're a god!* He didn't say anything. He didn't sign anything. He looked thunderstruck, as if he'd never experienced this sort of adoration, as if he'd forgotten the mobs of groupies blocking his entrance to the Rainbow Bar and Grill on the Sunset Strip in the hedonistic '70s or throngs of half-naked girls who'd slipped backstage after a Led Zeppelin concert—the girls bouncers deemed attractive enough to let stay. He looked distraught, anxious for escape.

I stood beside him, slack-jawed. I was blowing it. I realized that. While my arm was still pressed against his, I realized I was blowing it. The chance would never come again. I would never come here again—not to this space, this building, this moment.

Claudia, we're blowing it.

Jimmy's bodyguards . . . I saw them out of the corner of my eye stalking toward us. They pushed the lackeys away and grabbed his arms, practically dragging him onward.

I watched him go. He was getting smaller and smaller. Going down the hall, the hall that led from the VIP room to the vestibule. The moment, the *right now*—the protean *now*—was slipping into past.

Claudia, we're blowing it.

It was now or never. He was getting smaller and smaller. It was now or never.

I started to run, my backpack slapping against me like a riding crop, Claudia's anklet making a jingle-jangling sound.

There was a stairway at the end of the hall, before it curves around and leads back to the vestibule. A stairway, for chrissake. It didn't lead to heaven. It went down. To a car park, more than likely. The bodyguard in front began the descent. Jimmy was next. I was less than ten feet away from him. Nine. Eight.

I screamed his name. Again and again, until he stopped on the second step and looked up at me.

The only words I could think of were, "I came all the way from America just to meet you!" I heard the anguish in my voice. I said it again. "I came all the way from America to meet you."

Everything had led to this moment.

He has to speak to me.

I waited.

Please speak to me.

Everything had led to this moment.

His bodyguard—the one directly behind him—whispered something to him. Jimmy looked at me again.

"I'm sorry," he said, his English accent soft and soulful. He smiled, with his mouth and his eyes. I could see the hint of gray in his hair, the crinkles around his eyes, his glasses peeking from the top of his jacket pocket like an ill-kept secret.

He's grown older, Claudia. Not like you, your unblemished face locked in my memory. He's changed. Gone is the black satin dragon suit of years ago. He looks elegant, respectable, conservative, like somebody's father.

All the things I didn't say . . . I was choking on them. *You can't go. Not yet. What about my mother? Claudia. My mother. Remember her? The owls cried for her. The river ran red for her. Your guitar said so. What about my mother? What about me?*

"I'm sorry," he said again, as if he'd heard my thoughts. His voice was gentle. He actually sounded sorry. He started down the stairs.

"Wait!" I cried. I shuffled through my backpack and brought out the envelope with my letter and photographs and violently waved it at him. "Please take it. Just look at it. Take it. *Please.*" My eyes were wet. I was terrified I might cry in front of him. "Please take it," I said faintly.

"Mr. Page, the car's waiting," one of the bodyguards said.

Jimmy gave a curt nod then reached up and took the envelope from me. His hand touched mine, too quickly to tell if his skin was soft or coarse, chapped from the London wind and cold or moisturized and massaged into delicacy in a ritzy salon. He clutched the envelope.

"Mr. Page." The bodyguard. He sounded firmer this time.

Jimmy tucked the envelope underneath his arm and went down the stairs. I dropped my backpack on the floor and teetered against the railing. The world was spinning. I focused my eyes on the step where he'd just stood and held my breath until the spinning stopped. Then headed back to the hotel, to wait.

CHAPTER TWENTY-TWO

PETER BUNKED off work the next day too—my last day in England. I didn't know his phone number—Anna's either—or where he lived. Somewhere close by, with one of his mother's sisters and her flock of pre-teens, he'd told me. As far away from his dad and daft cow stepmummy in Finsbury Park as he could get on a hotel clerk's wages. His wanker boss had refused to divulge his personal information, so I had to wait alone. I'd enticed the old guy with five of my remaining thirty pounds to send up any messages or phone calls that might arrive from a Mr. Page or his associates immediately, and spent the morning and afternoon holed up in my room, watching the phone like a simmering kettle.

I tried to read. Someone had left a copy of *Beloved* by Toni Morrison in the lobby. I didn't get past the first chapter. My mind kept drifting back to Jimmy, the stairway, his hand clenching my envelope. Had he opened it yet, unsealed the flap and dug inside for the photographs, my letter? Had he read it? Surely he'd read it by now. He had to have read it. Why else would he have accepted it from me? He could have shooed me away and carried on with his bodyguards. But he didn't. He'd reached out to me. He'd touched me. There'd been a connection. It was all so poetic, surreal, like a Gothic fairy tale.

On a lonely London night, by a flickering fire in a gilded drawing room, he sits in silence, the dusty hands of an antique clock at rest, the door locked, his pregnant wife held at bay. He examines the photographs. He remembers the eyes, the mouth, the angles of her face, her elegant neck and translucent skin. He never really forgot. He reads the words, the story of the child by the child, the one who's made of water and of her and of him. The story of another lonely night, a Southern night outside a concert hall once upon a time, the pines crying, the owls crying, a river running dry, running red. He remembers. He always remembers, every time he hears the song that chronicles it all. Except the child. He didn't know about the child, the girl without a name. How could he know? He never returned. He left death in his wake. Life and death. The former came first. The former still lives. He cries in the night, by the flickering fire in the gilded drawing room. He'll have to tell the pregnant wife. He'll tell her in the morning about the woman in the photograph and their nameless child. In the morning he'll tell her. Then he'll come calling, a knight in black satin, violin bow raised like a rapier. He'll claim the child. He'll name the child.

That's not how it would happen—I knew that. But maybe something similar, a variation on the theme, but less theatrical. That would do. I could live with that.

I lay down on the bed, my hand on the cradle of the phone, wrangling the scenario from my thoughts. He'd contact me. I was positive. I just had to wait a little while longer.

****

The word *distraction* means a thing that prevents someone from giving full attention to something else—a diversion, like counting the number of scuff marks on a baseboard or stains on a bedspread. It also means extreme agitation of the mind or emotions—hysteria, madness, mania. Waiting for Jimmy Page was a distraction, in the second sense of the word, the worse sense of the word.

I was listing words in my journal, words that nettled me, like *distraction*, and words I found soothing, like *kitchen* and *hearth and home*. And *grandma*—the word, concept, and its physical manifestation. What irony, I thought—searching for Jimmy Page had been a distraction from thinking of her, and now thinking of her was a distraction from waiting for him.

I imagined another scenario, one I couldn't romanticize.

Grandma, sitting at the kitchen table at home, smoking a cigarette. Why not take up the habit again? She's dying. She knows that. It's morning in Full River. The cold spell has broken and her cracked hands are beginning to heal. She's worried about me. Girl, you could worry the hell outta the devil, she'd tell me if I were there. But if I were there, neither she nor the devil would be worried. She knows I'm coming back. She knows she's the one who'll be leaving for good, not me, not yet. Still, she's worried. Aunt Lorraine is with her. She doesn't want to leave her alone in her condition, and Grandma won't go back to Morganton with her. She has to stay on the farm, she says, to watch the driveway for Connie's car to bring me home, to listen for the back door to squeak open and my dirty sneakers plod into the kitchen. She has to wait, she says, just a little while longer.

It was three o'clock in London, ten a.m. in Full River. She would have already washed the breakfast dishes and wiped down the table and counter, put a load of laundry in the washing machine, then finished getting ready for church. Or maybe she was sitting in Claudia's room, not in the rose-colored beanbag chair; her knees would scream bloody murder if she did. Maybe she'd sewn new curtains for the naked window above the stereo and had Aunt Lorraine help her hang them. No, I couldn't imagine Aunt Lorraine setting foot in that room. She was probably furious at me for opening the door, not to mention for leaving home the way I did. But I could picture Grandma in there, communing with the bookshelves, the floor, that tainted window, the record on the turntable, all of them witnesses to the *abomination*, if my great-grandfather was to be believed. I don't think Grandma did. She'd render her child to a cremation chamber but not the eternal flames of hell. I don't know where she thought Claudia's soul had gone. Grandma was reticent about her religion. She went through all the motions of a good Christian woman like a blind person in a labyrinth—bumbling solemnly toward the exit, unsure if there even was one, accepting the futility of altering course. This was the path she'd been assured would save her. This was the path on which she'd remain.

I lifted the receiver and called the front desk. No messages, the old guy assured me dully. I could hear a group of American teenagers chattering in the background. They'd arrived that morning with three beset literature teachers, intent on making Anglophiles out of a bunch of doctors' and lawyers' kids who'd rather be eating tacos on a beach in Mexico than force-fed a matinee of *Hamlet* in London. I wasn't sorry I'd miss my class trip. I never particularly wanted to go to Mexico anyway. Had the circumstances been different, I would have loved to catch a matinee of *Hamlet*, take one of those Dickens walking tours, even do a Jack the Ripper night prowl through Whitechapel.

I would have liked to spend an afternoon at the National Gallery. I'd never been to an art museum. All I knew about the Great Masters was what I'd seen in books and on TV, and what I'd heard from Claudia. She loved Cezanne, especially *An Old Woman with a Rosary*, a bleak portrait of an elderly peasant woman enveloped in darkness, clutching her prayer beads as if they were an antidote for despair, her body stooped, her eyes downcast, submissive and desolate. She knows there is no such remedy. She knows her fate. I hated that painting. Even more, I hated that Claudia loved it. I wasn't especially fond of the Impressionists—too bourgeois for my taste, and definitely Claudia's—but I was always drawn to Monet's *Water-Lily Pond*, the bridge arching over a pool of sparkling water filled with a kaleidoscope of aquatic plants, nestled among fecund trees and reeds. To me, the painting spoke of hope, in all its ambiguity.

I hung up the phone and began to pace the tiny room. Time was running out. My flight was scheduled to leave at nine o'clock the next morning. *Now* would soon be *then*, and *then* would be too late.

There were four stains on the white bedspread, mostly brownish, as if someone had spilled coffee or tea on it. Two were rust-colored, the hue of dried blood. I didn't want to imagine how they'd gotten there. The scuffmarks on the baseboards were like smudges of black coal, some of them hiding behind the furniture, as if the room had been rearranged, perhaps to conceal its imperfections rather than refurbish it. I couldn't get an accurate count.

The elevator door clacked open. Footsteps, light like a woman's, coming my way. I stared at the door, looking through the door, into faint possibility. Whoever it was walked on by. I cursed savagely under my breath, *motherfucker* mainly. Why does no one say *fatherfucker*? I noted them both in my journal.

I turned on the TV. A rerun of *Monty Python's Flying Circus* was playing—the Minister of Funny Walks sketch.

What was Mrs. Page doing this minute? Pleading with her husband in her crude accent to forget the goddess in the photograph and her dark-eyed daughter? *Jemmy, you cain't call that girl. You just cain't.* Maybe she was the holdup. That had to be it. He was probably hard at work in the turret concocting an elixir to stir in her jambalaya that would put her into a deep sleep from which she wouldn't awake until long after he'd flown to America with me to fill in the *Father* blank on my birth certificate.

I lay back down on the bed. I wished Peter were here. I wished Grandma and Claudia and Connie and even my great-grandfather were here.

I wished Jimmy were here.

****

The phone woke me at five-thirty that evening. I'd fallen asleep clutching Claudia's anklet in my hand. The room was dark, except for the blue flicker of the TV, the Monty Python boys jaunting through the Spanish Inquisition sketch.

I lunged for the receiver then hesitated. Whose voice would I hear on the other end of the line? Who had something important enough to say to me they'd make the effort to pick up a phone, punch in my number, and wait for me to answer? Who was waiting for me? There were only three prospects:

Peter, his wanker boss, or . . .

I rubbed my sweaty palms on my jeans then answered the call.

"You asked me to ring if someone came round for you." Prospect number two.

I snatched the remote control and clicked off the TV. "What do you mean *came round*? Is he still there?"

"Yeah, he's got something you got to sign for. Very official, like it come from Her Majesty herself."

I slumped against the wall. For a second I couldn't remember where I was. "Who is he?" I asked eagerly.

"Some young chap. A messenger boy, I reckon."

"Did he tell you who sent him?"

"You want I should ask him?" He sounded annoyed. I was a nuisance to him, a distraction—in the first sense of the word.

"Never mind," I said stridently. "Be down in a sec."

The young chap was sitting in the lobby thumbing through the *Daily Telegraph*, a large manila envelope like the one I'd given Jimmy at the Hammersmith Palais on his lap. His navy trousers were wrinkled, his socks mismatched shades of brown, as if his employer's unexpected call had reached him in the midst of an afternoon tryst and he'd slipped on the least soiled professional attire he could scrounge from the laundry basket on such short notice. When he saw me coming, he folded the paper and stood up, combing his fingers through his tousled hair.

"Miss Luna Kane?" he asked with the bent smile of an underling who'd rather be anywhere but on the job on a Sunday evening.

I threw my shoulders back and cleared my throat. "Yeah,

yes, that's me. I'm Luna Kane," I said. I licked my chapped lips and reached fervidly for the envelope.

He pulled a slip of paper and a pen from his coat pocket and offered that instead. "Sign first, please." My hand twitched while I scribbled my name across an official-looking form I didn't bother to read. "Brilliant," he said, then passed me the envelope and scooted out without another word.

****

I didn't open it immediately. I sat on the edge of the bed in my room and stared at it. There was no address, no markings to indicate whom it was from, only my name typed in all caps and highlighted in glaring yellow on the front. Not very inviting, I thought with a growing sense of dismay. But then, I could hardly expect to receive a letter with *To Miss Luna Kane From Mr. Jimmy Page* stamped across it like an engraved invitation for a gossip rag to go on the rampage. Discretion was in order. He'd probably paid his errand boy handsomely to keep quiet.

All the waiting, all the wondering, the speculation and veiled signs. The answer to the riddle was looming like an oracle on my pillow. I could tear into it like a greedy raptor, or I could open it slowly, slide the tip of my finger gingerly beneath the flap, preserve its dignity the way I hoped its contents would preserve mine. Or I could keep waiting and wondering. Maybe I wasn't supposed to know who my father was. Maybe Claudia had wanted it that way. I staggered to the bathroom and splashed cold water on my face. The hell with what she'd wanted. I'd come here to get what I wanted.

I ripped open the envelope and dumped the contents on

the bed—the photographs, my letter, and another letter, that one on white parchment paper with letterhead, signed, sealed, delivered, my signature tucked in some horny kid's coat pocket proof positive.

Thacker & Jones, Solicitors
30 Old Broad Street
London EC2N 1HQ
+44 (0) 20 3320 4388

Sunday, 6th of March 1988

Dear Miss Luna Kane:

As legal council for Mr. James Page of Melbury Road, Kensington, London, UK, I am writing to inform you that Mr. Page has reviewed your letter and photographs, which you delivered to him unsolicited on the 5th of March 1988. In the aforementioned letter, you suggested that you are the biological child of Mr. Page and Ms. Claudia Kane, an American woman now deceased. I must advise you that your claim is invalid for the following reasons:

*   Mr. Page has never met nor had relations of any manner with Ms. Claudia Kane, who to Mr. Page's knowledge has never made a public claim to the contrary.

*   Neither Mr. Page nor Led Zeppelin, the musical group of which Mr. Page was a member from 1968 until 1980, was physically in the American state

of North Carolina or any other state or locality in the United States in late February 1969, the time in which your letter claims a meeting between Mr. Page and Ms. Kane took place in the aforementioned state. No documentation exists that corroborates your assertion that Mr. Page was physically in the United States during this time.

    * Before the 5th of March 1988, Mr. Page had never seen nor met nor had any contact with or knowledge of you, Miss Luna Kane of North Carolina, United States of America.

This instrument serves as a legal refutation of the claims posed in your letter based on the reasons stated above. Mr. Page requests that you immediately cease and desist making such false claims in public or private and refrain from attempting any further contact with him. Should you have questions about this matter, please phone our office at +44 (0) 20 3320 4388.

Sincerely,

Charles Thacker

Charles Thacker
Senior Solicitor, Thacker & Jones

Enclosures

Cc: Mr. James Page

I read it again. And again. One more time. Then again.

I turned the TV back on—BBC news. *Three IRA suspects shot dead in Gibraltar by SAS officers. Israelis kill two Palestinians. Soviet Union reports an arms buildup by Afghan rebels. More Armenians are attempting to flee the Soviet Union; the United States has drafted a proposal to admit twelve thousand as refugees.*

I turned down the volume and read the letter again, parsing every sentence, probing every word, looking for logical disjunctions, double-entendres, subliminal messages, watermarks, like rivers, like tears.

Claim: to state or assert that something is the case, typically without providing evidence or proof; a demand or request for something considered one's due.

Invalid: (especially of an argument, statement, or theory) not true because based on erroneous information or unsound reasoning; a person made weak or disabled by illness or injury.

Request: politely or formally ask for.

Cease: come or bring to an end.

Desist: cease.

I, Miss Luna Kane, a weak and injured young woman of North Carolina, United States of America, am politely and formally asked to bring to an end and cease, a redundancy signifying emphasis, my request for my due from Mr. James Page, a Rock music guitarist who has never met nor had knowledge—carnal or otherwise—of my mother, Claudia Kane, of . . .

Carnal knowledge: fornicate; shag; fuck.

Jimmy Page never fucked my mother.

Who the fuck lived down by the river?

Who the fuck was I?

A one-syllable word I was once punished for writing on the cloakroom floor in my sixth-grade classroom had determined my past and my future. It was the beginning, middle, and end of my story.

Jimmy Page never fucked my mother.

Nothing else made one fucking bit of difference.

****

How does that Shelley poem go—"The Witch of Atlas"?

Within the which she lay when the fierce war
Of wintry winds shook that innocuous liquor,
In many a mimic moon and bearded star,
O'er woods and lawns. The serpent heard it flicker

Too cerebral for the occasion.

Drink to forget but never forget to drink.

Much more appropriate, artfully direct, charmingly pedestrian.

I was standing at the pedestrian crossing between Bayswater and Kensington Gardens, sipping what was left of Bonzo's whiskey from a paper cup. I'd intended to get shitfaced at the duck pond, but I'd gotten started in my room and couldn't seem to make it any farther than the end of the block. Through fevered eyes, I could see two of Peter loping toward me, both of them waving that ridiculous turquoise fedora to get my attention. Curiosity must have gotten the better of him. He'd come to get the scoop.

"Land ho!" I shouted, amazed by the clarity and precision of the syllables, how perfectly they collided to form a whole new being, alive with rhythm and subtext. "Get it?" I said. "Land? Ho?"

He covered the rest of the distance between us in three or four lanky strides. "What's that you say?"

"We're standing on land, not water, right?" He cocked an eyebrow. "And who says *ho, ho, ho*? Santa Claus, that's who," I proclaimed before he could answer. "Fucking Santa Claus, a make-believe dude your parents tell you is real."

"Pissed again, I see," Peter said, taking my cup from me and pouring the liquid on the sidewalk. "Where'd this come from, aye? You gave Anna and me the rest of the bottle."

"I had another one."

"Blimey, Luna, how much did you drink?"

"Dunno," I said. "I spilled a lot of it on the floor in my room."

He crumpled the cup and tossed it into a trash bin. "What happened last night?"

"What happened today is a lot more amusing." I snorted. "You know what? I just thought of something. My mom would've *paid* Jimmy Page to fuck her, but *I* had to pay a boy ten bucks and a six-pack of beer to fuck me, and I don't even like the sonofabitch." I gave a venomous laugh. "I didn't even wanna do it, with him or anybody."

"You shagged someone today?" Peter exclaimed, his eyes, lined in black this time, bulging.

"No, no, no. Forget it." I teetered off the sidewalk and a taxi blew its horn. "Bite me, jackoff!" I yelled.

"Okay, mate, off we go." Peter took my arm and shepherded me toward the hotel. "Is the fat duffer still on duty?"

"You mean your wanker boss?" He grinned wryly. "No," I said. "That girl, the one with the buckteeth who chews her fingernails like a rodent. She's there."

"That bucktooth rodent is the wanker's niece, so don't repeat that when we get inside."

"Who cares. I'm leaving tomorrow anyway." I stumbled on a crack in the sidewalk. "Step on a crack, break your mama's back," I trilled.

Peter wrapped his arm around my shoulder to steady me. "Come on, Luna. Almost there."

He stood me up against a wall in the lobby while he filled a cup with tea, Rodent Girl behind the desk watching us dubiously. Peter whispered something to her I couldn't hear, and she looked at me askance.

"Horses for courses, I say." She shuffled a stack of papers and gave a smug nod. "I won't say a blooming thing. But Uncle Ted will have your head if you're not out of there before he gets here in the morning."

"No, it's not like that," Peter tutted. "I won't be long." He blew her a kiss then took my elbow again and led me inside the elevator.

"Goddamn, Peter," I slurred, swaying beside him while he punched in the floor number. "There are two of you. Are you both coming up with me?"

"You don't mind, do you? We both promise to behave," he said, putting the cup of tea to my lips.

I gagged down a few sips then pushed his hand away. "Why do I have to drink this?"

"Because, love, I don't want you to chunder all over me." We lumbered into the hallway. "Which room's yours?"

"I don't remember."

"This one? Number twenty-four?"

"Twenty-four."

"Right, then. Let's have your key."

I noodled through my jeans pockets then handed him the key. He opened the door and practically carried me inside the room. I plopped on the bed, kicking off my sneakers, and closed my eyes.

"That's good," he said. "Have a lie-down. You'll feel better soon."

"You think I can dream it away, disappear back into Kansas, like none of this ever happened? Go back to the way things were before?"

He eased down at the foot of the bed, crossing one leg delicately over the other. "I thought you were from North Carolina," he said.

I rolled over on my side, covering my face with my hand. "I'm not making any sense. I don't make any sense." I gestured feebly toward the letter on the nightstand. "See for yourself."

He seemed to waver, as if he were reluctant to enter the innards of my life, then took the letter and read vigorously. "Luna," he said gently when he was done.

"She lied to me. Everything she ever said or did was a lie." My voice broke and I began to sob, great gasping howls from the pit of my stomach, a violent purging of illusion. Peter pulled the hardback chair in the corner beside me, sat down, and began stroking my arm softly. "Feels nice," I said, once the wailing became a whimper.

"My mum used to do that when I was little." He gave a brittle laugh. "Even when I wasn't so little." He went to the bathroom for a tissue then placed it in my hand and sat back down in the chair. "She'd still be here if it wasn't for me," he said in a curious tone, devoid of any hint of sentimentality or equivocation. The confession was stone fact, not conjecture or rumor.

I blew my nose and pushed myself up on my elbows. "What do you mean?"

"That night," he said. "She was coming after me when she crashed her car. She was looking for me."

"Why?"

"I wasn't what they thought I was, or what they wanted me to be, anyway." He cracked his knuckles then clasped his hands behind his head. "The old man's a right bastard. He didn't bother to knock. It was my room, for fuckssake. He didn't knock. He just came right in, big as you please. I didn't know anyone was home."

"Oh," I said, fixing my eyes on one of those scuffmarks on the baseboards. "I think I know where this is going."

"Yeah, I figured you might. It was the first time, though. I'd never brought any blokes round before. It was a bit dodgy—especially with the old man. We'd never got on well, and he'd have lost the plot if he'd known."

"So what'd you do?"

"What do you think we did? Pulled up our trousers and ran before the old man could knock us arse over elbow. My mum was standing in the doorway, yelling for me to come back. But we kept running, popping into shops, ducking down alleyways, her following as best she could in the car. Made it to my auntie's in the morning, and she told me. I never went back home, not to stay. I picked up my clothes and such, and that was that. No more of the old man. He didn't even give her a proper funeral. Had her cremated. Don't know where he scattered her ashes or if he stuffed 'em in a closet." Peter leaned back in the chair and took a frazzled breath. "I never got to tell her goodbye."

I lolled against the headboard, unsure what to say, except the obvious. "It wasn't your fault, Peter."

"Not entirely, it wasn't," he said. "It was the old man's fault too. Duffer should've let me be. Why couldn't he just let me be? Called me a Nancy Boy, a no-good Nancy Boy. What's it got to do with him who I get a stiffy for?"

I slipped my sock feet underneath the covers, concentrating on the chill of the sheets—anything to divert my thoughts from the image of Peter with a stiffy. Anna suddenly came to mind—his girlfriend, Anna, who drapes her legs across his lap and calls him *love* and spits instead of swallows. "What about Anna?" I asked.

"What about her?" He brushed his cowlick from his forehead. "I've never lied to Anna. She knows what's what. That's the thing, Luna. I'm *not* a Nancy Boy, not like you think. That's what I'm trying to tell you. You're so hung up on names, labels, like you're only *you* if someone tells you who you are. Tell 'em all to piss off. So what if Jimmy Page isn't your dad? Why can't you just let yourself be?"

"You don't understand," I· said, crawling out of bed, wobbling on unsteady legs. "My mom made me think he was. She lied to me."

"She actually told you Jimmy Page was your dad? She said that? *Luna, Jimmy Page is your dad.* That what she told you?"

"Fuck off." Angry tears filled my eyes.

He looked wounded, then undaunted. "No, not fuck off," he said. "Tell me. Did your mum say that to you?"

"She did everything but say that. Don't they teach you guys about innuendo in school? Allusions, connotations? Reading between the lines?"

He scoffed. "Fancy words for wishful thinking, they are."

"The hell with you! You don't even know me."

He threw his head back and laughed. "Luna, you don't know yourself."

My stomach lurched. I tasted whiskey rising in my throat. I bolted for the toilet and vomited fiercely. Peter leaned over me, holding my shoulders while I retched. After I'd spewed the better part of a pint of John Bonham's liquor, I rocked back on my heels and sat cross-legged on the tile floor, my head in my hands.

"The room's got the jigglies," I groaned.

"Yeah, I hate when that happens. Up you go." He helped me back to bed and draped a blanket from the closet over me. "What time's your flight?" I held up nine fingers. "I'm setting the clock for six," he said, fiddling with the alarm clock on the nightstand. "You'll miss it for sure if I don't."

He stood over me, his hands in his pockets. "Look," he finally said, "I don't mean to upset you. I just think you should loosen up on your mum. Maybe something happened to her. Why else wouldn't she just come out with it? Maybe she thought some rubbish story was better than the truth. Sometimes it is, innit? Maybe she worked so hard to make you believe it she believed it herself."

"I don't wanna talk anymore," I muttered.

Peter shrugged. "Can I write on this?" he asked, holding the letter from Jimmy's lawyer.

"You can flush that piece of shit down the john with my upchuck for all I care."

He found a pen in the desk drawer next to a Bible and

wrote something on the back of the letter. "I'm leaving this right here. Luna? Look. Don't toss this, okay? It's my address and phone number. I have to go, but I'm leaving this. Ring me up when you get home." He nudged my hip. "Hear me? I want to know you got home safe. Don't forget." I pulled the blanket up to my chin and nodded with my eyes. He lingered by the door a moment, his coat hanging from a hooked finger, that turquoise hat perched inanely on his head. "One more thing," he said. "Did you ever ask your mum straight out about your dad?"

"No," I said.

"Howcome?"

"I didn't need to know then."

"How come?"

" 'Cause I had her. I didn't need anybody else."

"You don't need anybody now, not to figure out who you are, you don't." He tipped his hat and smiled plaintively. "You'll be all right, you know. You'll sort it out." He flipped off the light and opened the door. "Don't forget to ring me," he said, then faded into the darkness before I could assure him I would, before I could say goodbye.

I wiped my eyes and flopped over on my side. He'd left a nightlight on in the bathroom so I wouldn't take a nosedive the next time I had to vomit. I stared at the shadow on the wall, letting my eyes zoom in and out of focus, a game I used to play with Claudia. *Zoom in,* she'd say, pointing to a tree, the river, her face. *Now out.* I'd open my eyes wide, wider, until the image was an amorphous blur. *Which view do you like more?* she'd prompt. I'd always pick the *in* one. She'd always say *out.* She always preferred *out.* I didn't know when that preference had begun. I'd overheard Aunt Lorraine say the change had taken place after she got pregnant with me. *Sometimes things happen that change a person,* Claudia had once said of my great-grandfather. He wasn't crazy, she'd insisted. He was changed. He missed his wife. Part of him had died with her. But what had changed my mother? If it wasn't Jimmy, what was it? How had it happened? Where? I zoomed in on the wall, the white glare from the bathroom light stark, foreboding, cold.

A cold winter's night deep in the pines. Meet me down by the river on this cold Southern night. I've a counterfeit ticket to the star in your room. You want him, your talisman, come to me soon. You've kissed my face, touched my tawny summer skin, purred your siren's song into the sultry August wind. Like music, like magic, you wanted me then. Come to me now, on this anniversary of your birth. No one will hear us. Your daddy won't see. Just the owls in the mist, crying in the trees. Not a whisper, not a word, the word that is mine. Don't think it. Don't scream it, the word that is mine. No one will hear you. No one will believe. Come to me now, lie beneath the veil of the trees. Listen to the river, the ebb and flow of the river. Feel the rhythm. Feel the rhythm. Feel the river running dry. Feel the rhythm then forget—my face, my name—when the river runs dry. Brush the dirt from your hair, wash the blood on your thighs. Baptize your body, in the chimera of gold starlight. Birth your riddle, before I take flight, on the wings of the owls on this cold Southern night.

Was that how it had happened? The profane told in verse, a softening of the sword, taming of the tragedy. Then revised, the draft polished, the story retold, the imagery all that remained. Was that what Claudia had tried to do? Save me from her pain, her fate, share her myth, the one she clung to until her grip failed us both.

I'm just like you, Claudia. We're both marked, I'd told her. She knew I knew what I didn't yet fully know. The rainbow had ended, the curtain pulled back, not completely, but soon. The questions would follow.

Had she thought I would be better off without her—in the incognizant arms of Aunt Lorraine and Grandma? Had she sacrificed herself to save the fable?

I dug the heels of my hands into my eyes.

You're not like me, Luna. Say it. I'd said the words, but I hadn't believed them. And she'd known that.

She'd held my face in her eyes and her father's gun to her head. She was looking at me, not Jimmy. She'd chosen me.

When I was nine, my mother gave me a leather-bound journal with gold-tipped pages and placed a pen in my hand. *Write*, she'd said. *Tell me a story.*

Let me tell you a story. Spun together with scraps of old clothes and loose threads, a pattern all my own that changes on a whim, the loss of a needle, the prickling of a finger, unraveling of a spool. A story born of earth and sky, fire and water, of the living and the dead, rhythm and riddle. Some of it true, the rest always a mystery, like the beginning and the end, like the crisp Autumn night, the moon and the stars. A story in full flight.

Let me tell you my story.

CODA

THERE'S A GATE. Of course there's a gate. There's always a gate—this one more satirical than formidable. No elegant wrought iron spires or finials safeguarding well-groomed palatial grounds. Just a rotting split rail fence with a rusty metal barricade hemmed by a flimsy string of barbed wire that runs the length of the rails. Any relatively thin person could squeeze through the opening, and by the looks of the gate, forced awkwardly ajar, many have. I am more than relatively thin, and my hair, once a spiky black Mohawk that added an inch to my height, is now blue-dyed peach fuzz, an act of rebellion following a course of chemo. I'm not dying, so my doctors have assured me. The double mastectomy and aggressive treatment for one small tumor confined to one breast presumably guarantees my membership in the long-term cancer survivors club. The odds are more than in my favor. I don't think about them much, especially not today. In the eerie gray mist on this late January afternoon in 2018, I am standing outside another gate before another house daring entry. I am here to finish what I started nearly thirty years ago.

The property, overlooking Loch Ness in the Scottish Highlands a forty-minute's drive from Inverness, is privately owned, even after the conflagration that consumed the bulk of it in 2015, but no one could possibly live there. It isn't a home anymore. It's rubble, a scorched mockery of a home, barren and forlorn, a soul betrayed by its body. Sometimes I think the same is true of me, even though I am harbored by those I love. The feeling never lasts, that hint of the aleatoric uncertainty of life that sneaks up on me on rainy days. Like

obsession, emotions are protean, as is this moment, the now—
the magical, protean now.

"Can we go already?" Connie asks, shivering in her designer
wool coat. She's come along on the journey reluctantly, unlike
Peter, who was seduced by the thrill of a spooky jaunt to a
house that was rumored to have been the scene of many of
Aleister Crowley's nefarious deeds in the early twentieth
century. According to legend, Boleskine House was built
atop the ruins of a tenth-century church that burned to the
ground during a service, killing everyone inside. Jimmy Page
purchased the property in 1970, or '71, and sold it in '92. I
don't know who owns it now.

"No, we can't go yet," I say obstinately, surveying the
layout of the grounds and surrounding landscape. Boleskine
Cemetery, at the foot of the hill below the house and across
the narrow mountain road, is reputed to be linked to the
manor by a tunnel leading from the cellar to the graveyard
for the purpose of body snatching, or something else equally
distasteful. We explored the cemetery on our way up, and
Connie has exceeded her tolerance for all things supernatural
and gloomy. She turns up her collar and blows her warm
breath on her hands. She left her gloves in the rental car and
won't trek down to get them unless Peter or I go with her, but
neither of us is through torturing her yet.

"Aren't you cold?" she asks me, in that maternal tone she
still uses with her twenty-year-old daughter, my namesake
and godchild. She buttons the top button on my jacket—the
same Levis denim coat I wore on my first trip to the UK, pulled
out of mothballs for the occasion. She touches my chilled
cheeks with the backs of her hands. "Luna, you're gonna catch

pneumonia out here. Dr. Whatshisface should have told you not to go out any more than you have to in this kind of weather. What was your white cell count at your last appointment?" Her ex-husband, Martin, is a physical therapist, which, to Connie, is close enough to an oncologist to give her carte blanche to question the competence of my medical team. "In fact," she continues, "you really should have waited a little longer before doing this book tour. Three weeks post-chemo is just not long enough for a body to recover."

"She's fine, Mummy," Peter quips, throwing his arms around Connie playfully.

The three of us have been inseparable since Peter and I moved to New York City in the early '90s, right after my first novel was shortlisted for the National Book Award. Connie was pursuing her MBA at NYU and living in a cramped dormitory with sketchy plumbing and a roommate from Spain who masturbated with unabashed vigor every night. I sprang for a loft on MacDougal Street, and the three of us moved in together, until Connie graduated and landed a grunt job on Wall Street—not Goldman Sachs, but close enough, with health insurance and opportunities for advancement, of which she quickly availed herself. She and Martin found a brownstone in Lower Manhattan, and shortly thereafter, Peter fell in love with the receptionist at my agent's office and married her, eventually gaining US citizenship and a degree in accounting from Hostos Community College. After she and Peter divorced, he began a relationship with my agent, a jovial British chap named Ben whose claim to fame, after me, is that he almost boarded a flight out of Dulles bound for one of the World Trade Center Towers on 9/11. Serendipity intervened by way of a passionate phone conversation with Peter in an airport bar that ended with a gush of *I love yous* and a promise from Ben to trade in his first-class ticket to California for two coach seats on a flight to the Netherlands, where they could get married. At the time, Peter was with me in Richmond, having joined me on the east coast leg of my book tour for my third novel. We drove together to Dulles and the three of us made the trip to Amsterdam. The next morning, Connie joined us.

We're a family. They're my only family now.

Grandma died in the fall of 1988. She'd eschewed surgery and treatment and opted for palliative care at home, in spite of Aunt Lorraine's protestations. I understood her need for peace and comfort, her insistence on exiting the world on her own terms, in the house where she'd been born and spent her whole life. I held her hand while she died and thought of my great-grandfather and my mother, how I was glad Grandma didn't die in the icy blankness of winter or the anguished heat of summer. Mostly, I was glad she didn't die at night, tortured by spirits and superstition.

Aunt Lorraine and Uncle Jack sold the farm and asked me to come to Morganton to live with them. Instead, I returned to London and bunked with Peter and his auntie and her flock of pre-teens, all of us squeezed together in a small flat near Paddington Station. He managed to convince his wanker boss to take me on, and I worked the night shift and wrote my first novel on pen and paper sitting on a blanket in Kensington Gardens. Peter became a brother, the long-lost sibling I discovered instead of a father on my first soirée to England. And I was the little sister who encouraged the reconciliation, however subdued, between Peter and his dad after the daft cow stepmummy took what she'd stashed in Peter's mother's jewelry box and absconded to who-knows-where with his father's best mate.

When Aunt Lorraine and Uncle Jack were killed in a car crash in the winter of '92, Peter came with me to Full River to bury them near Grandma, my grandfather Hyram, and my great-grandparents. Afterward, I persuaded him to relocate to New York with me. I had the funds from my book sales to facilitate the change of scenery we both craved. And I needed to be near Connie again. She was the constant in my life. She was the one who held my hand in a sterile Planned Parenthood waiting room before my abortion the month after I returned to the farm from London the first time. I never told Denzel. No one else but Peter knows. I think Grandma had her suspicions. As always, she kept them to herself. She'd been a master at keeping secrets. I never asked her to reveal them, and there were no deathbed confessions. To her, that would have been a betrayal, and I couldn't ask her to sin before she entered the hereafter. That would have been a betrayal.

Peter jangles the gate, pulling it open another couple of inches. "If you're going inside, this is the way," he says to me. "You can't climb over this one."

A gust of haunted wind blows inland from the water and startles the trees. I tip my head back and stare into the leaden sky. Tomorrow night is a Super Blue Blood Moon, the first since 1886. The next one won't come for another twenty years. I'd wanted to change my London reading date from tomorrow to the day after and camp out at Boleskine House to moon watch by the mountainside Jimmy climbs in *The Song Remains the Same* to reach the Hermit at the crest, in search of Truth, Knowledge, and Light—the things my mother had redefined with such zeal—but Connie and Peter quickly nixed that idea. I didn't protest. High white blood cell count or not, I had to agree the idea was ridiculous, a fantasy as far-fetched as Jimmy's in the movie.

I'd followed his trajectory since 1988 from a respectful distance—the birth of his son James; his divorce from his wife Patricia; reunion with Robert Plant for a successful MTV special and subsequent albums and tours; Jimmy's collaboration with The Black Crowes; his marriage to an exotic Brazilian activist, with whom he had three children and joined in her fight to aid Brazilian street kids; his divorce from said wife; and his triumphant Led Zeppelin reunion concert at London's O2 Arena in 2007, with John Bonham's son, Jason, on drums. I never attempted any further contact with him, nor did I visit Led Zeppelin landmarks or Tower House or Old Mill House again, the latter of which Jimmy sold in the mid-2000s.

"Why do you want to go to this place in Scotland?" Connie asked when I propositioned Peter and her to join me.

"I don't like loose ends," I said.

"But why now—after all these years?"

I pondered the question. "Because I just got smacked on the ass by the Grim Reaper. I don't see a reason to wait until he kicks the shit out of me."

Peter wedges his lanky body through the opening then rubs his own peach fuzz with his *inside boy* hands. Much to Ben's chagrin, he shaved his head in solidarity with me once my hair began to fall out. His boss, another wanker, who manages the small CPA firm in the Bowery where Peter works as a bookkeeper, threatened to fire him until Peter told him why he'd done it. The guy backed off and even sent me a Get Well card.

Peter nudges the gate with the toe of his shoe and beckons me to follow. I slip through the gap and approach what's left of the house. "Come on, Connie," I holler over my shoulder.

I hear her suck her teeth. "Forget it. I'll wait here."

I turn around and give her a smirk. "Come on. I double-dog dare you."

She crosses her arms in front of her and purses her lips. "What are you, twelve? You dog-dare me?"

"I believe that was a double-dog dare, wasn't it?" Peter deadpans. He begins to cluck like a chicken.

"Oh hell no. Uh-uh." Connie squeezes through the gate. She tried everything from Weight Watchers to Jenny Craig to lose the baby weight after her daughter was born, then finally accepted the extra twenty pounds that padded her hips and belly and carried it as regally as she'd once sported the afro she'd sacrificed to the unspoken hair code in the world of high finance. She didn't shave her head for me. She couldn't. But she was with me at every chemo treatment and took care of me after my surgery. She's always taken care of me.

"Nobody here better say a word about this to my child," she says tartly, massaging her lower back muscles. "I don't wanna set a bad example."

"Oh right," Peter says. "You're meant to be the adult in the room."

"Honey, I'm always the adult in the room when I'm with you two." She trudges ahead of us toward the white plaster stone carcass. "Come on," she grumbles. "We're here now. Let's do this so we can go."

I catch up to her and thread my arm through hers. "Thanks," I say.

She gives a half-smile and bumps my hip with hers. "You're such a pain in the ass."

"Yeah," I say, "but you're stuck with me."

She rolls her eyes, feigning irritation we both know she doesn't really feel. "Well there you are, then," she says.

Peter peeks inside one of the broken windows and whistles. "What a bloody mess."

I cross the gravel, cluttered with debris, and look inside another window, careful not to disturb the precarious shards of glass that remain. "Looks like a bedroom, or a parlor," I say. The wallpaper is ripped and mildewed, carpet and matching valance over the adjacent window a sickening shade of pink. A chair remains in a corner, its front legs broken, body tilted forward, as if praying for mercy. It seems cruel to leave the place like this, a wounded animal begging to be put out of its misery. Why didn't the owners raze the structure, clear away the remains, rebuild, make a fresh start? That wouldn't change its history, but they could reclaim the space, make peace with the ghosts. Maybe the task had been too daunting for them, not worth the trouble. Maybe it was best they'd moved on, leave the house to scavengers and thrill-seekers. How oppressively sad.

"Okay," I say. "I think I've seen enough."

Peter pushes his glasses up on his nose and nods. "Me too." He gazes at the loch, the snow-capped mountains garrisoning it. "There's something heavy about this place—not just the house and cemetery. The lot of it," he says. "You can feel it." He sniffs the air. "You can even smell it."

"I guess that's what I wanted to find out," I say.

Connie crunches across the gravel toward us. "You wanted to find out what?"

"I don't know," I say. "I just wanted to see if I could sense something, energy of some sort."

"Do you?" Connie asks.

The breeze tickles the sprigs of hair on my head and neck. "Not really," I say, "at least nothing particularly enlightening."

"What then?" Peter asks.

I shrug. "Loneliness more than anything else. That and heartache." I start for the gate. "Damn shame, too," I say dreamily. "Before the fire, it must have been amazing."

****

Charing Cross Road, between Leicester Square and Tottenham Court Road, is home to some of the best bookstores in London. I always choose one of the funky indie shops on Cecil Court, an enclave of Charing Cross Road, rather than one of the mega stores, like Borders on Oxford Street, to give my readings. Tonight, a crowd gathers upstairs at Goldsboro Books, brandishing hardback copies of my new novel for me to sign later. The *New York Review of Books* gave it a lukewarm critique—*a quirky peregrination through the psyche of a schizophrenic doctor with an Oedipal complex and addiction to Monty Python's Flying Circus; funny and complex, in the vein of David Foster Wallace, except Wallace did it better. The author is a fine writer, but her latest offering fails to reach the heights of her first novel. Based on the quality of her oeuvre, with this one exception, I have no doubt she'll reclaim the magic again in her future work.*

I wrote the book during the Year of the Excrescence, as I referred to the grim period of my illness and treatment, and finished the final edits from my publisher during the first couple weeks of chemo. They put a rush on the release, hoping to cash in on public sympathy. Given the astronomical sales and size of the crowds at my readings, the strategy seems to have worked. Now that I'm on the mend, I wish I could take another year and revise. But as Connie said, "That's muddy Tar River water under the Greene Street Bridge. Move on, sister."

She and Peter sit on metal folding chairs in front of the podium, next to towering wooden shelves of first editions by the likes of Charles Dickens, Agatha Christie, and Daphne Du Maurier. Anna, who always shows for my London readings, unless her duties as a Literature professor at the same university she was attending when we met prevent her, nurses a glass of red wine in the second row, her husband and teenage son beside her.

Peter and Connie flash me the thumbs up. They know I'm nervous. I hate giving readings—the fraudulent solicitude of clerks, who deliver the same canned bio from my marketing director; the expectation of the crowd and inevitable disappointment they try to hide when they realize I'm a stiff reader, who lumbers through excerpts like a dyslexic android; and my feeble attempts at humor during the Q & A.

"What rot," Peter always tells me afterward. "The bit about [fill in the blank] was quite a laugh."

The worst is that no one really wants to hear the new work. They'll buy it and eventually fall in love with it—so far, anyway. But it's the first novel they want to hear, the scene at the beginning. I know the one before they request it. I've brought a photocopy with me tonight, tucked underneath the new book and the notes I've been making for the next one. Someone—usually a middle-aged woman, like me—will raise her hand during the Q & A and ask—

"Excuse me, would you read a bit from *Searching for Jimmy Page*?" Lady with the nose ring and tan sweater near the top of the stairs. She's standing under one of the overheads the store dims during readings to give the place a dramatic atmosphere. The people around her rubberneck to see who's asked the question they were contemplating.

Connie stifles a snicker, not very successfully, and Peter gives me a wink.

I take a sip of what the clerk thinks is water but is really Vodka from a paper cup, then clear my throat and give my stock response: "Which part would you like to hear?"

She tells me, and I watch her sit back down. My pulse begins to race. There's a man standing beside her, lurking in the entry, as if he's positioned himself to bolt down the stairs if necessary. He's not part of the crowd. No one seems to have noticed him. I didn't until right then. He's an older gentleman, trim and elegant, dressed all in black with a black scarf wrapped round his neck. His hair is gleaming white, pulled back in a neat ponytail. Blood drains from my face and I feel lightheaded. I clutch the edge of the podium. People are staring at me, perplexed. *Is she ill? Is she dying?* The questions are hanging in the air, unspoken but deafening.

He smiles at me. I smile back.

"Luna?" Connie whispers.

I look at her, my eyes wide.

"Are you okay?" she mouths.

Peter is standing, ready to help me to his seat if need be.

My eyes drift back to the man in the back, to the threshold, shadowy in the murky light. He's gone.

I take another sip from my cup, a gulp really. "Sorry about that," I say to the silent audience. "It's a little stuffy in here."

The clerk gives an awkward laugh. "No worries." Another awkward laugh. "Maybe it's that brilliant moon tonight that's making us all a bit wonky."

The crowd chuckles.

Ah, yes, the moon. *They say people go barking mad on a full moon.* What about on a Super Blue Blood Moon? What apparitions appear then?

I compose myself, then adjust the lamp strapped to the podium and begin to read:

She waited with him in his shack tucked deep in the pines. The autumn air, crisp and chilly, seeped in through the drafty windows. The fireplace remained unlit. It always did at night. He was a diviner, her grandfather, touched by the staff of a sage. He could see what wasn't there, hear what was silent. The fireplace was the medium, but only when cold and still, and only at the Witching Hour. Like a stoplight in a one-horse town, he'd miss it if he blinked. He'd miss it if he didn't listen with his whole consumptive body.

She was pregnant, heavily pregnant, a month away from giving birth. She was really just a baby herself. Her lover had gone away, the way lovers often do, the good and the very, very bad. She would bear the child alone. The music would guide her—another man's music, a man over the hills and ocean and far away. He had always been far away, but his music was near,

Christy Alexander Hallberg

hypnotic and soothing, like a seraph, eternal, suspended in time and space.

She placed a slip of paper and a pen in her grandfather's palsied hand. A question about the unborn child. What to name her? She knew it was a girl. She could see her face in her mind's eye, the dark hair and eyes, little pink fingers that would curl around her own. The child would shine like the moon, burn like the sun. But what would be her name? Not her last name. That didn't matter. What about her first?

"Do you know?" she asked her grandfather.

He spat tobacco juice into an empty coffee can. "Shh," he said. "It's almost time."

"But you'll tell me, won't you?"

He eased into his rocking chair and leaned forward, close to the fireplace, the invisible flames.

"Granddaddy . . . "

"Shh," he implored. "Wait a bit longer, girl. I'll tell you directly."

She sat on the wood floor at his feet and rested her head in his lap, breathed in his old man smell. He'd been ancient ever since his wife died, long before his granddaughter was born. This old man was all she'd known. Not the spirited boy who'd played the banjo and mocked his own father's superstitions—Don't eyeball the moon, do you get youself some bad luck; don't let nobody take up your footprints, lose your soul if you do. The boy would grind his bare feet into the dirt road by his house on musty summer afternoons just for spite. He'd float naked in the river, gazing straight into the moon, singing To the moon be the glory. He'd been what the Flower Children of the '60s would call a free spirit, without turning on, tuning in, or dropping out. He'd been like his granddaughter, the one he loved the most. She was a Flower Child, and she was sure her little girl would be a Moon Child, bright and beautiful and strong.

The clock on the mantle struck twelve. They both held their breath.

"Can you hear anything?" she whispered.

He nudged her head off his lap and pushed himself to his feet with his cane and stepped closer to the grate, his scraggly tabby cat trailing after him, the one that would run off one raw winter's night to die alone in the pines. She could hear the wind funneling down the chimney. Had her grandma come calling? Sometimes she'd catch him talking to her, softly, like a lover. He hadn't left her, though. She'd died in their bed lying next to him. There was nothing he could do to save her, he'd said. He'd rocked her dead body in his arms by the fire—to warm her, he'd said. She was cold. Then he went cold. His granddaughter, the one he loved the most, was afraid that would happen to her one day—grow cold, not die. She wasn't afraid to die. There were far worse things than that.

"Can you hear something?" she begged him, waddling over on her knees, cupping her belly in her hands. "Did you ask my question?" she said, pointing to the paper pressed between his fingers.

He looked down into her face. She favored his wife. She was more like him, he thought, marked at birth like him, but she favored his wife. He was glad. His love had been a beauty in her day.

"Granddaddy. Did you ask?"

He shuffled back to his chair and sat down with a humph. She touched his arm, kissed his cheek. He began to write, his hand scuttling across the paper in a shaky script. He folded the paper and gave it to her.

She clutched it in her hand. "Do I open it now?"

He gave a gummy smile, his cheek bulging with tobacco. "Don't matter. Now or later, it's all the same."

She stared into the empty fireplace. "Who was it in there? Who told you?"

"Ain't for you to know, girl," he said, then closed his eyes.

She covered him with the quilt her grandmother had made and left him there with the decrepit tabby. She'd tried to usher him to bed once before, and he'd stomped his cane on the floor and growled like a hellhound. She let him be now.

When she reached the clearing in the pines, the Hunter's Moon drifted from behind the clouds and bathed the yard in light. It's perfection, venerable, she thought. Valhalla. You catch a glimpse if you're lucky, but nobody believes you when you tell them. It might as well not be true. Maybe it wasn't. The music was, though, she thought. The music was in her soul—that man's music, the one who's over the hills and ocean and far, far away. She could see him. She could hear him. Even when no one else could. In a way, she'd created him, just as someone else had created Valhalla. But the music, the moon, her little girl—they were true.

She opened the paper and read the words, accepted the fable. She welcomed it:

Ecclesiastes 6:10: That which hath been is named already.

ACKNOWLEDGMENTS

The seed that would become this novel was first sown during the final months of my mother's battle with cancer in 2003, and reaped, in a very different form, as my Goddard College MFA creative thesis two-and-a-half years later. Thanks so much to my Goddard professors Martha Southgate, Jan Clausen, and Nicola Morris, who guided me during that turbulent time and helped me begin to discover my voice and vision. Also, thanks to my Goddard classmate Elizabeth Thorpe, who urged me to maintain writing deadlines and send her drafts during the two semesters I took off from the program when grief held me captive, and for helping me plot my 2005 UK vision quest, to search for Jimmy Page, in an effort to break free.

My MFA thesis was largely abandoned after my graduation, until the death of my husband, William "Bill" Hallberg, in 2014. Again, I sought solace in art, revisiting some of the scenes from the original story, re-imagining the narrative, reinventing old characters and inventing new ones, bringing my own story full circle with another UK Led Zeppelin vision quest in search of healing and hope. How bittersweet and amazing to finally fulfill the vow I made both Bill and Mom that I would finish my novel. As promised, Mom, it's dedicated to you.

And there are others I want to recognize:

My dear friend and esteemed colleague Dr. Margaret Donovan Bauer, who read every chapter of this book in draft form and offered valuable feedback and even more valuable encouragement throughout this journey. Special thanks to another dear friend and esteemed colleague, Dr. Liza Wieland, for her generous input and advice on the complete manuscript.

The love and support of my family was crucial to me throughout the writing of this novel: my brother Greg Alexander; father, S. Rudolph Alexander; sister, Martha Alexander Montgomery, who was a champion for me during those times of devastating loss and continues to be a rowdy partner in crime during our weekly wine and chat phone dates. An extra shout-out goes to my brother Steve Alexander, who introduced me to the music of Led Zeppelin and Jimmy Page when I was a kid and who will always be my favorite Rock drummer. Huge thanks to Amanda and Meredith Campbell, my sisters in soul if not blood, for their unconditional love, infamous Hallberg "deck times," unforgettable New Year's Eves, and for being the best aunties my beloved Chihuahua, Corniglia, could have. I am grateful to Garth Risk Hallberg.

Thanks to Ric and Elizabeth Goodman for their incredible support and encouragement of my writing endeavors and for their steadfast friendship, and to Amy Parker and Rebecca Tucker.

My love and appreciation to Herbert "Hub" Respess, IV, for entering my story in the last stages of this book's gestation. What an amazing gift you are. Thank you for believing in me and for being such a steadfast, wonderful partner.

I am grateful to Joe Taylor and the team at Livingston Press for their integrity, expertise, hard work, and creativity. You guys rock!

And finally, thank you, Jimmy Page, for your gift of music and magic, my constant through love and loss, offering epiphany and truth, mystery and passion. "Inspiration's what you are to me/Inspiration, look see"—"Thank You" by Led Zeppelin.

Thank you all.

Christy Alexander Hallberg teaches literature and writing online at East Carolina University. She serves as Senior Associate Editor of _North Carolina Literary Review_. Her short fiction, creative nonfiction, book reviews, and interviews have appeared in such journals as _North Carolina Literary Review, storySouth, Main Street Rag, Fiction Southeast, Riggwelter, Deep South Magazine, Eclectica, Litro, ST-ORGY Magazine, Entropy,_ and _Concho River Review_. Her flash story "Aperture" was chosen Story of the Month by _Fiction Southeast_ for October 2020 and was selected by the editors of the annual _Best Small Fictions_ anthology series for the 2021 edition. She lives near Asheville, NC.